D 4/11

AUTUMN'S PROMISE

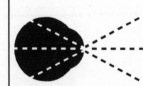

This Large Print Book carries the
Seal of Approval of N.A.V.H.

AUTUMN'S PROMISE

SHELLEY SHEPARD GRAY

THORNDIKE PRESS
A part of Gale, Cengage Learning

GALE
CENGAGE Learning™

Detroit • New York • San Francisco • New Haven, Conn • Waterville, Maine • London

LIBRARY OF CONGRESS CATALOGING-IN-PUBLICATION DATA

Gray, Shelley Shepard.
   Autumn's promise / by Shelley Shepard Gray.
      p. cm. — (Thorndike Press large print Christian romance)
  (Seasons of Sugarcreek ; bk. 3)
   ISBN-13: 978-1-4104-3568-2 (hardcover)
   ISBN-10: 1-4104-3568-7 (hardcover)
   1. Amish—Fiction. 2. Large type books. I. Title.
PS3607.R3966A95 2011
813'.6—dc22   2010050567

Published in 2011 by arrangement with Avon Inspire, an imprint of HarperCollins Publishers.

Printed in the United States of America
1 2 3 4 5 6 7 15 14 13 12 11

"I do not mean that I am already as God wants me to be. I have not yet reached that goal, but I continue trying to reach it and to make it mine. Christ wants me to do that, which is the reason he made me his."

— Philippians 3:12, New Century Version

"You make a living by what you get, but a life by what you give."

— Pennsylvania Dutch Saying

CHAPTER 1

"I'm pregnant," Lilly Allen's mother announced at breakfast. Calm as could be — just as if she was asking for someone to pass the bacon.

Lilly almost choked on her juice as she stared at her mother in shock. *"What?"*

"You heard me. I'm pregnant," she said again, her voice overly bright. "The doctor said I'm four months along. By Valentine's Day, we're going to have a wonderful new addition to the family."

Ty, all of ten, grinned. "Now I won't be the youngest anymore!"

Their mother laughed. "You sure won't. Now you'll be a big brother. I'm really going to be depending on your help, too." She looked at all of them. "I'm going to need all of your help."

"We already have a crib, don't we?" Ty chirped. "The one we bought for Lilly?"

Her mother's smile faltered. "Yes."

As Ty continued to chatter, Lilly felt her world flip on its side. Her mother was four months along? It was the beginning of September, which meant she got pregnant in May.

Right after Lilly had miscarried.

Waves of nausea coursed through her. Warily, Lilly looked her dad's way. He was eating his bowl of cornflakes like he didn't have a care in the world. As Ty kept chattering, she glared at him. "You knew about this, didn't you?"

Slowly, her father set his spoon down. "Of course," he said.

Her older brother Charlie scowled. "How come you two waited so long to tell us?"

With a helpless — almost sheepish look — their mom shrugged. "At first I just thought I had the flu. Then, well, I put two and two together."

For the first time in what felt like forever, Lilly stared at her mom. And as she did, she started seeing all the changes that should have been obvious. Her mother's cheeks were fuller, and her usually neatly tucked-in T-shirt was gone. Instead she wore an oversized button-down loosely over a pair of knit slacks.

She should have noticed the signs. After all, she'd been in that same condition just a few months earlier.

Beside her, Charlie was frowning. "I'm glad I won't be here to deal with it." Tossing his napkin on the table, he turned to Lilly. "You should have applied to college. Now you're going to have to take care of it."

"The *baby*," their father corrected.

"Whatever," Charlie retorted.

As their dad chastised Charlie, Lilly zoned them out. Her brother was right. She was going to be expected to help. It was inevitable.

She couldn't imagine a worse chore. The last thing she wanted was to be around a baby. It still hurt to see a baby in the grocery store. And even on TV.

Now she was expected to be excited about living with one?

Abruptly, she stood up. "I've got to go to work."

"Right now?" Her dad looked at his watch. "You've got over an hour before you have to be at the Sugarcreek Inn."

"I told Mrs. Kent I'd come in early," she lied. "I'm, um, already late."

"I think you're being awfully rude, Lilly," her father chided. "This is a wonderful event. It's something to celebrate."

Struggling to hold herself together, Lilly

bit the inside of her cheek. Anything to keep all the feelings from bursting out. "It's not my fault I have to work."

Face pale, her mother stood up, too. "Please don't leave. I think we should talk about this. Lilly —"

"There's nothing to talk about."

"Of course there is. I know you're still upset about —"

"Don't," Lilly interrupted, the pain inside making her voice hard, clipped. "Don't mention that. Ever."

"But —"

"Let her go, Barb," her dad said quietly.

Before her mother decided to have some kind of creepy heart-to-heart, Lilly set her plate in the sink, picked up her purse and keys from the kitchen counter, and raced out of the house.

Two minutes later, she was pulling onto the quiet state road that led to Sugarcreek. She hardly looked around her. The surrounding leaves, just beginning to change to gold and bronze, meant nothing. The cooler, crisp air with the hint of pine and apples failed to penetrate her awareness. Only pain surged through her as her eyes welled with tears and began to fall.

When her vision blurred, she pulled into an empty storefront's parking area and collected her thoughts. How could her parents be expecting a baby . . . just months after she'd miscarried?

And they'd looked so happy, too. How could they be happy? Her mother was forty-five years old! Charlie was twenty-one. Nobody had a baby when they had a twenty-one-year-old.

Except her parents.

Putting the car in park, she covered her face with her hands and breathed in and out slowly. She had to get a hold of herself. There was no way she could function if she didn't.

A knock on her window startled her.

"You okay?" the Amish man said, looking curiously through the glass at her.

Lilly nearly jumped out of her skin when she saw who it was. *Robert Miller.*

Robert, who came to the Sugarcreek Inn on a regular basis and always sat at the same table. Who hadn't said more than a handful of words to her the first five times he came to the restaurant.

Who knew she'd had a miscarriage and had asked if she was all right.

Who had volunteered to help look for her brother during a horrible storm this past April.

And there he was, standing outside her

door, as if he wandered around Sugarcreek and looked in car windows all the time.

As his blue eyes continued to examine her, she nodded. Perhaps then he would go away.

She wasn't that lucky.

He stood there, strong and still — waiting for her to roll the window down.

She did one better and got out of the car. Though she knew her tears had blurred her mascara — most likely making her eyes look like a raccoon's — she looked at him directly and smiled. "Hi, Robert."

"Are you all right? You've been sitting in here cryin' for a good ten minutes."

"Has it been that long?" she murmured, not actually expecting an answer. There was no way she was going to tell him about the latest development in her crazy, mixed-up life. She hardly knew him.

Lilly decided to ask a question of her own instead. "Why are you here?"

His face didn't even crack a smile. "You answer my question first. Pulling over and crying is not good."

"I know. I'm just upset about something."

"Well, I can see that." He stepped closer. For a moment, she thought he was going to reach out and touch her arm. But he didn't. Instead, he folded his arms across his chest, mimicking her, and murmured, "Sometimes talking helps."

"Talking won't help this problem."

"You sure?"

"Positive. It's something to do with my family."

Alarm entered his eyes. "Is someone sick?"

Lilly remembered hearing that Robert Miller had lost his wife to cancer a few years back. "No, everyone's healthy." She tried to smile. "It's just something to do with me, really. And I'll get over it. Now, why are you here in the parking lot?"

"This is my shop."

He was looking at her curiously, thought Lilly. With a hint of disappointment?

"I thought you knew that."

The plain wooden building was decorated by only a beautifully carved sign. *Miller Carpentry,* read Lilly, and then she shook her head. "Honestly, I've never noticed it before," she said. And besides, Miller was a common name in Sugarcreek; it was common anywhere, actually. She wouldn't have had any reason to guess it belonged to him. "It looks nice."

"*Danke.* My cousin Abe helped me start this business three years ago, in honor of my twenty-first birthday."

So he was twenty-four. She'd just turned nineteen — only five years separated them.

She'd thought he was older.

For a split second their eyes met. Again.

But this time it wasn't concern and alarm that filled his gaze. No, it was interest. Awareness.

Unbidden, a flash of hope hugged her tight. Knowing this was the road to disappointment, Lilly squashed the feeling down. "I, um, need to get to work. I'm sorry I bothered you."

"You didn't."

She just pulled open her car door and got back inside, not daring to reply. If he thought she was being rude, then that was just fine.

Anything would be better than Robert guessing the truth — that, for a brief moment, she'd been tempted to reach out to him for a hug, with the hope that he'd never let her go.

"Caleb Graber, you must stop being so lazy and fulfill your duties," his father said. "Now that Timothy is married and you are sixteen, you need to do your part." Looking around the barn, his father glowered. "Why haven't you mucked out the stalls and watered the horses yet? It's already eight in the morning."

"I don't know."

"That's no answer."

Caleb knew it wasn't. But he also knew he couldn't tell the truth. The truth was that the six pack of beer he'd drunk the night before with Jeremy was making his stomach sour, and the last thing in the world he wanted to do was rake up horse manure. Reaching for the rake, he muttered, "I'll do it."

Under the straw brim of his hat, his father's eyes looked him over. *"Gut,"* he said, then turned away.

As soon as he was alone, Caleb let go of the rake and leaned against the barn; closed his eyes against his pounding head. Wished he was anywhere else.

He hated his life.

"Still sitting around, doing nothing?" his sister Judith chirped.

He opened one eye. "Yeah."

"It won't help, you know," she murmured.

"What do you mean?"

Moving the basket of eggs to her left hand, she scowled at him. "I mean, that no matter how much you wish you didn't have to do things, it doesn't make responsibilities go away."

Judith Graber, the font of wisdom. "Can I wish you'd leave?"

Instead of turning away in a huff, she eyed

him with disdain. "What's wrong, Caleb? Too much partying with your crazy English friends last night?"

"Shut up."

"You better get over that soon and grow up. We need you around here, you know. With Joshua busy at the store and Tim now farming Clara's land and ours, Daed has to depend on you."

"It's not fair that I have to do everyone else's chores just because they found something better to do."

Pure amusement lit her face. "Found something better? Well, that's one way of puttin' things, I guess. Caleb, Joshua, and Tim got married."

He hated it when she made him feel like the dumbest person in the room. With a sigh, he turned away from her, filled a bucket with fresh water, and poured it into Jim's stall.

The horse perked up its ears and came to him for a pet. Caleb complied, rubbing the horse around his ears in the way Jim had always loved.

"You don't have a choice about your future, you know," Judith murmured. "Daed expects you to take over the farm since Joshua is in charge of the store. You might as well accept it."

Turning from the horse, Caleb angrily eyed his sister. "What if I don't want to?"

"Don't want to what? What are you talking about?"

"I'm just saying that maybe I don't want to work in fields and barns for the rest of my life. Maybe I don't even want to work in the store."

"What else is there?" Pure confusion emanated from her. Judith really had no idea how he felt.

"A lot."

"Not that I can see."

That was the problem with his family. They loved being Amish. They loved their way of life. They never contemplated anything else. Never longed for decent work, or meeting other people, or living other places.

Slowly, he said, "There's a lot other things outside of Sugarcreek. One day, I aim to see it all."

Just a bit of her superiority slipped. "Caleb, what are you saying?" she whispered.

For a moment, he was tempted to tell his sister everything. To share his dreams of escaping Sugarcreek and the endless rules that caged him in.

But he didn't dare. Judith would tell his parents. "Nothing. Leave me alone so I can get this done. And tell Anson to come out

17

here and give me a hand."

"All right," she said quietly. "But I hope you know what you're doing."

He didn't. But that was okay. Anything was better than doing what was expected of him . . . than staying.

All he had to do was wait just a little longer.

Then he could leave. Yes, just as soon as he was able . . . he was going to get out of Sugarcreek for good.

CHAPTER 2

"You're here bright and early," Gretta said when Lilly walked into the kitchen of the Sugarcreek Inn.

Lilly shrugged as she put her jacket and purse in the storage area. "I thought I'd try and get some things done before work."

"Like what?"

"Oh, you know. Filling salt shakers. Wiping down tables."

Gretta nodded solemnly. "Yes, those are important tasks, to be sure."

"Oh, stop." Chuckling, Lilly said, "Actually, I couldn't wait to get out of the house today. My parents were driving me crazy."

Her friend grinned. "I hope not too crazy."

"Just enough." Not eager to discuss anything more about what was going on in her house, Lilly looked around the kitchen. "What can I help you with?"

Gretta lifted two pitchers. "These need to be filled. Also, Miriam made several dozen cookies last night. Could you refill the trays in the bakery case?"

"Sure." Without another word, Lilly set to work. As she made tea and prepared the drinks, she observed Gretta kneading bread at the wooden butcher block table. Gretta's sleeves were rolled up, but, as usual, she worked as efficiently as ever. Her cornflower blue dress looked neat and spotless. So did her apron.

But even more apparent was the sense of peace that seemed to surround her. Gretta was expecting her first baby around Thanksgiving. Lilly couldn't help but contrast her excitement for Gretta's pregnancy with the feeling of betrayal and sadness she felt for her mother's.

But really, what was the difference?

Lilly knew she wasn't making any sense. Actually, she had a feeling all her happiness about Gretta's baby might vanish when she saw Gretta holding her newborn.

Jealousy and despair might cloak her again and plunge her into depression.

After a time, Gretta's hands stilled. "Lilly, is anything wrong?" She looked at the front of her dress. "Am I covered in flour and I didn't know it?"

Lilly laughed. "Not at all. Sorry I was staring. I was just thinking you looked pretty."

Gretta blushed as she waved off Lilly's words. "I'm as big as a field horse."

"Not quite that big," Lilly teased.

Gretta smiled too, then turned serious. "Lilly, truly, if you ever want to talk, just let me know. I am your friend."

"That's sweet of you. But really, I'm fine," she answered as the front door chimed. "Who could that be? We don't open for another hour."

"Not everyone cares about our signs, you know. They just look for the lights on."

"I'll go," Lilly said as she turned around and pushed through the swinging door into the dining room, already saying, "I'm sorry, but we're not open."

"That's okay. I don't want anything to eat. The only reason I'm here is to see you," Cassidy Leonard said.

Lilly stopped in her tracks. "Cassidy?" she murmured, stunned. "I can't believe you're here. I never expected to see you again."

"Obviously," she said, in a voice thick with sarcasm. "You might as well have moved to Tibet or something. You never come back to Strongsville to visit. You just couldn't fit it into your busy schedule?"

Lilly supposed she deserved that. She and Cassidy had been friends since grade school. Though they hadn't been quite as close her last year in high school, Lilly knew much of the reason was because of lack of time. They had both had busy schedules and boyfriends.

And then, of course, she'd become pregnant and started keeping secrets.

It had become easier to drift away from Cassidy and the rest of her friends than continue to lie. Which was why Cassidy hadn't known that Lilly had become pregnant, planned to give the baby up for adoption, miscarried, and was now floundering in her life.

No, all Cassidy knew was that Lilly Allen had moved less than three hours away and never looked back.

But still . . . Lilly couldn't believe one of her friends from Strongsville had come to Sugarcreek. After staring at her in shock, she ran over and hugged her tight.

Thankfully, Cassidy's arms wrapped around her, too. "Finally! I thought we were going to just stand here like frenemies for ages."

"I'm sorry. I'm just having a hard time adjusting to the fact that you're standing across from me in Sugarcreek, of all places. What are you doing here?"

"I missed you," she said simply. "When you never wrote me back, I decided to come and see for myself why." Still holding Lilly's arms, Cassidy looked her over. "Hmm. So far, you look pretty good."

"Not as good as you." Just as Lilly remembered, Cassidy was the picture of preppy perfection. Her brown hair was neatly combed and secured in a headband. Her light brown eyes were skillfully outlined and highlighted with subtle makeup. And her casual button-down and tailored jeans looked like something out of a J.Crew catalog. "How come you aren't in school?"

"Today's a holiday. Labor Day, you know." Cassidy looked at her curiously. "Don't you have the day off, too? Where are you going to college?"

"I decided to wait a while to go."

"What? But all you ever used to talk about was becoming an English professor."

"That dream came and went," she lied. Realizing that they were standing awkwardly near the door, she said, "Hey, want to sit down?"

"Sure. Any place?"

"Any place you want." As soon as Cassidy took a chair, Lilly moved to the coffee bar. "Would you like something to drink?"

"I just wanted to see you. Lilly, what's wrong with you? You're acting so nervous."

"Nothing. I'm just not used to having

guests here," she replied, thinking that the lies were coming easier and easier. "My boss is pretty strict."

"Maybe we should do this later. When do you get off?"

"Not for eight hours."

"Oh. I can't stay that long. Can't you take some time off now?"

"Not really."

"Oh."

The tension rising between them was becoming incredibly uncomfortable. "You should have called."

"Your number's unlisted and you're never online. Besides, I have a feeling you probably wouldn't have even called me back."

Lilly winced, though she knew that it was a fair assessment. She had been avoiding her friends. "How did you even know I was here?"

"Megan's little sister is still friends with Ty. He told her you were working here. She told me."

Megan had been part of their circle of friends. And was yet another person she'd pushed away. Still not sure what to do with herself, Lilly said, "Let me go get us something to eat." She scurried back into the kitchen before Cassidy could say anything.

Gretta's hands stilled when Lilly flew into

the kitchen. "Who is that girl?"

"A friend of mine from Cleveland."

"Oh, *wonderbaar!*"

"Yes, it is." Without hardly looking, Lilly pulled open the door to the walk-in fridge and chose the closest pie. A dutch apple. She sliced two pieces and set them on plates. "I'm going to sit for a minute with her, then I'll be back."

"Take your time. We're *gut* until others get here."

Cassidy grinned when Lilly set down the plates. "Yum. What kind of restaurant is this?"

"Amish."

"Ah." Instead of launching into the usual questions about the Amish, Cassidy played with her pie, cutting off a small portion and pushing it to one side. "You know . . . Alec still misses you."

Alec. Even hearing his name sometimes caused her hands to shake. "I doubt that," she said slowly. Their last conversation had been pretty final.

"He told me he thought about you all the time when I saw him two days ago. Actually, he couldn't believe it when I told him I hadn't spoken a single word to you since you left." Looking vaguely accusing, Cassidy murmured, "And I couldn't believe it

25

when he told me that you two had kept in touch."

"We only spoke a few times." When she told him she was keeping the baby. And then when she'd told him that she'd miscarried.

"But I thought you had broken up weeks before you left?"

Lilly's hands were shaking so much now, she kept them clasped tightly in her lap. This was why she hadn't ever called Cassidy. She had too many secrets — and she still wasn't much of a liar. "It's complicated."

"How complicated?"

"Well . . . you know . . ."

As self-assured as always, Cassidy risked challenging her friend. "No. I don't. What are you talking about? What exactly happened between you two?"

"I can't really talk about it." Though her stomach was in knots, Lilly picked up her fork and made herself eat a too-big bite of pie.

Something flickered in Cassidy's eyes. Remorse? Disappointment? "I see."

No, she didn't. But Lilly's nerves felt so taut, she was sure if she said another word, she'd tell Cassidy everything. And then Cassidy would tell all their friends in Strongsville.

And then she'd really never be able to go back again.

"You do good work, Robert."

"Danke." Robert looked over at his cousin Abe, who'd stopped by the shop under the pretense of examining his latest pair of kitchen chairs. Robert knew there was another reason he'd stopped by. He was out for information.

Dipping his rag in the oil, he let the cloth soak up a good amount, then carefully ran it over a chest of drawers he'd just finished the day before. His customers were due by that afternoon to pick it up, and he wanted the piece looking its best.

Abe watched him for a moment. "It's been too long since you've stopped by the house. Weeks."

"I've been busy. You know that."

"Not too busy for family? Come over soon, why don'tcha? You could meet us for supper. Mary would like that."

"I'll do that soon." Not too soon, he added silently to himself. Lately Robert had gotten tired of Abe's constant questioning about his business.

"Tonight, perhaps?"

"Not tonight." Robert rested on his heels as Abe became more visibly agitated. "But I do appreciate your askin'."

"Tomorrow?"

"Maybe another week."

Abe looked him over, chewed on his bottom lip for a bit, then shifted. "You know, I was asked to stop by and visit with you. By your father."

"There's no need for that. If my *daed* needs to speak with me, he can come himself."

"He told me that the last time he stopped by, you hardly had time for him. Or your mother."

Robert remembered that visit well. His parents had shown up after suppertime one evening, and had been full of unwanted advice.

"You shouldn't be working this late, Robert," his *daed* had chided. "There's a time for work and a time for rest, *jah?*"

He'd had no need to go home. There had been nothing there except memories. "I'll leave soon."

"Why don't you leave now?" his mother suggested. "We'll help you clean up."

There had been something in their voices that had grated on him terribly. He was a grown man. He'd not only taken care of his wife, but he'd cared for her as she passed in front of him from this earth. His business was making a profit. He neither needed their assistance nor their advice.

"Nee," he'd said with a bit too much force. "I'm not ready to leave."

"Robert. We came all this way to get you."

"And we have someone we'd like you to meet . . ."

As he'd turned to his mother, the piece of paper he'd been holding fell to the floor. *"What?"*

After glancing his father's way, she'd continued. "We invited Edith over for dessert."

"Edith Beachy?"

"Jah." His mom stepped forward. Took his hand. "She's anxious to meet you. She's a widow, you know."

"Do you actually think I want to meet a woman?" He pulled his hand away from her grip. "Do you actually imagine I will ever want to meet another woman?"

His father stepped forward, and to Robert's amazement, he put a reassuring arm around his mother's shoulders. Comforting her. "Robert, you will mind your tone."

He'd been so angry, Robert had barely been able to look at them. *"Nee.* This is my place of work. This is my life. I don't need your interference."

"You are being disrespectful."

"I am being honest." Inside of him, words rushed forth, begging to be uttered. For once, he gave in. "Grace was my life —" Tears choked his voice, then he repeated himself. "Grace was my life and now she's gone. Now there is nothing else."

"Robert!"

He turned his back to his parents. Unwilling to see his mother's stricken expression. Unwilling to see his father's disapproval. "I have much to do. I'd appreciate it if you would leave."

For a moment, they'd stood there. Even though his back was still turned, he could imagine their look of disappointment. They slowly, deliberately, turned and left.

Since then, they had only the most mundane of conversations when they'd see each other at church. It was obvious they were still nursing hurt feelings over the way he'd treated them.

But what they didn't understand was that he, too, still hadn't forgotten.

Abe waved a hand in front of his face. "Robert? What should I tell your *daed?*"

"Nothing. There's nothing to tell."

"I think differently. People are concerned about ya. Robert, it's been a fair amount of time since Grace passed. Three years."

"I know." He never forgot how long she'd been gone.

"You need a wife. If not Edith Beachy, then some other woman."

"My parents spoke to you about her?"

Abe only looked slightly shamefaced. "They're only thinking of what's best for you. Robert, you've got a nice home and good business. It's time to think about getting a new partner."

Abe talked like it was as easy as going to an auction for a new horse.

The idea of being set up with a dozen different women from their community turned his stomach. He just wasn't ready.

"I appreciate your concerns." Robert set his rag down and faced his cousin. "Abe, I am grateful for your time, I am. And I am grateful for Mary's invitation. But I'm not in any hurry to start visiting folks' homes for suppers. Not yet."

"Grace . . . she's not coming back."

Abe's words hit him like a blow to the chest. "I realize that. Now I've got to get back to work." Smiling weakly, he added, "It won't get done by itself, you know."

"Robert —"

"Leave me be. Please. Just tell Mary and my father you tried, cousin."

31

Abe stood frozen in his spot. "But one day? Will you ever be able to move on?"

"Perhaps."

"Perhaps?" Hope entered his voice. "*Sehr gut!* Is there anyone special?"

"Nee." Although, as soon as he disclaimed it, a sudden vision of a blond woman with curly hair flashed into his head.

After Abe left, Robert sat down and stretched out his hands. They'd been clenched in an effort to control his emotions.

Yes, he was finding it difficult to be around friends and family and talk about life like he had nothing more on his mind than the recent weather report.

But, fact was, he had a great many things on his mind . . . the least of which was his disturbing attraction to an *Englischer.* To Lilly Allen.

She was as unsuitable for him as Grace had been perfect. Of course, Grace had been everything proper and good. She made him happy and centered. They'd believed in the exact same things and seemed to bring out the best in each other.

Lilly, on the other hand, was too young. She was too beautiful, with her curly blond hair and chocolate-colored eyes. She'd had a relationship out of wedlock and had even had the misfortune to become pregnant.

And then, of course, she'd lost the baby.

So why could he not look away from her? She drew him to her like a shining star in the dead of night. He'd found himself thinking of her when he fell asleep.

And sometimes, while working in the silence of his workshop, he'd found himself imagining her by his side. Speaking to him. Looking at him like he interested her — more than as just a customer in her restaurant.

Even the thought of that was shocking. But what could he do to stop it? So far, he'd tried staying away from her.

Even tried to concentrate on her unsuitability. But nothing worked.

The only blessing was that she obviously didn't think of him at all.

He couldn't help but remember how terribly surprised she looked when he'd checked on her in the car that morning. She'd never even noticed his shop before. To her, he was just another man eating at the inn. An Amish man.

She probably had a fair amount of men eyeing her, wishing that she'd smile their way.

It embarrassed him that, at the moment, he yearned for a smile, too.

CHAPTER 3

Caleb had just finished sweeping out the back storeroom when his father called out to him.

"Caleb, I need you to walk Mrs. Miller's groceries to her at the boarding house."

After replacing his broom and dustpan, Caleb entered the main store. It was one o'clock, and the place was busier than ever. Two women, friends of his mother's, were buying trail bologna and cheese. Another Amish lady was in the bulk food aisle, examining seasonings.

Everywhere else he looked, there seemed to be tourists and *Englischers* talking noisily and filling shopping baskets. His *daed* had left the double front doors propped open. In blew a cool breeze, along with the unmistakable scent of autumn leaves. Caleb nodded to a few curious people, then stood in front of his father. "Busy today."

"Jah. Sehr gut," he agreed.

"Do you want me to wait to run the errand? Maybe you need help?"

"I don't. Joshua's here — he just went upstairs for a moment. This is more important, I think." Pointing to a pair of boxes on the counter, he said, "Mrs. Miller already paid for both of these. She'll be looking for them. There's eggs and fresh bread in there. Have a care with them, now."

Before Caleb could say a word to that — that of course he wouldn't crack the eggs or smash the bread — his father turned away to wait on a customer.

Without a word of thanks.

He did his best to shrug off disappointment. He knew better than to look for praise for something so minor. It wasn't the Amish way to tell someone thanks for expected tasks.

Caleb picked up one of the boxes. It was heavier than it looked, which would mean he'd either have to take two trips down the street or use a wagon of some sort.

There was no choice. No way was he going to pull a red wagon down the street in Sugarcreek. His English friends would never let him live that down.

After readjusting his grip, he strode toward the front door.

"You forgot one," his father called out.

"I'll be back for it," Caleb threw over his shoulder as he raced out the door — before his *daed* told him to pull out the wagon.

It was just after lunchtime and the streets had emptied a bit. Wednesdays were like that. Thursdays, Fridays, and Saturdays brought tourists and traffic jams; Sundays were almost empty. Monday was filled with busy workers — the day for many to get their business done at the bank, the printers and such. On Tuesdays, people came out for lunch but otherwise stayed away, doing whatever their busy lives needed them to do.

Caleb knew the town's routine almost as well as he knew the schedule at his own home. He'd grown up with both. But now he was so sick of the sameness, and of the constant worry about doing what was right — what was expected. He could hardly stand it.

He was so lost in thought, he almost ran into a lady and her little girl. "Excuse me!" she blurted. "Watch where you are going. Understand?"

"Sorry," he mumbled, then, unable to help himself, he glared at her back. She hadn't needed to yell at him. His hearing was perfectly good. He was sick of people thinking he wasn't smart — or couldn't hear too well — because he was Amish.

Finally, after another block, he turned right, then walked up the steps to Mrs. Miller's house. Luckily, she opened the door as soon as he reached the stoop. "You made it!"

"I did."

"Here, let me get this from you."

"*Nee,* Mrs. Miller. It's a heavy box. I'll bring it in." After depositing it on the counter, he wiped his brow. "All right. I'll go get your other one."

"I feel bad, making you do all this work."

"It's no trouble. I like getting out of the store."

"Could you spare a few moments when you get back for a soda? I just bought some root beer."

"I can." He grinned. She knew he loved root beer. "I'll be back in a jiffy."

"Great. We'll sit and have a soda and you can tell me what your plans are."

That made him pause. "Plans?"

"You, Caleb Graber, have a look about you that's new. I sure would like to know what has put that glint in your eyes."

"I'll be back soon." But as he turned, he wondered if he could trust her. Or better yet, if he could count on her. He needed someone from the outside world on his side.

The Allens had become too close to his parents to go against them. But maybe Mrs. Miller would. The Mennonite lady had something of a mysterious past, at least to Caleb's way of thinking.

Rumor had it that she'd been engaged once, but the man had jumped the fence and taken off with an English woman. After that, she married but it hadn't lasted long. Her husband passed away after only a few years of marriage.

Now Mrs. Miller seemed content to straddle two worlds with ease. She was everything proper on the outside, but she also had a great understanding of how it felt to not fit in.

Caleb had even heard it whispered that she'd helped a pair of brothers leave their order, against their parents' wishes.

As he walked back to the store, Caleb wondered just how much he dared to open up.

"You could have taken the wagon and been done in half the time," his father said when he strode through the shop's doors again.

Caleb said nothing, just picked up the box and left again. Only retorts and sarcasm were on his tongue. And if he'd said either, it would have been a foolhardy decision.

Luckily the second box was a little lighter and shorter, therefore easier to see around. He made it back to Mrs. Miller's in no time at all.

After she put her eggs away, she brought two mugs of root beer to the kitchen table. "Have a seat, Caleb. Are you hungry?"

"I'm fine," he murmured as soon as he took a long sip of root beer. "I need to get back to work soon."

"And how are things at the store?"

"The same." It took all the effort he had not to grimace.

She searched his face. "Nothing new?"

He had a choice. He could either lie . . . or come clean. "I've been thinking about leaving," he blurted out.

Then he waited. Waited for her to ask why he wanted to leave. Tension filled him as he struggled for the words to describe the deep need he had to leave everything. The store. Sugarcreek.

Being Amish.

But instead of asking anything of the sort, she merely sipped her soda. "I see," she said after staring at him for what felt like forever. "Well, if you're thinking of leaving . . . I suppose we ought to talk about where you want to go."

In a flash, all the anxious, dark thoughts

that Caleb had been doing his best to keep under wraps came flooding out. "You don't think I'm terrible, to be thinking such things?" he prodded.

"It's not my place to judge you."

Again, the rumors of her past swirled between them. Had she been judged before? Had she been found lacking? He was dying to ask her, but didn't want to offend.

Or, perhaps, she was only pretending to be on his side? Suspicion rose inside him like bile. "Are you going to tell my folks now?"

"Tell them what, Caleb?" Reaching out, she squeezed his arm. "So far, all you've done is brought me my groceries and shared a cold drink with me." She stood up then. "One day soon, stop by again. When you trust me."

Her statement made him flush. "It's just . . . I'm not sure what I want to do."

"Perhaps you don't have to know yet," she said gently.

As the silence between them lengthened, she gestured to his half-drunk bottle. "Why don't you finish up your drink? That's enough for now, yes?"

Without a word, he slurped the rest of his drink, then left with only a terse goodbye. As he walked back to the store, with his head down, his thoughts jumbled together.

So jumbled, he almost missed sight of two of his English friends standing on the corner. Watching him.

Jeremy raised a hand. "Caleb. You busy tonight?"

They meant later. When it was dark. When they'd go out drinking and driving. When they were free from too many watchful eyes. "No," he called back.

The boys grinned. "Good. We'll see you later."

Caleb grinned, too. No, he didn't know what he was going to do in the future. But maybe he didn't have to. All that mattered was that he had plans for later.

That was enough to get him through the rest of the day.

Miriam peeked into the back workroom, where Lilly liked to sometimes take her break. "He's back," she chirped.

Lilly put her novel down. "Who?"

"Robert Miller, that's who. I just seated him near the windows." She winked. "He asked if you were here."

Lilly folded a page down to mark her spot and stood up. "Do I look okay?"

Never one to shy away, Miriam looked her over with a critical eye. "Perhaps you need to tame your hair a bit?"

"I'll do that."

She grinned. "Then I'll deliver Robert his coffee . . . and the news that you will be right there."

After stuffing the book in her backpack, Lilly ran to the bathroom and turned on the light. Looking at her reflection, she winced. As usual, her blond curls looked like she'd stuck her finger in a light socket. She pushed the worst of the wayward curls from her face, washed her hands, then ran out the door.

Afraid to question why she was so excited to see him, she walked quickly through the kitchen and right out to the dining room. She paused when she caught Robert's eye. He'd been watching the kitchen door. Watching for her. "Hey," she said as she pulled out the chair across from him and sat. "You taking a coffee break?"

"Actually, I wanted to see you. I was worried . . . are you still upset?"

Lilly wondered if she'd ever get used to Robert's forthright ways. Though sometimes it felt like he was shy around her, when he did say something, it was exactly what was on his mind. "No." She shook her head. "I was being silly."

"Are you sure?"

She didn't blame him for being skeptical. After all, she'd had to pull over into his parking lot to cry! "Really. You know how it goes . . . sometimes things seem worse than they are. Once I settled down, I realized I shouldn't have been so upset."

Blue eyes examined her again. She felt his gaze as clearly as if he'd been running his fingers along her skin. "Well. I'm glad of it, then."

An awkward silence percolated between them. Yes, they'd talked . . . but rarely had she ever sat with him for any length of time. "Well . . . I guess I better get back to work."

"Is that what you were doing when I came here? Working?"

"Actually, no. I was taking my break. I was in a backroom, reading." She rolled her eyes. "I'm a fan of western romances."

But instead of looking horrified, the corners of his lips lifted. "Do you have time to tell me about your book? Are you still on break?"

She looked at her watch. "I have time." She wrinkled her nose. "Are you sure you want to hear about it?"

"Mighty sure," he murmured.

A flash of warmth settled in her as she began to talk all about the book. And as Robert Miller gazed at her like she was the most interesting person in the whole world.

The following Tuesday, her work shift ended much too soon. With leaden feet, Lilly walked to her car. She wished she had somewhere else to go, but at the moment, the only place she really knew to drive to was home.

What a day it had been. First her mom had been chirping all about her pregnancy. Again. Then the restaurant had gotten incredibly busy and she'd hardly had time to clear tables before more customers were seated.

Now she was running on fumes. Barely holding on.

When would her life ever settle down and get back to normal? Of course, what was normal?

After pulling out onto Main Street, Lilly noticed the slow changes that were taking place around Sugarcreek. Some gift shops had fall flags out and other festive displays. Around them, mums were in bloom. A beautiful display of black-eyed Susans waved in the distance. And one or two elm trees had already begun to switch colors. The air was cooler . . . soon corn mazes would be advertised and pumpkin patches would be filled with children searching for their perfect jack-o'-lantern.

No matter what happened, it seemed as if the seasons really did move on. She was just thinking about that when she noticed Miller's Carpentry and Robert's buggy parked to the side.

Whether it was because she was willing to do anything to delay going home . . . or because she'd felt drawn toward Robert since the day she'd met him, or because she'd enjoyed their last conversation so much . . . Lilly made a sudden decision and pulled into his lot.

Maybe it wouldn't be too awkward if she simply went in and thanked him for his concern the week before? After all, it had been really nice of him to visit the restaurant just to see how she was doing.

That would be the Christian thing to do. Right?

The light was dim and the air smelled like oil and sawdust when she opened the door. She found him easily enough. He was sitting hunched over a desk, glaring at a stack of papers.

His head popped up when she opened the door. The stunned look on his face when their eyes met was almost comical.

"Hi," she said. "I hope I'm not bothering you?"

"*Nee.* I mean . . . no." His chair scraped the floor when he stood up. "Did you need something?"

Since he looked glued to the ground, she walked forward. "Maybe."

That seemed to set him in motion. Clumsily, he walked around the desk. Cleared his throat. "Very well. Um, what may I show you?" He pointed behind him to a beautiful chest of drawers made out of oak and stained a rich walnut. "A bureau? Or maybe a rocking chair."

"It's all beautiful, but I didn't come here for furniture."

A line appeared between his brows. "No?"

He looked so flustered, she almost smiled. Almost. "I just wanted to stop by to thank you."

"For what?"

"For what you did last week, of course. Not only did you not mind that I pulled in here and cried, but you even came by the restaurant." Because he was still looking at her so intently, she stumbled over her next words. Panic was setting in. Maybe stopping by had been the completely wrong thing to do? "I mean, I'm glad you stopped by and we talked."

Only one kerosene lamp aided the waning natural sunlight illuminating the room. But even in such conditions, Lilly spied a faint blush stain his cheeks.

He swallowed again. "No thanks is necessary."

"I think otherwise." Anxious to not belabor her mini crises to death, she gestured toward his desk. Papers and account books littered the surface. "Looks like you've got your share of paperwork."

"I do. One of my supplier's statements didn't add up. I've been sitting here for the last thirty minutes trying to figure out if it was their mistake or mine."

"Any luck?"

"No. All I'm discovering is that I still don't have the head for numbers that I wish I did."

"Math isn't my strong point, either. But if it was, I'd try and help you," she said with a smile.

"Well, then," he mumbled. Still looking uneasy, Robert stepped a little closer.

With some dismay, she realized he was probably about to show her to the door.

He probably couldn't wait for her to get out of there. To leave.

He looked ill at ease. Tense. Was she making him feel that way? Wow. Maybe she'd completely misread things at the restaurant. Maybe when he'd asked her about her book he was just being nice?

But, she could have sworn when their eyes first met that he hadn't looked upset to see her . . . merely surprised.

"Hey, how about a tour?"

"Sure." Half smiling, he pointed to his desk. "This is my least favorite part of the operation. My desk."

She laughed. "Show me your favorite part."

"Gladly." He walked her through a doorway and down a small hall. When they turned left, it was into a backroom, one that was far more brightly lit and large. "This is my workshop."

Lilly inhaled. "It smells like heaven in here."

"I'm not quite sure what heaven smells like, but I doubt it smells like this." Meeting her gaze, his expression warmed. "I wouldn't mind if it did, though."

As he guided her through a maze of wood, saws, benches, and toolboxes, Lilly looked in amazement at the wide assortment of furniture that was displayed everywhere. "Robert, it's all beautiful."

"Danke."

"What's it all made out of?"

"Oak, mostly. But there are a few things built from cherry. One customer just asked me for a dresser out of pine."

Unable to help herself, she ran a hand over a cherry dining room table. "I like this."

"You have good taste. That piece took me a whole month to build."

"Is it sold?"

"I thought it was. But the people who ordered it backed out."

"That's rude!"

He shrugged. "I don't think so. The man lost his job. I feel bad. I had to keep his deposit because I bought the wood special for him. But I don't blame him."

"I'm sorry. I guess I'm the one who's being rude." As she heard her words echo in the vacuous space, she groaned. What in the world was she doing? Flirting? Just being friendly?

Sometimes she didn't even know herself anymore.

To her relief, he only shook his head slowly. "No, Lilly. I don't think so."

The way he said her name, almost reverently, made her skittish. She turned away before he saw how it affected her. "I like this rocking chair."

"It's a *gut* one. Sit down."

She sat, and let her hands slide over the smooth wood planes. "It's lovely. It really is."

He looked fondly at it. "This one here is

for a mother in Berlin. She's expecting a *boppli*."

Whether it was his kindness or the reminder, she blurted, "My mom just told us that she's pregnant. That's why I was crying last Monday."

"Ah."

Catching his eye — still not very sure why she was even telling him so much — she added, "I was really upset. Devastated, really."

"Because you lost a baby of your own?"

She started. Over the past few months, she'd done her best never to talk about the miscarriage. Most everyone else she knew never mentioned it, either. But now, here was Robert, bringing it up in conversation. Like it was something that they should talk about.

Something that she should share. "Yes," she said slowly. "Because of that."

Robert regarded her a long moment before walking to stand next to another chair. The additional space between them gave her breathing room. She watched his brows furrow as he gave the rocking chair a little push. And then he looked directly her way. "Life isn't fair at all, is it?"

"No. I guess I shouldn't expect it to be, huh?"

"I wouldn't say that. All of us want happiness. Don'tcha think?"

Before she could come up with a reply, he turned and walked toward the door. Lilly scrambled to follow as they meandered their way out of his workshop, and then back into the open front room of his shop.

Suddenly, she was incredibly aware that only the pair of them were in the room. Alone. Together. And she'd just told him about her mother, and about her feelings about losing her own baby.

All without him asking. All without even being invited over! For sure, it was too much information, too quickly, and too soon.

Her cheeks burned. He probably couldn't wait for her to leave. Couldn't wait for her to stop acting like they had some kind of connection. They didn't. They were hardly even acquaintances, let alone friends.

It was a huge mistake to even have stopped by. She should have just kept driving. Gone home. Tried to make things better with her mother . . .

She should have stopped trying to imagine that there was something between her and Robert, something that counted. Stopped trying to think that they had anything at all in common . . .

51

"Lilly, do you have plans on Saturday?"

Her mouth went dry. "Saturday? No."

"Perhaps . . . maybe . . . Would you like to go to the farmer's market with me?"

"Sure," she answered. Fast. Probably too fast? "I mean, that sounds like fun." Robert looked pleased with her answer, though he wasn't smiling. No, the only difference was a twinkle in his eye. "Would you like to meet there?" she added.

"The farmer's market is a big place. How about you come here instead? Say, at two o'clock? The booths will still be busy then. After we see the shops we could maybe walk to the maze."

"All right. I'll be here at two. On Saturday."

He looked relieved. "*Sehr gut.* I mean, that's good. I'll see you then."

"All right." Without looking his way again, Lilly turned and ran out the door before Robert could take back his invitation.

Or before she could wonder what in the world had just happened.

CHAPTER 4

"Lilly, you've been running out of the house so fast these days. We haven't had a chance to talk," her mother said. "I think it's time we did."

"What is there to say?" Lilly murmured under her breath.

"Plenty, don't you think?"

Was that a question? It was phrased that way, but underneath was the steel thread of determination that nineteen years of experience led Lilly to believe was really a command. Biting her lip, Lilly sat down on the couch next to her mom. "We can talk now if you want."

"I think we should."

When Lilly had gotten home, the house had been suspiciously quiet. She'd found a note on the counter saying her family was attending a program at the grade school building.

It was a welcome relief. She'd showered

and pulled on a pair of old sweats. Then spent most of the evening watching old sitcoms on Nick at Nite.

Just as she'd been thinking about making popcorn, her parents had come in with Ty. He'd gone off to bed, and with hardly a word in her direction, her dad had walked to his office.

Looking her over, her mother's own blond hair glinted in the dim glow from the lamp on the table. "So . . . I'm sure you have feelings about the baby."

It was all Lilly could do not to roll her eyes. Uh, yes, she had feelings. But no amount of talking was going to help her sort them out. And no amount of talking was going to make her suddenly feel all excited and happy about her parents' new addition. "Not really. I was just surprised. But now that some time has passed, I'm okay with it."

Her mother laughed. "Dad and I were surprised, too. More than that, really. Shocked. Floored." She curved her hands around her tummy. "I never thought something like this would happen to me."

Lilly knew the feeling. "I bet." She shifted uncomfortably and mentally crossed off her original snack idea. This conversation needed something far more than popcorn.

It called for serious amounts of chocolate. As her mother sat there, all dreamy eyed, Lilly wondered just how much ice cream there still was in the freezer.

Completely unaware of the turn in Lilly's attention, her mother stretched out on the couch, looking like she wanted nothing more than to sit together, side by side. Chatting.

"I know you must be still mourning your loss. Even though —"

"Don't say it," Lilly interrupted.

"Don't say what? How do you know what I was going to say?"

All of her good intentions left her. Needing space, Lilly strode across the room and opened the freezer door. Peering inside, she mumbled, "Do we really have to play this game? I thought we were all going to try to be honest with each other."

"I'm trying to be."

Right behind two packages of frozen steaks, she found her goal. A brand-new, unopened container of Häagen-Dazs. Chocolate. After putting the pint on the counter, she turned back to her mom. "Mom, don't even think about telling me that my miscarriage was a good thing."

"I wasn't about to say that."

"But you thought it, didn't you?" As her

mother looked at her guiltily, Lilly said, "Mom, I wanted the baby. I'm sad it's gone. I will never think what happened was 'for the best.' "

In the span of two seconds, her mother's confident expression fell. "I know."

"Then why do you keep acting like I should be fine by now? That I should be over it?"

"I'm not. I'm just trying to get you to see my side of things."

"I do see. And I promise I'll do my best to be happy for you, but I'm not going to pretend it isn't hard." Softening her voice, she turned toward her mother. "Mom, all my life, you've been telling me to smile when I'm not happy. To chat with people I don't want to . . . to pretend everything is fine when it isn't. That might be how you want to live your life, but I can't do it anymore."

"Lilly, that's not how we act."

"Mother, we moved to keep my pregnancy a secret."

"We moved here for your father's job, too."

"Don't rewrite history. We moved here to hide my pregnancy. You're good at hiding things. You've known about this new baby for weeks and didn't think to tell me."

In a flash, her mother got up. "Lilly, we

didn't know how to tell you because I was afraid of having a conversation just like this. I was afraid to make you upset."

For the first time, Lilly noticed the fine lines around her mother's eyes. Noticed the new vulnerability in the tilt of her chin. And as she saw those things, she felt some of her anger fade.

And recalled what Robert had said. *Life wasn't fair.*

She needed to come to terms with that. No matter how much she complained, Lilly wasn't going to be able to make things the way she wanted them to be. She could never go back to just being Cassidy's best friend. She could never go to college and pretend that everything was fine. That she was just a typical nineteen-year-old with regular problems.

She was way older than that now. No, those days of being a carefree teen were behind her, no matter what the calendar said her age was.

That knowledge left her exhausted. "Listen, I'm going to take some ice cream and go to my room. I've got to work tomorrow."

As Lilly turned back to the counter to fill a bowl, her mom piped up, "Honey, things will get better. They always do."

The words resonated. "Do you really think that?"

"I do. I truly believe that time heals all pains." After a moment, she added, "And I truly think it's in our power to make positive choices. We can make things better, if we want them to be."

Lilly ached for her mother's words to be true. "Do you really think that we all have the ability to do something about our situation if we want a change?"

"Of course. What brought this on?" Her expression brightened. "Are you thinking about college? Because it's not too late to get you registered for the spring semester."

"I'm not thinking about college."

"Then what?"

"Nothing. Nothing, really. Don't worry about it. It doesn't concern you." Lilly turned away before she could see her mother's crestfallen expression.

Luckily, she didn't follow Lilly. Just let her run off with her ice cream to her room.

Whether she realized it or not, her mother's words had found their mark. She did have the power to make choices.

Maybe she was even getting strong enough to move on.

"Robert, shall we pick you up for the

farmer's market this afternoon?" Abe asked. He and Mary had stopped by the shop on their way to pick up some items at the Grabers' market.

"No. I'll see you there."

"No reason to go by yourself, Robert," Mary murmured. "We always enjoy your company. How about we stop by here at three o'clock?"

Taking a deep breath, he plunged in. "That's no good. I won't be here. I'm leaving here at two."

"Why are you going so early?"

"I'm taking someone."

"Robert! That's most exciting!" Mary exclaimed. "With whom are you going?" Before he could even open his mouth, she chattered on. "Is it Edith?"

"No." When would his family ever stop mentioning that widow?

"Who, then?" She gripped Abe's hand. "Is it Amanda? Amanda is a dear girl and she's always fancied you."

"Not Amanda." Because he knew Mary could continue the game for hours, Robert plunged ahead with the truth. "I'm taking an English girl."

Mary dropped Abe's hand as he scowled. "What are you talking about?"

"You heard me. I'm taking an English girl

to the market. Her name's Lilly Allen."

"The name sounds familiar . . ."

"It should. Don't you remember her parents? We met them when Lilly's brother Ty and Anson Graber got lost during the storm in the spring?"

"How could I ever forget that day? That was a terrible time. But I also remember hearing talk about her." A line of consternation formed between Abe's brows. "Wasn't she with child once? Out of wedlock?"

"She was."

"Then why would you spend any time in her company?"

"Don't act so judgmental, Abe. You know nothing about her."

"But do you?"

"I know some." He knew that she needed a friend as much as he did. He knew there was a spark in her eyes that drew him closer.

But he certainly wasn't in any hurry to share his thoughts.

Plus any talk about her pregnancy was her business, not his. Certainly not his cousin's.

Like a magpie, Abe kept pecking away at him. "Surely you don't know enough about her."

"I know that I asked her and she accepted," he said simply.

Mary looked alarmed by the way he was

shrugging off their concerns. "I think you're making a terrible mistake, Robert. If you are seen with Lilly Allen, people will talk."

"Then let them."

"But your parents will be most disappointed . . ." Her voice drifted off as she turned to her husband. "Abe, say something."

"*Nee*. Don't," Robert said sharply. He was doing his best to remember that his cousins were saying such things because they cared about him. They wanted him happy. But in truth, he was having a difficult time keeping his temper. "I thank you both for your concern, but it is unwarranted. I'm simply taking Lilly to the farmer's market. That's all."

"There's got to be more. She probably wants something from you."

Mary's words held a distrust of outsiders. A distrust that some kept close to their hearts, because they feared people who were different. But he'd never been one of those people who didn't want to visit with those who are different.

"She doesn't want anything from me. Now, I didn't ask you for your opinion, did I? Nothing is wrong with this. It surely doesn't feel that way. Right now, it feels like I'm finally doing something correct." He laid a hand on his cousin's arm. "I appreciate your concern, but don't pester me about this, Abe. I'm not trying to do anything funny. I just want to spend some time in the company of someone new. That's all."

Under Robert's restraining hand, Abe's arm stiffened. "Let's hope that is all."

"Goodbye, now. I have work to do."

They left, reluctantly. The moment the door closed, Robert walked to the workroom and picked up a hammer and a handful of nails. He'd been working on a rocking chair all morning and he meant to get it assembled by lunch.

But as his hands ran over the smooth grain of the wood and Abe and Mary's words echoed back to him, Robert found himself gazing into nothingness. Were Abe and Mary correct in their worries? Was he about to be inviting gossip and talk? Was it wrong to not only be thinking about an English woman, but one with a past like hers?

Had he completely lost all sense of right and wrong? Of who he was and what he wanted in life?

Or was it simply grief?

Though three years had passed, perhaps he hadn't moved on at all. Maybe his judgment was impaired by the pain of Grace's death. After all, he had been pushing his parents away.

He had ignored Abe and Mary's efforts to set him up with women. Suitable women.

Could he not be trusted any longer?

But as he carefully hammered a copper nail into a joint, a new clarity settled in.

No, he wasn't on the brink of making a terrible mistake. If anything, he was on the verge of grasping something more. Reaching for something more inspiring than he'd ever dared to hope for. If Grace were sitting by his side, counseling him, he knew what she'd be saying. *Finally, Robert.*

He smiled in spite of himself. Oh, but Grace had been an impatient woman! She'd hated to wait for anything, and watched the clock as closely as the busiest *Englischer* in the city.

He'd often thought that Jesus had asked her to join him early because He was afraid she'd chastise Him for calling her late.

No doubt she would've called such thinking fanciful. But she would have agreed it had merit.

No matter what, she had enjoyed living, and had lived each day to the fullest. No way would she ever have let other peoples' gossip keep her from what she wanted to do.

And no way would she have ever questioned something that she knew in her heart was right.

"I don't know why I can't stop thinking about Lilly," he said to the empty room. "It just happens."

Slowly, he picked up another nail and prepared to hammer it in. "For once, I am happy about the day. After weeks and weeks, and months, of only seeing a black cloud, now I'm looking forward to the day."

Of course, nobody answered him. But as he dug deep and smoothed the plane of wood again, he felt lighter.

For it had occurred to him that he didn't need anyone to reassure him. He was stepping out into his own self.

Just like it was a brand-new day.

CHAPTER 5

"I'm sorry you have to work all day, Caleb," Gretta said when she came downstairs from her apartment with her purse and cloak. "There's sure to be a lot of people at the farmer's market. After weeks of rain, everyone's eager to be outside."

Caleb looked at his sister-in-law with genuine fondness as she lumbered slowly down the stairs, holding the rails on both sides of the steps with a steady hand. With every day, she seemed to get a little bit bigger. Joshua had privately told him he was worried Gretta was carrying triplets.

"I don't mind working," he said when she joined him at the counter. "I wasn't planning to go to the farmer's market, anyway. Besides, Judith will be here soon to help."

"And Anson, too, I suspect."

"A lot of good that will do," Caleb muttered. "Anson is still more trouble than not."

"I hate to say it, but you are right about

that," Joshua said as he approached, stopping just short of Gretta.

Caleb watched as his brother curved an arm around his wife's stomach and held her close. They were a picture of contentment, which was good to see. Just months before, they'd had their own struggles.

After brushing Gretta's cheek with his lips, Joshua shook his head. "That Anson is a terrible lazybones, and that's the truth. Why, when I was ten, Daed had me here every Saturday morning with the dawn."

Those memories were still vivid. "I remember. Because then I had to take over your chores in the barn."

"Now our spoiled brother plays with Ty Allen while Cousin Tim waters the horses and cleans out the stalls in his stead."

"Mamm and Daed would have never let us be so lazy," Caleb agreed.

Gretta leaned into Joshua's arms as she grinned. "Oh, you two. Stop being so judgmental. Anson's fine. He's just his own person, you know."

"He's his own *lazy* person," Caleb corrected.

"It's time he accepted more responsibility." Joshua looked at Caleb. "You want me to say something to him?" asked Joshua. "I *could* stay."

66

"No, I've got it. Besides, Judith's just as irritated with his lazy ways. Carrie is following Anson's lead, so she's not doing much around the house, either."

Joshua grinned. "Hearing that makes me glad I have a home of my own." After kissing Gretta's cheek again, he murmured to his wife, "You ready?"

"Not quite yet. Don't forget, Margaret is going to meet us . . ."

As if on cue, the door opened, and in walked Gretta's little sister. "I'm sorry I'm late. Daed didn't want me driving the horse, so I had to walk." When she turned his way, she blushed. "Hi, Caleb."

"Hello, Margaret," he murmured, trying his best to ignore her stare. For a time now, he'd been aware that she had a crush on him. The idea was embarrassing. The last thing he wanted was an Amish girlfriend. However, she was nice and pretty, and Gretta's sister, so he didn't want to hurt her feelings. "Have fun at the market."

"Danke."

As Margaret cast another too-long look his way, Gretta winked at Caleb. "I think it's time for us to go."

Right before leaving the store, Joshua paused. "Caleb, I don't know if Daed has told you, but we've all noticed how much

67

you've taken on. You do a lot here, and you do it well. It's *gut*," he said simply.

Caleb didn't reply but, inside, he felt warm. Hearing praise was rare. It didn't happen too often. But when it did, he was as gratified as could be.

It was moments like this — when he and his perfect older brother Joshua felt in sync and his efforts were noticed — that Caleb wondered if he was making a huge mistake, wanting to leave the order. Maybe he already had everything he should want? Maybe he fit in more than he'd thought. The idea that he was settling into everything he'd been fighting so hard made his stomach knot.

But, then, he remembered the conversation he'd had with some boys at a recent singing. They had talked about the rumors circling Mrs. Miller. How she'd helped those Amish brothers make their way out of Sugarcreek. Those rumors had spiked his interest. Made him imagine the possibilities that could be in his life.

The door opened. "Good afternoon!" a trio of ladies chirped as they scattered through the store. Five minutes later, another crowd of tourists flew in.

And then finally, from the back, came Judith and Anson. Right away, Judith was all business, darting over to customers and helping them look at fabric. Anson, however, wore a disgruntled look. "Do I have to stay, Caleb? A bunch of kids are at the market."

"Of course you have to stay here and work," he replied. "This store is full."

"But you and Judith are here."

"Accept your responsibilities, bruder," Caleb snapped. "Both Joshua and I are tired of you acting like you're five." Before Anson could whine, Caleb pointed to a group of customers near the bulk food aisle. "Now, you go offer your help."

"But —"

"Now. And don't you dart off, either. You're going to need to help unbox the latest shipment of spices."

He wrinkled his nose. "I hate doing that."

"That hardly matters. You'll do it, and do it well, too. I'll be watching you."

With a scowl, Anson folded his arms across his chest. "You don't have to be so mean, you know."

Caleb mimicked his brother's militant stance. "You haven't even seen mean . . . yet."

When Anson finally did as he was told, Judith beamed and, moments later, walked over to join Caleb. "I can't tell you how happy I am that you said all that. He bellyached the whole way here."

"Joshua and I agree he's gotten lazy. I've had enough of everyone pampering him."

Judith chuckled, then smiled warmly. Two women began to ask for her help in the baked-goods section just as three people came to stand in line at the cash register.

Caleb rang them up with ease. Unlike Anson, he'd never been given the choice of how to spend his days.

Unlike Anson, he'd always had to do what was expected of him. Always. For a moment, he couldn't help but let envy float over him. What would his life be like if he'd had more chances to play? If he hadn't felt the strictures of this way of life so tightly? Would he still yearn to go away?

Of course, none of that mattered now. Dreaming about what-ifs didn't get things done. They only led to regret.

After practically slamming the front door behind her, Lilly rushed into Robert's workshop in a panic. "Am I late?" she asked. "If you've been waiting forever on me, I'm so sorry. First my mom started asking twenty questions about where I was going. Then I had to change clothes, and then there was traffic . . ." Lilly let her voice trail off as she caught hold of Robert's look. It was full of amusement. "Sorry."

"Don't be. I enjoy the way you always go on and on."

"*Always?* I don't always talk about nothing nonstop." A sinking feeling settled in as he continued to grin. "Do I?"

"Not so much." Right away, he led the way outside. After locking the front door, he walked her to his horse and buggy. "At least, not that I've noticed," he teased.

Lilly smiled right back at him for a moment before stepping carefully on the small metal platform that hung midway between the buggy and the ground. She swayed a bit. It was higher than she'd realized.

Robert reached out and took her arm. "Easy, now. Some say this step takes a bit of getting used to."

Feeling more secure now that he was holding her elbow with a firm grip, she scooted onto the bench covered in leather and tried to acclimate herself to the unfamiliar sensation of sitting in a contraption attached to a horse. When Robert easily hopped in next to her, he let go of the brake, then gave a low whistle to the horse. In no time, they were off.

As they clipped along, she felt the air flutter the curls in her hair and luxuriated in the first signs of autumn. Oh, she loved the way the leaves on the trees changed colors and the crisp scent of fall permeated the air.

"Your buggy's different than the Grabers'."

"How so?"

"There's no top. And no Plexiglas."

He smiled. "I have one of those at home. This here's called a courting buggy."

That caught her off guard. "Courting?"

A faint haze of red colored his cheeks. "Um, 'courting' is just a descriptive term," he mumbled. "See, this size is smaller than the one you see at the Grabers', and it's a bit spiffier."

Something told Lilly that he wasn't being completely honest. But since she already was feeling a little self-conscious by his side, she latched onto another descriptor. "Spiffier, huh?" She bounced a bit in the seat experimentally. "I like it."

"Me, as well." Just like he was in a car, he waited for a break in traffic, then turned right on the road. A flick of the reins brought them moving at a fairly quick pace. Of course, it was far slower than the cars zipping by.

Scooting toward him a bit, she murmured, "Hey, Robert? Can I ask you something?"

"Of course."

Now that she had his attention, she almost didn't dare ask it. But how could she not? "Robert . . . why did you ask me to go to the market with you?"

He glanced her way, before guiding the horse to a stop at a traffic light. "Truth?"

"Truth." She never failed to enjoy pushing his words right back at him. "I'm glad you asked me. I'm just curious."

"All right." For a moment, he looked to be gathering his courage. Lilly watched in some amusement as his cheeks puffed up. Finally he blurted, "The fact is, I don't know."

That surprised a laugh from her. "What?"

When the light turned green, he flicked his horse's reins. With a jerk, the buggy rolled forward. "That's the truth. There's something about you that has struck my fancy. I wanted to see you more. I wanted to get to know you more than just at work. There's only so much coffee a man can drink."

"Have you been coming to the inn so much because I worked there?"

"Did you really doubt it?"

"I never thought about it."

"If you never thought about it, why did you say yes, Lilly?"

His question was legitimate. What they

were doing wasn't a common occurrence, and no amount of pretending would change the fact that most Amish men and English girls did not go out together on a whim.

"Probably for the same reasons as you. I wanted to spend more time with you." Daring to be even more honest, she added, "When you asked, I didn't want to say no."

"I thought you might refuse me. A friendship between us, it would be unusual . . ."

"Probably." She fingered the denim fabric on her jeans. They were loose and dark. Far from the slim-fitting jeans she used to wear in high school. But they were jeans all the same. The long-sleeved T-shirt and fleece jacket were modest enough . . . but again, a far cry from the clothes Robert wore. From the dresses the women in his life wore. "On the surface, I'd say we are pretty different."

"We *are* different. But that is no surprise." He cleared his throat. "Even though I don't know why I asked, and you don't know why you said yes . . . even though we are so very different . . . I'm still glad you came."

"I am too," she murmured.

She said nothing more as they turned right again, and slowly made the way to an open barnlike structure lined with a large maze of booths, tables, and displays. As Robert guided his buggy, the buzz of people and activity sounded like a beehive.

All the activity was exhilarating. And a relief. The market was going to be too noisy to have another serious conversation. Too crowded to even try.

As she glanced at the array of people in attendance, Lilly was struck by the many differences among them. Amish. English. Young kids. Grandparents. Most were grouped in clusters of two or three. With the exception of families, most were walking with their own kind. Teenagers with other teens. Amish men together. She saw no pairs of English women and Amish men walking together.

Perhaps it was a natural thing to look for commonalities and be suspicious of differences. That's what she and her girlfriends had been taught to do. Look for friends who lived in the same area. Who attended the same schools. Who liked the same activities. Belonged to the same churches.

Although it wasn't said outright, it seemed the message was to stay away from people who were too different.

"We're here," Robert announced, shattering her reverie. He hopped out easily, then wandered over to his horse and tied her reins to a post.

Lilly slowly scrambled down and swung

her purse on her shoulder. As an after-thought, she picked up Robert's basket and looked out at the orderliness that was an Amish market.

Just beyond was a large cornfield. A hand-painted sign was posted at the front, inviting all gathered to try the maze. Smells of horses and hay and popcorn filled the air, reminding Lilly of a carnival.

She was excited. More excited about going with Robert on this simple outing than she had been about any activity in ages. "Where do you want to go first?" she asked in a rush. "What are you looking for? Anything special?"

He almost smiled. *"Nee."*

"Should we plan our route? I, for one, am hoping to find some quilt fabric. I'm going to give quilting a try."

"You'll find plenty of fabric and quilting supplies here." They walked two or three steps, then he suddenly stopped. "My cousin is here. With his wife."

"Okay," she said slowly. Robert looked incredibly ill at ease. "I'll look forward to meeting them."

If anything, he looked more pained. "They might not be *verra* kind. They tried to persuade me not to bring you here."

Lilly didn't have to ask why. "What do you

want me to do if they approach you?"

"Do? You can do whatever you want. Just be Lilly."

He looked so perturbed, she couldn't believe it. "Are you sure?"

"Very sure. I just wanted to warn you, that's all. They may not be especially friendly. I didn't want you to be offended."

"I won't," she promised. "Besides, I'm sure they're just curious about us."

"Oh, they're curious, all right."

His sarcastic tone made her laugh. "I get it. They don't want you keeping company with me."

"It's nothing personal."

"Then I won't take it personally. I'll smile and say hi. And nothing else."

To her surprise, he chuckled. "Again, it's not your behavior I'm worried about."

Together, they joined the throng of people, and as they walked from booth to booth, looking at Amish-made baskets and crafts, stacks of homegrown fruits and vegetables, and rows and rows of canned jams and jellies, they wandered slowly and pointed out little details. Lilly spied a puppy. Robert grinned at an old man enjoying a bright red licorice whip.

As the minutes passed, Lilly became less aware of how the pair of them must look to others and more focused on the man at her side.

Robert was a thoughtful man — seemed to have a kind word for most people — but he was also kind of standoffish. She knew instinctively that his behavior wasn't just because she was by his side. It was his nature to be a bit removed from the others.

They'd just purchased cups of freshly squeezed lemonade when he stiffened by her side. "Oh. Hello, Abe. Mary."

A group of five people, three men and two women, stopped right in front of them. "Robert," one said, completely ignoring Lilly. "So you decided to come after all?"

"I told you I would be here. It's no surprise."

"Robert, would you like to join us for dinner?"

"I already have plans." When he looked toward her, his gaze softened. "As you can see."

Though Lilly had just promised that no one's rude behavior would bother her, she slowly felt her nerves start to fray. It was awkward, standing there, half smiling. Waiting for someone to introduce her. Or, for them at least to acknowledge that she was standing there. But not a one of them did. Actually, all five of them seemed to be staring straight through her. As if she didn't exist.

Beside her, Robert looked uneasy. It was obvious he was embarrassed about their rudeness. "This is Lilly Allen," he blurted.

She raised a hand. "Hi."

Slowly, they all turned her way. One of the women nodded in her direction. Then, practically in unison, they looked away again. It would have been comical if she hadn't felt so bad for Robert.

A man about Robert's age spoke up. "So, Robert, will we see you at church tomorrow?"

"Of course."

"It's at the Grabers', you know."

"I haven't forgotten."

"We could pick you up."

"There's no reason to do that," Robert replied, his voice turning sharp. "I know my way to the Grabers'. I've never been late for services." Abruptly, he turned to her. "Lilly, there's some kittens down the way. Would you care to see them?" The look he gave her was almost pleading.

"Of course." She tried to smile at his friends again, but her lips froze as she caught their cool glares.

Continuing to look irritated, Robert led her down a row of booths. When they'd walked a good twenty steps, he stopped. "I know they were discourteous. However, I cannot apologize for them. I'm embarrassed, too. And, I promise, I had no part in their actions."

His honesty made her insides melt a bit. "I didn't mind. Well, not too much."

"Not too much?"

There was so much hope in his voice, so much doubt. So much of the same confusion she was feeling, Lilly knew she'd say anything to help ease the situation. "Actually, I think . . . I think I kind of understood." When he gazed at her in confusion, she attempted to explain. "The Grabers hadn't liked my friendship with Joshua at first. They were sure he was going to leave them all to be with me. But once they understood I wasn't a threat, they settled down. I, um, bet your friends will come to the same conclusions. Once they realize we're just friends. Now, are there really kittens over here?"

"Of course. I wouldn't lie to you."

"Then let's go see them. I have to tell you, I'm a sucker for kittens and puppies."

"What girl isn't?" He grinned, then pulled her toward the end of the row, pausing finally as he greeted an elderly man sitting next to a crate of eight kittens. "Eli, hello."

"Robert. Good day. And to you too, miss."

"Hi. May I step in and pet the kittens?"

"That's what they're here for." He waved a hand. "Come on in. They are desperate for a little bit of affection."

Lilly didn't need another bit of coaxing. She crouched down and gently petted a tiger-striped ball of fur.

Interested, the tiny cat turned and pounced toward her hand. Before long, the others had decided to play, too. Next thing she knew, she was sitting on the ground holding three cats. Another two were playing with the laces on her boots. "I love them," she murmured. "Thank you for taking me here."

As Robert watched Lilly, her expression turning soft and sweet, he was struck by the rush of tender feelings that were pooling inside of him. She was lovely, sitting there, holding two kittens up to her face.

She looked so happy.

"Would you like one?" he asked impulsively.

She blinked. "I couldn't —"

"Why not? Cats are not much trouble."

"My parents would probably get mad . . ."

"You sure? A kitten seems like a small enough thing." He smiled at his quip. The tiny kittens were definitely small.

Lilly looked at him for a moment, then, to his surprise, tears formed in her eyes. "You're right." Looking to Eli, she smiled. "Actually, I think I would like one. How much are they?"

"Not much. I only want reimbursement for the shots they need." He shrugged. "Twenty-five dollars?"

Robert pulled out his wallet. "Sold."

Lilly scrambled to her feet. "Wait! This is too much. I can't let you buy a cat for me —"

"I think he already is, English," Eli said.

Robert laughed. "Her name's Lilly."

"It's a fine name." Holding out his hand, he took the money and promptly put it in a wooden box by his side. "Get you a cat, Lilly."

Around her, the kittens were meowing and each looking at her with wide eyes. One tried to climb her boot. With a laugh, she pulled it off her laces, then held it up to her face. "Are you my cat?" She picked up another one, this one almost all black. "Or are you?"

Its four legs hung limply as it looked at her pleadingly. "Oh, Robert, they're all so cute! I can't decide." As a curl fell across her brow, she tried to blow it away. "I'm sorry. I bet you're ready to go . . ."

He was enjoying himself more than he could remember in years. It was a pleasure to watch someone be so happy over something so little. Leaning back against the fence, he grinned. "We're in no hurry. Take all the time you want, English."

Lilly wrinkled her nose. "You know, I should be upset with you for calling me that."

"Are you upset?"

She shook her head. "I'm not sure why, though."

He had a feeling he knew. There was a spark between them that pressed the bounds of the usual budding relationship. There was a connection between them that was tenuous.

No, what was forming between them wasn't all tender and sweet. Instead, there was a healthy dose of nervousness and ambiguity. Just standing next to her made his skin feel extra sensitive. Made all his senses a little bit heightened.

He was finding, with Lilly, even the smallest thing made him happy. Even talking with her. Or sitting by her side.

Luckily, Lilly seemed to be oblivious to all of that. No, he seemed to have slipped her mind as she sank back to her knees and gave each tiny fur ball her attention. "I just can't decide."

Eli laughed. "She might be needin' two, Robert."

"Maybe so." He'd buy her all the kittens, if that was what it took to keep that expression of pure bliss on her face.

"I heard that. I definitely won't need two cats." She worried her bottom lip as both kittens purred and played. "Robert, I promise, I'm almost ready. I just need a few more minutes, that's all."

"Take your time."

"They'll probably decide for you, *jah?*" Eli said. "That's what usually happens, I think. The right things find us instead of the other way around."

"I have a feeling that is true," Robert said.

Around the corner, four children scampered close. "Kittens!" Without waiting to ask permission, they barreled in.

The look of panic in Lilly's eyes was priceless as the eager balls of fur rushed to the children in excitement. All except for the little black kitten. It stayed by her side. After pawing at her jeans, it hopped on her lap. Seconds later, Lilly was cuddling it close to her chest.

"Ah. She's found you, Lilly," Eli said with an especially pleased smile. To Robert, he winked. "Told you it would happen."

As two children looked about to reach for it, Lilly placed one arm over the cat protectively. Slowly, she stood up. "Robert, this is the one. If you're sure . . ."

"I'm sure. It's bought and paid for."

"She's going to be well loved."

He grinned at that.

After another moment, they walked away, much slower now that Lilly was cradling the tiny cat. "Oh, Robert. Look how she's just sitting here. I think she's about to fall asleep!"

Making a sudden decision, Robert led her to another booth, where baby blankets had been hand-tied in a fuzzy flannel. "We'll need one of these, Gwen," he said, and handed over a ten-dollar bill. Then, he led Lilly to a spot away from everyone.

As she watched, he carefully stuffed the blanket into the basket he'd been carrying, and put the sleeping kitten inside. "Now she's snug."

Lilly's eyes glowed. "You're doing too much for me."

"Not so much." Robert paused as he caught a whiff of Lilly's cool, clean scent. His pulse beat a little bit faster as it surrounded him.

Ach, but she was getting it all wrong. In truth, he was the one who was getting so much out of their time together. For the last few years, he'd felt hollow inside. So empty of emotions that he'd sometimes wondered if he was never going to feel again.

But Lilly's appearance in his life had changed that. Now, when he looked at her, he felt a longing that was so strong, it took his breath away. A part of him wanted to hold her close, protectively, so she never would feel pain or hurt again.

But yet another part of him wanted to do far different things than simply hold her close. He wanted her in his arms. He wanted to kiss her. He wanted to run his hands through her curls. He wanted to press his lips to the pulse point on her neck. To wrap his arms around her . . .

He wanted to feel love. But of course, he could never say such things. Certainly, he could never act on them.

"Buying you the cat makes me happy," he said simply. "I'm glad you like it."

"I love it. This is the best day ever."

He agreed. He was glad he'd ignored Abe's warnings and had followed his instincts. "There's popcorn over there. Maybe caramel apples, too. What say you we get some?"

"I'd like that very much."

Lifting the basket, he handed it to her.

"You carry the cat. I'll lead the way."

For a moment, their eyes met. Her usual laughing brown eyes clouded for a moment. Filled with something more . . . something full of promise. Her lips parted slightly.

He couldn't look away. It had been too long since he'd kissed a woman.

It had been so very long since he'd kissed Grace.

Then she swallowed and hugged the basket. "That's a great idea," she murmured. "You lead and I'll follow."

Robert turned away and walked ahead. Perhaps if he did that, he wouldn't catch her scent again.

Or dwell on his sudden urge to hold her hand.

On his sudden urge to taste her lips.

CHAPTER 6

Used to be, she would have called home to ask for permission to have a cat. And, if her parents had told her no, Lilly would've listened and told Robert that she couldn't accept his gift, no matter how badly she wanted to cuddle a tiny six-week-old kitten.

But that was not the case anymore. She'd grown up. And though she'd only recently turned nineteen, and though she was still living with her parents, Lilly felt as mature as any other woman in Sugarcreek.

Having a miscarriage did that to a person.

After sharing a bag of piping hot popcorn, but skipping the caramel apples, they wandered down another aisle of the market. Every so often, they stopped and inspected a homemade craft or a farmer's fall bounty.

As she cuddled the tiny ball of fur close, Lilly knew she needed that cat more than she'd needed just about anything else in her life. And as it looked at her with its sweet black-as-midnight face, her heart melted. In mere seconds, she'd fallen in love.

Beside her, Robert fidgeted. "What would you care to do now?" he asked.

"Anything. I'm happy doing whatever you want to do now."

"Now? What do you mean?"

Finally depositing the kitten into the basket, she shrugged. "Oh, you know. First, you bought me a kitten, and then you bought us popcorn. Just a few minutes ago, you stood there patiently while I looked at quilting material. I'm sure there's other things you'd like to do."

When he still looked confused, Lilly explained, though she was starting to feel pretty silly. "I just don't want you to be bored." But even as she said that, she knew she meant something far more personal. What she really meant was that she didn't want him to regret taking her out.

His blue eyes gleamed. "This trip to the market is my gift to you. I am happy just being by your side."

His words were so earnest, her mouth went dry. "I see."

"*Gut.* Now, where would you care to go next?"

His complete attention on her needs made her flustered. Never before had she been with a man who was so focused on her happiness. "So it's all about me?" she joked.

"Of course."

If she was more comfortable with him, Lilly would have grabbed his hand and dragged him to the stall selling handmade Amish dolls, just to watch him attempt to look interested.

If things between them were different, she would have told him that she wanted to look at the home remedies for colds — and the newest home cleaners, too.

She would have laughed and teased him, and done her best to make him laugh, too.

But that wasn't who they were. And because he was Amish and older and widowed . . . because she was just nineteen and English and had become pregnant out of wedlock . . . things between them could never be much more than what they were. She didn't want to indulge fantasies that could never come true.

A keen sense of loss rushed over her until she shook it off. Really, it didn't matter what they were to each other. She didn't need another boyfriend. And Robert could sure do better than her.

Finally Robert made a suggestion. "Perhaps you'd like hot chocolate?"

She wasn't really in the mood for a hot

drink. But perhaps he was? "OK. I mean, thanks, that sounds great." After checking that the kitten was still happily asleep, Lilly walked by his side down the crowded, busy paths of the market.

"Do you ever sell things here, Robert?"

"I used to."

"What did you sell? Your furniture?"

"Oh, no. Nothing that big," he replied with a wry smile. "Those chairs would have been hard for me to cart back and forth. No, when I was younger, I used to carve smaller, less practical items for places like this."

As they passed a booth selling wooden trains, she grabbed hold of the idea. "Toy trains?" she prodded. She really was interested. She wanted to know everything she could about him. The way he rarely spoke about himself intrigued her. The way he never bragged or sought to be the focus of conversation made her want to know every little thing about him that she possibly could.

He chuckled. "No trains. I leaned more toward coat hooks and bread boxes." He shrugged. "I did fairly well with that."

"But . . . not anymore?"

"No. When Grace and I got married, she encouraged me to follow my dreams."

91

"Which was furniture making."

His voice warmed. "Yes. Grace, she was right beside me when I made my first table and chairs. She led me to believe that they were good enough to show off and sell, too." He paused for a moment, looking far off, into his memories.

When Robert looked at Lilly again, there was a hint of sadness in his gaze. "Grace was so happy when I sold that set, she spun in a circle with her arms stretched out. It was . . . it was a sight to see."

"I bet she was really proud of you," Lilly murmured.

"Perhaps she was."

Without her hardly realizing it, they'd stopped and were standing at a booth in front of a pair of teenage girls. "Two hot chocolates, Katie," Robert said, pulling out a pair of dollars.

One of the girls carefully poured their drinks into Styrofoam cups, the other took the money, then squirted whipped cream on top.

After exchanging a few words with them in Pennsylvania Dutch, Robert handed a cup to her. "Thanks." She took an experimental sip. The drink was piping hot and creamy and smooth. She was glad she'd gotten some after all. "Oh, wow. It's been ages since I've had homemade hot chocolate."

"You should make some, then, *jah?*"

"I guess you're right." She was just about to add something more when she spied Josh and Gretta. "Hey, Josh is my neighbor," she said when their eyes met. "Robert, do you mind if we go say hi to them?"

"Of course not."

But Lilly noticed that he didn't rush to see Gretta and Josh the way she did. Was it because he had no need to hurry? Or because he was worried about what they would think about them being out together?

"What brings you here?" Josh asked when she and Robert made their way over to them.

"Robert asked me if I wanted to come and I said yes. It sounded like fun."

Josh blinked. "I didn't realize you two knew each other."

"Oh, we do. You come to the restaurant all the time, don't you, Robert?"

"Only sometimes . . ."

Before he could stumble out more words, Gretta spoke again, smiling at Lilly and Robert. "And are you two having fun?"

"Yes," Lilly replied. "Very much so." When Joshua simply stared, she looked from one man to the other. "You do all know each other, right?"

"Jah."

"We do," Robert said.

Again, it was Gretta who seemed intent on smoothing things between them. "We all know each other, of course, Lilly. Now, what is that in Robert's basket?"

"He bought me a kitten."

Gretta's face softened as she reached out a finger and gently rubbed the kitten's fur. "She's a sweetheart, for sure. And look how glossy and shiny her black fur is! Why, I don't see a speck of white."

"Jah," Joshua agreed. "It's a right, fine cat." But Lilly noticed his voice was strained . . . and that there was a thick coat of tension between him and Robert. Josh kept looking at Robert in a funny way, and seemed almost tentative toward her.

"Josh, is everything all right?" she asked.

"I'm not sure."

"What are you talking about?"

"Nothing that can be said here."

Gretta's chin lifted. "Everything is *perfectly* fine. Joshua is being silly."

"Perhaps," her husband murmured.

When Robert said nothing, only continued to look pained, Lilly stepped toward Josh. She knew what was wrong — he didn't like her with Robert. He didn't like the two of them as a pair.

But he wasn't her father, and she sure didn't need his permission or acceptance to go to the farmer's market with a friend. "Stop acting like this," she chided. "I'm not doing anything wrong, you know."

"Perhaps not."

"Perhaps?" She placed her hand on his arm. "Josh, I can't believe you're acting like this. I've done my best to be supportive of you, you know. I thought that's what friends did."

"Friends do . . . but there's other things to think about, too."

"Such as?" But instead of replying, he turned away. With the movement, her hand fell. "Josh. Gretta. You've got to tell me, what's wrong?"

"Nothing at all," Gretta said. "Joshua is just being silly. Don't mind him, Lilly. Please, don't."

Gretta sounded too reassuring, making Lilly feel completely off balance. Just earlier that year, it had been Joshua who had been struggling with his relationships. He'd leaned on Lilly for support, and she'd been happy to be there for him. But now it felt like he was completely abandoning her.

Just as Lilly was struggling with what else to say, Josh spoke again. "Gretta, we must get going. Margaret is with her friends at the other side of the market, isn't she? We best go check on her, especially since we said she could stay with us tonight."

After giving an apologetic glance toward both Robert and Lilly, Gretta nodded. "Yes, I suppose we should go check on Margaret. I'll see you all later." She treated them to another apologetic smile, then followed her husband back down the row of shops.

Robert handed Lilly the basket. "Perhaps we should leave now, too."

He looked distressed, and Lilly knew it was because of Josh's reaction. Josh could hardly have been ruder, and she knew Robert was perfectly aware of how he'd sounded.

Josh's attitude irritated her to no end. She really thought they were better friends than that. In addition, she was sick and tired of everyone casting judgments on everything she was doing. Life was too hard to constantly monitor what everyone was saying about her. Especially when she hadn't been doing anything wrong.

Determined to salvage the afternoon as best she could, she nudged Robert's shoulder. "Hey, I thought this little outing was all about me."

"You're not worried about what Joshua and Gretta are thinking?"

"No. At least not right now. Robert, I was having fun with you. Can't we just try to go back to having fun? I haven't had a whole lot of fun doing anything lately."

At first Robert looked flabbergasted. But then seconds later, humor filled his gaze again. "Of course, you're right. What do you want to do?"

She'd had enough shopping. What she really wanted was to erase the lines of worry and stress that had popped up on his brow. "Perhaps we could go to the corn maze?"

"You still want to go?"

"Of course. Let's go before it gets dark."

"All right, then." Robert led the way, but she couldn't help but notice that he didn't seem especially enthusiastic.

After his relatives' cold looks, and now Josh and Gretta's strange reaction, Lilly had a feeling he would have felt relieved if they'd just left. But she was determined to lighten his mood. At least for a little while.

Robert paid the farmer the three dollars each to enter the maze and, with a basketful of kitten, walked in. Almost immediately, they had to choose between going right or left. "Which way should we go?" he asked.

"I don't care."

Already, the noise surrounding them became muted. The high rows of corn prevented them from seeing anyone else. For the first time ever, it felt like they were the only two people in the world.

Lilly's pulse raced as a new kind of friction fluttered between them. This one had nothing to do with awareness of their differences.

Or of how their relationship was viewed by others. No, this time, it had everything to do with a surprising feeling of promise that rose between them. A hint of suspicion that something more was destined to take place . . . that like a runaway train, it was going to happen, no matter what.

"Left," she finally said.

"Then left we shall go."

Beneath their feet, the hard-packed dirt was strewn with hay and corn husks. The dusty smell mingled in the air. Soon, they came to another fork in the path. This time it was Robert who made the choice. "Left again."

Their pace slowed as over and over again they made decisions about turning left or right. Laughter from other maze adventurers floated up toward them. Once, they almost crashed into a cornstalk when two boys raced around a curve and nearly knocked them over.

The vivid blue sky overhead gently faded

into a lapis hue; and the moon appeared in the distance, bright and orange. A true harvest moon.

Soon it became obvious that they were nowhere near the exit. "I fear we're lost," Robert murmured when they took a break on a pair of upturned barrels in order to try to get their bearings.

"Hopelessly," she agreed.

"Should we try to go back to where we came from?"

She laughed. "Do you even know any longer? I feel like we've been everywhere in this maze except the right direction."

His lips curved upward. With a shrug, he said, "Let's continue, then. Sooner or later, we'll get out."

"I'm okay with it being later . . . I'm not in any hurry." And she wasn't. This was the first time all afternoon that they'd actually relaxed. It was the first time she felt like they could do what they wanted, say what they wanted . . . without a dozen pairs of eyes and ears taking notice.

"You know what? I'm not, either."

They got up from the barrels and walked farther, this time worrying less about the right ways and caring more about companionship. As the sky darkened and almost all traces of other voices disappeared, Robert reached out for her hand.

She took his immediately. "You lead the way."

His hand tightened on hers as they wandered some more. "Would you think it strange if I said I was having a good time? We're lost and confused and carrying around a cat." He shook his head. "By all accounts, I should be feeling completely at a loss. Irritated," he murmured after they made another two right turns.

As they stood in front of a row of corn and looked at the tiny opening, Lilly grinned. "I feel the same way. I've never really enjoyed corn mazes. I always thought they were too tame."

"And I found them frustrating. I've been the kind of man who likes a straight path to where I'm going."

His words shook her. *The kind of man.* As they continued on, walking slower and slower, Lilly found herself examining Robert from the corner of her eye.

Yes, he was a man. A grown-up. Mature. As far away from the boys she used to date as possible. With some surprise, she realized that she no longer even thought about boys her own age. She had no interest in boys whose whole world revolved around studies and football games. The last year had shaped her into a woman far older than her years. She'd gained wisdom and also a bit of impatience for things that didn't matter to her.

Now, though she was only a waitress, she seemed to relate best with other people who were working, too. Who were struggling to find themselves, or who were attempting to make something productive out of their dreams.

"I'm having more fun getting lost than just about anything I've done in a long time," she said as they crossed through another narrow opening and only came to another two routes. "This is the most complicated corn maze I've ever seen in my life. Whoever designed this should get a prize."

Beside her, Robert looked bemused. "I'm afraid the complications are all of our making, Lilly. Listen."

Sure enough, a steady stream of cheers erupted as yet another batch of people steadily found their way out.

When they heard a boy shout that it had only taken him four minutes to go from start to finish, Lilly giggled. "Well, that's humbling, I suppose."

"Terribly." With a new look of intensity, Robert stopped and fingered a stalk to his right. "Does this cornstalk look familiar to you?"

He looked so earnest, she couldn't help but laugh. "Oh, Robert!"

"I'm serious. I think I recall this ear of corn —" His voice was cut off by a fluttering of wings overhead. In a flash, a black crow flew near, almost dive bombing them in its hunt for tasty kernels.

Lilly ducked. "Oh!" she cried, impulsively leaping toward Robert.

Above, the bird squawked.

She was afraid of birds. Especially big, bold black ones that were out of cages. Heart racing, she reached for him, pressing her forehead to his chest in an effort to hide from the bird. Clung to him in a burst of panic. Positive that bird was going to come back and swoop down close again.

But it, of course, was already out of sight.

When the quiet settled in again, Lilly closed her eyes in mortification. "I'm so sorry," she murmured, lifting her head to meet his gaze. "I don't know what I was thinking."

"Perhaps that you were afraid?" he said gently.

Then she noticed that the kitten-filled basket was on the ground.

And that his hands weren't at his sides.

No, they were resting on her back. And his arms were holding her close. Protectively.

And he didn't seem to be in any great hurry to let her go.

She shivered. But it wasn't from fear. It was from his touch. And the rush of emotion that flew through her. Her muscles turned languid. Her body relaxed.

All of its own accord.

He misread her trembling. "It's all right," he murmured. "It was just a bird, and it didn't harm us. And it's long gone, now."

"I . . . a crow pulled at my hair when I was a child," she said, doing her best to concentrate on their conversation. Not the turmoil of emotions that was sweeping through her. "Ever since then, I've been unnaturally afraid of them."

Instead of releasing her, he rubbed a reassuring hand along her spine. "Especially blackbirds, I imagine."

"Yes." Then any further talk stuck in her throat as she realized she was still pressed against him. So close that her feet were in between his — which he must have spread in order to hold her more securely.

Robert was taller than she was. Taller by a good four or five inches. His arms around her were strong enough to make her feel like she was the most protected woman in the world.

But it was his eyes that took her breath away. He was gazing at her in such a way that she couldn't look away at all. "So blue," she murmured. "Your eyes are so blue. Like Ty's marbles," she added, trying to find a proper way to describe them. Like they needed describing.

Like a man even cared about what exact color his eyes were.

Especially when he was about to kiss a girl. Robert brushed his lips against hers, carefully, as if she would break if he wasn't careful. His beard grazed her cheek and jaw, bringing a tingle.

She was startled for a moment.

But then she kissed him back. His lips were firm and cool and tender. She tilted her head and relaxed against him. Enjoying the feel of his lips on hers. Enjoying the feel of his arms around her. Of being held.

A squeal in the distance broke them apart.

Stumbling backward, Lilly pressed a hand to her lips. But that hand did nothing but remind her of the way he'd made her feel. Like she was desirable.

No, that wasn't it, exactly. That one kiss, so chaste in many ways, had made her feel like she was special.

Worthwhile. A trembling sigh escaped her.

Lowering her hand, she met his eyes.

He was staring at her in shock and breathing deeply.

His hat had gotten displaced. He rearranged it without a word. Lilly reached down and picked up the basket. Miraculously, the kitten was still sleeping.

"I . . . I think the right way to go is left," he finally said. "We're near the outside now. Most likely, minutes away."

"I . . . I hope so. We've been in here too long." She averted his eyes, afraid to look at him now. "If all else fails, we can just cut through a row of corn."

"*Jah.*"

Feeling off center, she started chattering. "I bet, before we know it, we'll be out of here. I don't know about you, but I am glad about that. All of a sudden, I'm feeling kind of warm."

Ahead of her Robert kept walking, saying nothing.

Nerves took over and she chattered again like a magpie. "It is so warm in here, I bet it will be twenty degrees cooler as soon as we get out. I bet that breeze is going to feel so good, too."

He pointed. "I think we go through this opening, and then turn right. We're almost out."

"Great. I mean, that's good. I mean, it's about time."

He looked at her before disappearing through the stalks. "Yes. It is."

She felt stunned and embarrassed and her heart felt like it was going a mile a minute. Regrets poured through her like water. She shouldn't have gotten so scared of a bird. She shouldn't have clung to him.

She shouldn't have even agreed to go to the market.

She shouldn't have accepted the kitten.

She shouldn't have kissed him back.

This date of theirs was such a mistake. A mistake of huge proportions, and she was probably going to regret it forever.

Walking behind him, she finally saw the exit. Robert was already standing outside, his head tilted slightly up in the breeze, his face as solemn as if they were at a funeral.

When she joined him, she did the same thing. Closed her eyes and enjoyed the fresh breeze that floated around her — cooled her off. But though her skin felt relief, her insides didn't.

Because . . .

She knew if he turned and pulled her close, she'd kiss him right back. Already, she was eager for his touch again.

The thought shamed her.

This was not a good thing. Not good at all.

CHAPTER 7

"What in the world is going on with you, Caleb?" his mother asked as soon as he came in from gathering eggs. "Nowadays, it seems I must ask you something twice or even three times." One eyebrow rose. "Sometimes even more than that. And still you do not listen."

Stunned by his mother's harsh words, Caleb halted in the doorway of the kitchen. If his mother's glare had been full of fire, he would have been charred in his steps for sure.

Most of the time when she fussed, he knew exactly what she was upset about. But not in this instance. Today, for the life of him, he couldn't imagine what he'd done wrong.

Caleb was sick and tired of being yelled at. Carefully, he set the metal pail of eggs on the countertop. He used to gather eggs before school. Now it should be Anson or

Carrie's turn. He was too old for the chore.

But his mother had seen no reason for the others to take it on, even though all of them knew the hens had a special dislike for him.

The feeling was mutual. Three of the hens were so ornery, he continually hoped he'd be eating them for dinner. "Now what are you upset about?"

His *mamm*'s already thunderous expression turned darker. "That tone is unnecessary. You best take care with how you talk to me, son."

Well, he didn't appreciate her tone, either. No one liked getting yelled at the minute they walked in the door. "I would take care, if I was even sure what to say."

"What is that supposed to mean?"

"It means I'm not even sure how to talk to you anymore. You find fault with everything I say and do."

"That is not true." She pointed to a spot not a full foot from where she stood. "And come closer, Caleb. I don't care to yell at you across the room."

Though that had been exactly what she'd been doing, he complied. Almost. He stepped into the always clean kitchen but not nearly as close as she'd indicated. "Mother, what specifically is wrong?"

"*Specifically?*" She scowled. "What is

wrong is that you promised your father and me that you would chop wood this morning and then deliver it to the store. You have not."

Guilt passed over him, hot and stark. She was right. He'd completely forgotten to chop wood. He'd gotten hung up in the barn, cleaning up the stalls and watering the horses. And then he'd realized that Anson had not filled the grain and oat bins for the chickens like he'd been told to.

Which had led Caleb to inspecting the other animals' cages and discovering other places of neglect. Caleb was more than ready to wring his little brother's neck . . . but not so prepared to tell on him. Joshua had rarely told on him when he still lived at home and Caleb had always appreciated that.

"I'll go chop the wood now."

"Gut." She turned away and picked up a handful of vegetables from the sink without another word. And though Caleb was hungry enough to snatch that carrot she was chopping, he turned away and left again.

Two hours later, sweaty and practically starving, he drove the wagon to the store and stacked wood. Joshua was helping a customer, but nodded his thanks.

Then, before Anson showed up or his

father caught sight of him, Caleb walked down to Mrs. Miller's home. He needed a break from his family so badly he could taste it.

Only after knocking on the door did Caleb look at himself. He was covered in wood chips and dirt. His hands needed a good scrub, and he most likely smelled, too. He shouldn't have rushed to the woman's house without so much as washing his hands.

He was just about to turn around when Mrs. Miller opened the door.

Instead of looking put out by his mess, she stepped backward. "Caleb, what a nice surprise! Come in."

Conscious of his dirty boots, he hesitated. "Maybe I shouldn't . . ."

"Why not?" Looking him over with concern, she murmured, "What's wrong? Are you all right?"

"I'm fine. But I just realized the state I'm in." Now even more embarrassed about his appearance, he mumbled, "I've been doing chores all morning, but didn't realize I look the worse for it. I, um, shouldn't have come over like this."

"You don't look so bad." A trio of lines formed around her eyes as she looked him over. "Just in need of a wipe down, maybe."

"Yes. I'll go do that."

"You can get cleaned up here. And, Caleb, what is it that you need?"

"I was hoping that maybe you could spare me some time."

To his profound relief, she chuckled. "I have lots of time for you, always. That is, if you don't mind watching me can for a bit. I've been making applesauce all day."

"I don't mind." He followed her into her kitchen, wondering what it was about this woman's home that calmed him. His sister-in-law Gretta often said that she couldn't think of a better home than the Grabers'.

Why was he always so discontented there?

In a matter of moments, Mrs. Miller placed a large chunk of banana bread and a glass of milk on the wide kitchen table. "Grab a towel and clean up, Caleb. Then come have a snack. And you may tell me what's on your mind."

After washing his hands, he wolfed down the bread in just four bites. Instead of chastising him, Mrs. Miller merely cut off another generous portion and placed it in front of him.

"Now, then. Relax."

Her gentle manner always soothed him. Finally, he took his time about eating. Enjoying the silence of the room and the lack of tension as well. After what seemed like an eternity, after his last gulp of milk, he spoke. "I've still been thinking about leaving Sugarcreek. About leaving my order."

"Do you know where you want to go?"

He liked how again she didn't start telling him how horrible he was. How he didn't know his own mind. "I was thinking of Cleveland. It's close. Our neighbors the Allens are from there."

"Ah." She efficiently filled another three jars, and then used tongs to pull the lids out of boiling water. Then, with a cloth, she tightened the metal lids securely. "And what do you plan to do when you get to Cleveland?"

"I'm not sure."

After a pause, she said, "You might want to do some thinking about that."

"What is there for me to do? I guess I'll have to work."

"Yes. Or maybe you could go to school for a bit. If that interests you . . ."

"There's no place for me in the school. I only finished the eighth grade, you know. Lilly and Charlie Allen told me that they learned a lot in high school." He knew his lack of schooling would stick out like a sore thumb. Plus, he figured a person had to have a nearby address in order to attend. He didn't have anything like that.

"What kind of work would you do?"

"Work in a store, I guess. Or maybe help with carpentry or something."

"So you know a lot about woodworking?" His shoulders slumped. "No. Not a lot."

"Why are you so determined to get away? You're still in your *rumspringa*."

"Even right now, I'm finding things to be awfully confining. And no matter how much experimenting I do, things around here aren't going to change anytime soon."

With another pair of tongs, she carefully placed a line of jars in boiling water. Caleb knew that after five or ten minutes, she'd take them out, then they'd hear the telltale pop that signified that the seals were secure.

As the jars boiled, Mrs. Miller darted a look his way again. "Caleb, a few years ago, I helped a pair of brothers leave their order. I suppose you heard about that?"

He nodded.

She sighed. "It's not something I'm proud of doing. But, well, I knew the boys were going to leave anyway. With or without my help. They were having an awful time at home. Their father was abusive, and they had a lot of anger. In short, they were desperate. Do you know what I'm saying?"

She peeked his way.

"I do."

"I guess what I'm asking is — is that the state you are in? Desperate?"

"Desperate? No." All he really wanted was a break from his family. Nothing at home was horrible.

But if things weren't that bad, then why did he want to leave?

Slowly, Mrs. Miller said, "When I helped those boys, their parents were upset with me, and rightly so."

"Is that why you're not Amish anymore?"

"Partly. Nothing was said outright. And . . . you, Caleb, are the first person I've actually told. So I wasn't exactly shunned, but I definitely was out of everyone's favor." Haltingly, she added, "I've been lucky that I've had no trouble keeping boarders through the years. They've kept me company. But, it's not the same as being a part of the community."

"So you won't help me leave?"

"Right now? No. I don't think you're ready." Her voice softened. "But perhaps you should speak to your parents about how you're feeling. Your parents are good people. They might have some ideas for you. Maybe even more ideas than you can imagine."

"Like what?" All Caleb thought they'd do

115

was tell him to go gather more eggs and chop wood.

"Perhaps they could let you leave for just a time? Some teens do that, you know."

"And do what?"

"I don't know. Maybe stay with some friends of the Allens for a month? Then you would know if living with the English is the right thing for you."

"I could never do that." Just the thought of being somewhere temporarily gave him a stomachache.

Still working, she carefully lifted jars out of the water and placed each one on a row of folded towels. "Could never or don't want to?"

"It's the same thing, really."

She walked around the counter and rested a hand on his shoulder. "I don't think so."

"I had hoped you would make things easier for me."

"I know." A sad smile lit her face. "But I promise you this, everything you are considering *is* difficult. If you imagine not living at home is going to make your life easy, you are much mistaken. If you leave your family, your home, and everything you hold dear, you should be prepared to know what you intend to reach out and grab a hold of."

"How can I know? How am I supposed to know? This — working in Sugarcreek, working on our farm — this is my life. I don't know much about the outside world at all."

To his surprise, she didn't soften. "Don't play me for a fool, Caleb Graber. Ignorance and naiveté can only go so far. And I've never thought you were full of either trait. If you leave here, you will be leaving all your security and protection. You'll be an outsider, and subject to much more than you are dreaming of now. And everyone you meet won't care about your confusion. All they'll do is attempt to take advantage of it." A hint of a secret pain darkened her eyes. "And they will. Trust me on that one. They will."

For a second, he was tempted to ask what had happened to the brothers she'd helped. If their lives had become even harder after leaving.

But part of him was afraid to know. Before, all he'd cared about was that two boys had gotten out. Now, though, she'd given him something more to think about.

What if things weren't any better in the outside world? What if they were even harder? The thought of that made his stomach churn.

"Thank you for the banana bread," he

mumbled.

"You are welcome. Come back anytime, Caleb. You are always welcome here."

He turned away before she could see the flush he knew was staining his cheeks. The things she had told him didn't make him feel any better. If anything, they'd only made his situation worse.

Right at that moment, he didn't know if he'd be in any hurry to stop over there again.

He'd come to the restaurant again. Lilly fought a suspicious onslaught of nerves as she approached his table. It didn't help that he seemed to be silently watching her every move. "Hi."

"Good morning," he said politely.

"Would you care for some coffee?" She felt slightly silly. The two of them were acting like they hardly knew each other. But she didn't feel comfortable enough yet to gauge his moods.

"Sure."

"And pie or a cinnamon bun?"

"Just coffee, Lilly. And, perhaps, you could spare me a few moments?"

"Of course." She waved a hand around. "There's no one else here. I'll, um, be right back."

She hurried to the drink station and poured Robert a mug of coffee. On the other side of the picture window leading into the kitchen, she heard Miriam chuckle. Oh, her friend would have a lot to tease her about when he left!

"Here you go, Robert," she said, trying to find the right combination of friendliness and warmth in her voice. "It's fresh."

He took the cup from her as she sat down across from him. "It's hot," he said with a smile. "Though . . . I don't suppose it really matters."

"Why is that?"

"I came here to see you, of course."

She felt her skin flush. Okay. So they were being honest. "I'm glad you stopped by. I had a good time at the farmer's market. And I love my kitten."

Those clear blue eyes of his warmed. "I'm glad." A moment passed. He sipped his coffee, looking like he was searching for something else to say. "I got an order for a hope chest today. In oak."

"You are certainly keeping busy."

"Jah." He frowned. "I mean, yes." He sipped his coffee again.

Behind her, the bells at the door rang. More customers arrived. "I better get to work."

"Yes. I guess you should."

She stood up. "I'm glad you came by, Robert. I'm very glad." She turned away before she could see his expression. But she hoped it was happy. And more than that, she hoped he would stop by again. Walking up to the couple standing at the hostess desk, she smiled. "A table for two?"

"Three. My husband's parking the car."

As Lilly walked them to their table, she passed Robert on his way out the door. She could have imagined it, but she thought he reached out and brushed her shoulder with his hand as they passed.

It was the simplest of touches. But she still felt it all the same.

Robert Miller knew he was mooning over Lilly Allen like a lovesick pup. It was embarrassing. But he couldn't help it. From the time he'd asked her to accompany him to the market and she'd said yes, he felt like he was suddenly woken up from a too-long self-imposed sleep. Everything seemed a little clearer now. Brighter.

Their time spent together made him feel younger. Made him feel things he'd thought had died when Grace had taken her last breath.

All day long, he'd found himself smiling

— as he recalled the flash of pleasure in her eyes when she'd first spied him at her restaurant that morning; and as he remembered getting lost in the corn maze with her. But then, when he recalled their kiss, his smile would fade.

It had been a foolhardy thing to do, to kiss her. But for the life of him, he couldn't regret it. He'd been married. He'd enjoyed a loving relationship with Grace. And if he was honest with himself, he missed affection. He missed that spark of awareness that had burned brightly whenever he and Grace had been together.

Of course now, he had no idea what he should do. Continue to see Lilly? But to what end? She wasn't Amish, and sure didn't seem interested in being that way. But if she never became Amish, then he would have to leave his order.

And that might mean leaving everything he'd always held dear.

When the front door chimed, it was a welcome relief from his thoughts. "Hello, Frank. Do you need something?"

"I hope so," Frank Graber said. "I need to order a hope chest for Judith."

"Does she have a beau?"

"No, but she's looking around at all the boys in the area something fierce now that

Gretta and Joshua are married and in a family way." With a teasing smile, Frank added, "Careful you don't get caught in her clutches."

Frank was chuckling, so Robert did, too, though a thousand questions were forming in his head. Was their age difference really not much of a worry for her parents?

What would Frank think if he'd seen him out with Lilly?

What would he think about two such different folks courting? If, of course, that was even what they were doing?

Frank snapped his fingers. "Ah, Robert? You all right?"

"*Jah.* Sorry, my mind went drifting." He pulled out a pencil and paper. "Do you have time to go over designs and dimensions?"

Frank pulled out a paper of his own. "I did one better. I asked Elsa to help me with our order."

Robert took the paper with relief. The way his thoughts were flying around, he doubted he'd be able to make much sense of anything. "I'll figure out the costs and will let you know by the end of the week."

"I'll stop by on Friday, then," Frank said. He turned away, but two beats later, looked at Robert again. "Are you all right, *freind?*"

"Of course. I just have a lot on my mind

today, and a lot to do."

Instead of taking the hint, Frank sat down. "You know, I heard from more than one person that you were walking with my neighbor at the market on Saturday."

"Yes, I took Lilly to the farmer's market."

"Some people are wondering why you are spending time with a girl who's English. And younger than you . . ."

With a sinking heart, Robert prepared to be judged. "I'd be surprised if everyone didn't talk. It seems people do enjoy worrying about things that are not their business."

"Sometimes it seems that way, I guess." Slowly Frank added, "Though we both know that the interest comes from caring. People want each other to be happy."

"Perhaps," Robert allowed, though he kind of doubted it. Not all gossip was from the best of intentions. Still stung from his cousins' veiled accusations and obvious disapproval, Robert braced himself for a lecture. "What do you have to say?"

He raised his hands in mock surrender. "Not a thing."

"Truly?"

"Of course." Frank looked a bit put out to be doubted. "Truth be told, I was just going to tell you that I am fairly well acquainted with Lilly. I know her parents as well. They are good neighbors."

Robert waited for the other shoe to drop. "And?"

"And nothing."

Robert shook his head. "I'm sorry, Frank. I'm a bit sensitive about Lilly, and I don't know why. No, that's not true. I know why," he said in a horrible, rambling rush. "I'm touchy because I know she's the last person I should be thinking about. But I can't seem to stop."

"She's a pretty thing."

"She's more than that. There's a depth to her that I admire. And a joy that comes from her, too. I've sorely missed that."

"You've had a difficult time."

Difficult didn't begin to describe it. Watching a spouse slowly fade away through a blanket of uncertainty and pain wasn't something he'd wish on anyone. "I loved Grace . . . but she's gone."

"Where do you see things going with Lilly Allen?"

"I don't know."

"Maybe you should? You know what I mean, Robert." Looking almost amused, Frank folded his arms over his chest. "I'm old, but I've still got my wits about me. People are talking, and they're talking loud enough for me to hear what's said between the lines. There's something going on."

Stung, Robert retreated more into himself. He was tired of being judged. Tired of men stopping by and offering unsolicited advice. "Lilly, she's my friend. There's nothing wrong with that." Unable to help himself, he murmured, "She's *gut* friends with Joshua, I know."

"She is, but there's more between you two than just friendship."

Robert bit back a sharp retort. It didn't matter that Frank was right. He still didn't like being the subject of community gossip. And he sure didn't want to be forced into thinking about what was happening between himself and Lilly. "I don't know what the Lord has planned for me and Lilly Allen," he said. Giving away a bit more of his private thoughts than he'd intended. "Once more, I don't know why it is of your concern. I'm not a child, Frank."

"You're right. You've been married and have known great trials. But for all that, taking advice from friends isn't a bad thing."

"As long as it's just advice . . ."

Frank didn't even flinch. "Perhaps it is. But since I'm already saying too much, I'm gonna offer you some more wisdom . . . Robert, you should do some thinking about your interest in Lilly Allen. She's young, she's English, and she became pregnant out of wedlock."

"You're not telling me anything I don't already know. And let's not cast stones."

"I don't want to do that. I'm not saying that her pregnancy is something to be scorned." He swallowed. "However, it is something to weigh and balance."

"Ah, and is that what you're doing?"

"You know, it may surprise you to find out that I don't necessarily think she is the wrong person for you."

Robert snapped his head up. "Truly?"

Frank shrugged. "This has been a most unusual year. Things have happened I never imagined. I've kind of thought it was our Lord's way of reminding me that I can't always be in charge. He is, you know?"

"I know."

"Perhaps the thing to do would be to pray a bit and ask Him for guidance."

"That is good advice."

"I thought so." With two slaps to the top of the desk, Frank stood up. "I'll see you on Friday. Judith will be pleased with this gift, I'm sure."

His mind far away once again, Robert barely waved him goodbye.

CHAPTER 8

Lilly heard her mother groan when she passed by her parents' room in the hall.

When a bout of coughing followed, and then the flush of a toilet, Lilly frowned in sympathy. Her mother was suffering from morning sickness.

Though she hadn't suffered that malady too much, Lilly had had it enough to be in complete understanding. Some mornings, her symptoms had been bad enough to make everything in the world seem green. Her body had felt weak and her hands had shook. Her skin had felt hot and flushed. Only the comfort of a can of soda, a handful of crackers, and the welcome relief of an ice cold washcloth on the back of her neck had enabled her to continue her day.

And here, her mom had been going through the same thing in silence.

When she heard the telltale sound of her brushing her teeth, Lilly knocked quietly.

"Mom? Are you all right?"

The faucet turned off. "Of course, honey." She cleared her throat. "Did . . . did you need something?"

Instead of answering, Lilly asked a question herself. "Can I come in?"

"Of course."

Though their house still felt new, her parents' bedroom and bath still seemed the same as always. She'd know her father's cologne everywhere. On his bedside table was a pile of change from his pockets and a few business cards.

On her mother's side lay two books and her reading glasses. On their dresser was a ceramic vase Charlie had made for them in fourth grade, as well as a family photo, taken when Lilly was just fourteen.

Memories and familiarity hugged her hard as she walked into the brightly lit bathroom. Her mother sat on the edge of the bathtub, both hands braced on her knees. "I'll be out in a minute. I'm just trying to get my bearings."

"Mom, how about a cold washcloth?"

For a moment, Lilly thought her mom was going to refuse the offer, but a grateful smile lit her face. "Thanks. That sounds heavenly."

Lilly ran out to the linen closet, picked up a clean washcloth, then, back in the bathroom, placed it under the faucet. A few wrings and two folds later, she placed it on the back of her mother's neck.

She smiled weakly. "I don't know why this feels so good, but it does. Thanks, honey." She closed her eyes and sighed.

Lilly sat down beside her.

As they sat together in silence, Lilly knew it was time to stop avoiding her mom. It was time to grow up a little more and think about someone else's needs. "Do you need anything else? A Coke or something?"

She slipped the washcloth off her neck. "No, honey. This did the trick." Their eyes met in the mirror's reflection. "Did *you* need something?"

"No. I just heard you and got worried . . ." Lilly's voice drifted off as she realized how lame she sounded. She shouldn't have waited so long to reach out.

Ever since she'd blown up at her parents, Lilly had done everything she could to have as little to do with them as possible. She'd left the house early for work and come home only after she could find nothing else to do. On Sunday, she'd even driven Ty to his friend's birthday party so she wouldn't have to spend time with her mom.

While her mom never said a word about her absence, her father had. His voice had been stern as he'd cautioned her to stop feeling so sorry for herself.

But even that talking-to hadn't encouraged her to change her ways. Actually, if anything, it had only increased her desire to avoid her mom. Obviously they didn't understand how hard it was for her to watch her mother plan for a baby.

Her mother, on the other hand, had been doing everything but avoid her. She'd tried to talk to Lilly about her life. About her job at the Sugarcreek Inn. Even about how Charlie was doing at Bowling Green. Never once did she talk about how she was feeling. No, she'd continued to put Lilly's needs first. In addition, her mom had been doing her best to hide everything about the pregnancy so Lilly wouldn't be hurt.

But Lilly had hardly bent at all. No, she'd done her best just to stay away and ignore her feelings, to talk about everything but what was most important to her mother.

Funny how pretending nothing was wrong was continuing to be a family trait. Her parents had been champions at doing that when Lilly had been pregnant. And here, she'd done her best to act the same way during the last few weeks.

"I bet your stomach will settle down

soon," Lilly ventured. "All the books say it does."

"I hope you're right. The doctor said I need to gain a little bit of weight." She shook her head wryly. "Imagine that! After all those years on Weight Watchers, now I'm supposed to be gaining weight! It's hard to wrap my head around."

"I bet." Lilly leaned against the gray marbled counter and watched her mom brush and curl her hair. Her mom had worn the same hairstyle for ages.

So much was different . . . but still the same, too.

When their eyes met again in the mirror, her mom inquired, "You okay?"

"Oh, sure. I was, uh, just thinking how nice everything looks in here."

Smiling, her mom ran a finger along the wall. "I like it, too. I thought I'd never get all that dust out of the carpet, but now that everything's back to normal, I think it was worth the mess."

Her parents had recently finished sprucing up their master bath. Boring eggshell white walls were now painted a deep grayish-blue. Shiny bright hardware had been switched to a burnished silver. Gray and blue and ivory towels hung from hooks and towel rods.

And a beautiful watercolor of lilies hung above the bathtub.

"Did I tell you that Cassidy came out here the other day?"

Turning, her mother faced her in surprise. "No. What brought her?"

"Me. She got tired of me not answering her phone calls."

"I wish you could have encouraged her to stay for dinner. I always liked Cassidy."

"Actually, she stopped by the inn. I was working, and she had to get back, so her coming over wouldn't have been possible." Lilly didn't even know how to admit that she had been less than friendly, anyway.

"Oh."

"I think I might go see her soon," she blurted, wondering where in the world that had come from. "When we started talking, I realized that I should have called her or emailed her or something. We used to be really good friends."

"You know what? I think you're right. It might do you some good to take a few days and go see all your friends. You deserve some days off."

"You wouldn't mind if I went to go see her? Really?"

"Of course not, dear. Lilly, I think we both know that the days of me telling you what to do are over," she said dryly. As she bent down to close two drawers, her mom winced a bit. "I tell you what, I've got cramps on top of cramps!"

Immediately, concern for her mother's health overrode everything else. "Mom, you should go lay down. I had cramps right before I lost —"

Before she could say anything more, her mom enfolded her in a hug. "Oh, no, honey. They're in the muscles in my stomach — and everywhere else. It's called being forty-four and pregnant."

Pure relief filled her. As did embarrassment. "Oh. Sorry."

"Please don't be sorry for caring." Her arm still around Lilly's shoulders, her mother walked her into the master bedroom. "I appreciate it."

"I care. I've just been having a hard time."

"I know you have. I promise, we'll get through this."

"I'm sorry I haven't tried to help you more."

"It's okay. I'm just glad we're talking. I told your dad I was afraid you were going to be mad at me for six more months."

"I haven't been mad at you. More like stunned."

"You and me both, honey."

"Can I make you something to eat?"

Her mother grimaced. "I don't think I can stomach food right now. But do think about planning a trip to see Cassidy. Spending time with friends would do you good. You spend too much time working, I think."

"I think I will." Before she lost her nerve, she blurted, "On Saturday, when I went to the farmer's market and got the kitten . . . I went with somebody."

"Actually, I heard something about that. You went with a man, didn't you?"

"Yes. He's just a friend, though," she said quickly. "His name's Robert."

"And did you have a good time?"

"We did." Lilly's mouth went dry as she recalled their time in the corn maze. Kissing him, being in his arms — even for a few minutes . . . It had been very good.

Then she noticed that her mom wasn't acting all that surprised. "Hey, Mom, how did you know?"

A secretive smile played on her lips. "Elsa told me. She heard all about it from Gretta."

"Not Joshua?"

"She said Gretta, but it could have been both of them, I suppose. I guess you saw them at the market?"

"I did. Um . . . actually, Josh didn't act real thrilled to see me there with Robert."

"Why was that?"

"Because Robert's Amish."

"I heard that, too."

Again, her mother didn't seem all that shocked by any of what Lilly was revealing. Lilly wasn't quite sure what to make of that. She so wanted to be able to talk to someone about everything she was feeling . . . but she sure hadn't expected it to be her mom.

Could their relationship be finally mending . . . ?

"Robert is older than I, but not that old. He's twenty-four."

"Still pretty young. And you're eighteen."

"Nineteen now," Lilly corrected. "I just had a birthday, remember? Anyway, Robert has been through a lot. He's a widower."

"Well, you've had your share of difficulties. It's nice to know you made a new friend." She paused significantly. "Is that what you are? Just friends?"

"Maybe. Maybe more . . . I don't know."

With a tender smile, her mother murmured, "Don't worry, Lilly. I'm not going to lecture you. I'll just say that I hope you won't get hurt."

She knew what her mother meant. Alec had said he'd loved her, but he obviously hadn't. When he'd rejected her, and her pregnancy, it had been especially painful. "I don't think he's like Alec. I don't think he would ever say something and not mean it. But we're not anywhere like that," she said in a rush. "All I know is that I like his company."

"He must like yours, too, if he bought you that little kitten that's been scratching up our couch . . . and cuddling on my lap."

"So, Elsa told you that he bought me the kitten, too?"

"I'm afraid if you go to the farmer's market with Robert, you're not going to return with many secrets."

She hoped her mom was wrong. Having everyone know about the kitten was one thing. But if anyone ever guessed that she'd kissed him, Lilly knew people even as sweet as Elsa Graber wouldn't be so kind. They walked into the kitchen. "As I said, I, for one, am glad you're making some friends. That's important. Just take care that you're choosing good ones, right? You deserve to be around people who will be nice to you."

"Robert is."

"Good. And that's probably another reason that you should go back to Cleveland. You need to be around some more kids your age and have some fun. I can't expect you to only go to Amish farmer's markets!"

Her mom was right. Suddenly, Lilly felt

silly. Had she really been thinking that spending her weekends at a farmer's market was something she wanted to make a habit of? "I better get ready for work."

"Me too." Her mom hugged her again, and said, "I'm so glad we talked, honey. Everything's going to be just fine for all of us. I know it."

"I bet you're right." Lilly smiled as she turned away and walked to her room.

She was so glad things were ironed out between her and her mom.

But now, all she could think about was a twenty-four-year-old man with a light brown beard and icy blue eyes. A man who was kind and nice. And who could kiss like a dream.

A man who made her think that being in a relationship again might be just what she needed.

CHAPTER 9

To Lilly's way of thinking, the fields beyond her house heralded each approaching season. Rarely used for planting, the rolling hills that stretched for two miles to the creek were left for Mother Nature's care.

Spring brought wild raspberry bushes, short, fresh, bright green grass, and buds on the maple, ash, and oak trees. Summer arrived with an abundance of wildflowers and lazy bumblebees, each meandering from bloom to bloom.

Now, at the end of September, the colors of fall were chaotic and bright. Illuminating even the darkest spirits.

A beautiful last burst of vibrancy before winter arrived, bringing with it gray skies, dormant plants, lone deer, and snow.

Over the last few months, Lilly had begun to walk as much as possible. It gave her time to connect with nature and give thanks for her many blessings.

And she did have many blessings, even if sometimes she took them for granted.

Feeling in need of another bit of quiet time, Lilly went out after dinner. She'd just stopped to inspect an abandoned bird's nest when she spied a neighbor sprawled out on one of the logs that lined the creek. "Hey, Caleb."

Instead of looking happy to see her, he just stared. "What are you doing here?"

"Nothing. I just felt like going for a walk. Why? Am I bothering you?"

"No."

She came closer. Noticing that his boots lay in a pile beside him, she added, "What about you? Why are you out here this time of day? It's kind of cold to have bare feet, don't you think?"

"Not really." He wiggled his toes for emphasis. "We Amish like to run around barefoot, you know."

Lilly detected more than a hint of bitterness in his voice. "I've heard that," she quipped as she sank down on the grass beside him. "I, on the other hand, need layers of socks and thick boots when I'm out here. I'm too afraid of snakes to go barefoot."

Sitting up, he shook his head. "You know nothing, Lilly Allen. There're no snakes right now. It's almost October."

"I'll file that bit of information away." Studying him closer, she noticed his shoulders were hunched and his expression grim. "Seriously, Caleb, what's wrong?"

At first, she didn't think he was going to answer. "I'm thinking of leaving Sugarcreek," he said bluntly. "What do you think of that?"

"I think that's a pretty big deal." By now she knew enough about the Amish to know that some kids went out at night and drove cars and experienced the outside world during their running-around years. Some left their families for a time. Some did crazy stuff — crazy even for English kids.

And some never came back.

As Caleb's words hung between them, Lilly had to admit that she wasn't all that surprised. Caleb had been hinting about wanting to leave ever since she'd first met him. He didn't seem to have the same connection with the land and the family business that his older brother Josh had.

"I'm also thinking that I'm too afraid to do more than just think about it," he mumbled.

Caleb was a handsome boy with an easy smile and an almost bulletproof exterior. Even when she'd known he was unhappy, she'd never seen him rattled.

And Lilly would have never guessed that he would admit to a fear. "Oh."

He wrapped his arms around his knees as he eyed her coolly. "*Oh?* That's all you have to say?"

"What do you want me to say?" She paused for emphasis. *"Don't go, Caleb?"*

His eyes crinkled. "Probably. Most people are shocked."

"So . . . you've told a lot of people?"

"No. Just one or two others."

"Well, it's good I'm not most people, then."

He looked her over before lying back down again. "Maybe so." After a moment, he stretched his arms behind his head and stared at the sky.

The sun was setting and bands of red and yellow coated the horizon.

He looked so comfortable, Lilly gave into temptation and fell all the way back. The cool grassland felt like a bumpy cushion under her head. For a moment, she worried about bugs. Then looked up to the sky and all worries about earthly problems faded. "The sky's pretty. I don't know why it always looks so pretty to me in the autumn, but it does. There always seems to be less clouds and haze."

Beside her, he shifted. "I suppose."

As the quiet trickle of the creek floated over them and the gentle rays of the sun warmed her skin, Lilly felt herself completely relaxing. Rarely did she ever sit and watch the sky anymore. Or sit with anyone and just enjoy the moment.

Perhaps it was a result of being older. Or maybe it was because she always felt so alone? It was hard being in between two worlds. She didn't quite fit in with most teenagers she knew . . . and the girls her age at work were Amish, and therefore looking toward marriage and babies.

But as she thought of Robert, Lilly almost smiled. Perhaps she had more in common with Miriam and Gretta than she'd imagined? "I've got a secret, too."

"Yeah?"

"It's a pretty big one . . ."

"Let me guess . . . is your secret that you fancy Robert Miller?"

Startled, she propped herself up on her elbows to get a better look at him. "You knew?"

"Of course." His voice sounded smug.

"I've only told everyone that we're just friends. You know, like me and Josh. But lately, I've been thinking that maybe there's more to us than that."

"I've seen how the two of you act when he comes to the restaurant for coffee. Nothing between you and Robert Miller is like what's between you and my brother."

"It's that obvious?"

"Maybe not to everyone. But it doesn't take a genius to see that you fancy him. It's been in your eyes."

"I'll have to watch that."

He chuckled. "Don't think it would make a difference. I think Robert fancies you, as well. Sure enough, the two of you were looking mighty attached at the market."

"He bought me a kitten. I named her Midnight."

He snorted. "Now, that's a dumb name."

"Only to you. I think it's a great name. Anyway, he bought me a kitten and he carried her around for me." She stopped herself before she told him about walking with Robert in the corn maze. Before she mentioned kissing Robert.

"If he's buying you pets, I'm guessing the two of you must be mighty serious. You could practically say you two are courtin'."

His quip surprised a laugh out of Lilly. "I don't know. Maybe one day. We've only gone on that one outing. Otherwise, he just visits me at the restaurant."

"For now. . . ."

Oh, but Caleb was bold. And, he kind of had a point, too. The future was in her hands, and the idea that she had at least some control over it felt exhilarating.

"I really hope you don't decide to leave Sugarcreek. I'd miss you, Caleb. You've been a good friend to me. I like your sense of humor."

"I'll miss you, too. If I even decide to leave." Beside her, Caleb closed his eyes. "For so long, I've been obsessed with the idea of being someone different. I've imagined being English . . . imagined doing all the things I'm not allowed to do now."

"Having more freedom doesn't necessarily make life easier," she warned.

"Perhaps. But it might."

As a breeze brushed another batch of clouds in motion overhead, Lilly tried to be helpful. "Where do most Amish kids go when they don't want to be Amish?"

He thought for a moment. "Here and there. Usually some *Englischer* takes them in. Helps them get social security cards and a driver's license." Shifting again, he pulled himself up to a sitting position. "I've heard of some kids getting more learning, but most go get a job."

"That's a lot to take on. Especially at sixteen." Lilly already knew from experience how hard it was to start over in a new place without friends. She couldn't imagine how difficult it would be to attempt to do that without any family as well.

"It is." He paused. "Becoming a new person is a long process, I think."

Becoming a new person. Lilly's mouth went dry as she realized that was exactly what Caleb was talking about.

Did he even realize all he would give up?

"Are you going to tell your parents?" Already she was bracing herself for that burden. She loved his family and admired his parents. It would be extremely nerve-racking to keep his secret from them. Actually, deep inside her, she knew without a doubt that she would have to divulge his secret. If they had no idea where he was, they'd be frantic. Lilly knew she'd never be able to keep silent if they were hurting.

Picking up a stick, Caleb drew lines on the ground. "I don't know what I'm going to do," he said quietly. "My friend, Mrs. Miller, says I haven't thought things through. She says it's not enough to just want to run away from something. You have to know where you want to run toward."

"What she says makes a lot of sense. You know, when my family ran here to Sugarcreek, we didn't do all that much thinking about the consequences. It would have been easier if we had."

"If I leave, my parents are going to be upset."

"Yes, they are."

He jabbed at the ground again. "And angry."

"Yep."

Meeting her gaze, he frowned. "Why are you being so tough? I thought you of all people would understand how I'm feeling."

"I do understand, but there's no way I am going to let you imagine that I completely agree with everything you're doing."

He looked away. Shutting her out.

Though she understood his frustration, Lilly knew she had to say her piece. "Listen. I know you're going to do what you want. I can't stop you, and I don't want to try. But I think you should tell your parents what you're thinking."

"So far, there's nothing to tell them."

"But maybe you could tell them how you're feeling? Ask them for advice?" Even as she said the words, Lilly winced. What was she talking about? She, of all people, knew just how hard it was to tell parents something they didn't want to hear.

She also knew that parents didn't always want to be open minded, either.

"They're not going to sit in a circle and coddle me, Lilly." His voice came out harsh. In emphasis, he jabbed hard at the ground again, whether in frustration or anger, she didn't know. After two strikes, the stick broke.

"I know."

"I love my family," he mumbled. "I do. But I also don't want to get *stuck* doing something — stuck *being* something for the rest of my life — that I'm not sure about."

"I can see your point." Lilly felt sorry for him. Racking her brain, she tried to help Caleb come up with some other solutions. Really, if he was determined to leave and his parents were against it, there would be little else for him to do besides leave his house in the middle of the night and never look back.

What he needed was some time away in a safe place. "Hey, Caleb, what about if I found you somewhere to stay just for a while?" she said slowly, thinking of Cassidy. "I've got some friends who live outside of Cleveland. In Strongsville. Their parents might not mind you staying with them for a few weeks."

"Just a few weeks?"

Oh, he was so impatient! "It's better than nothing! Besides, who knows? Maybe that will be long enough to figure out your next step."

For the first time, his eyes filled with something besides contempt. "Do you really think you could ask your friends if I could stay at their house?"

"I wouldn't have suggested it if I didn't."

"Will you be able to ask them sometime soon?"

Oh, why couldn't she ever keep her mouth shut? Now he was going to be so upset if Cassidy and her parents shot down her idea. "I'll call them . . . but if I do that, and if you decide to go to Strongsville, I think you should talk to your parents about your plans."

Scrambling to his feet, a look of fresh pain filled his eyes. "I can't tell them I want to leave."

"They love you. Telling them the truth about how you feel is the right thing to do." As she stood up as well, she added, "Caleb, you're going to have to say something to them sooner or later."

"They're going to get really mad —"

She cut him off. "Then they'll get mad. Caleb, I had to tell my parents I was pregnant. Don't act like you're the only person who's had to deal with bad stuff."

After another moment, he stared at her.

"What if they kick me out?"

She couldn't imagine Elsa and Frank doing such a thing. But she also knew the power that worst-case scenarios had on a person's emotions. "If they kick you out, then I guess you'll go."

When he looked like he was about to start arguing about it all again, she shook her head wearily. "Let's go back. I don't want to argue with you."

For a moment, Caleb stared hard at her, then finally nodded, picked up his shoes and stepped into pace beside her.

As they walked the well-worn path that led back to their homes, Lilly breathed deep, needing a cleansing breath of the cool air.

Fall had brought a fresh look to the meadow. The tall grasses had faded to a yellow-brown and rustled against their feet as they walked. Bushes and shrubs had turned golden and orange, bringing a welcome batch of color to everything.

Every so often geese flew overhead, their squawks telling one and all that they were headed south for the winter.

And a new calm passed between her and Caleb. Perhaps everything would work out for him after all . . .

When their two houses were in sight, Caleb broke the silence. "So, what are you going to do with Robert Miller?"

"I'm not sure."

"You must have some idea."

"I might." Like Caleb, she was afraid to voice her dreams. They seemed too outlandish. "Hey, did you know his wife?"

"Only a little bit. Robert's a lot older than me, so we've never been close. But I do remember that they seemed real happy. When she died, he wasn't around much. Now hardly anyone ever sees him besides at work or when we have church." He waited a beat. "Or when he visits you at the restaurant."

"He told me he keeps to himself nowadays." Before she lost her nerve, she murmured, "Caleb, have you ever heard of an *Englischer* marrying an Amish person? Of joining the Amish church?"

"Uh-huh."

"Was it easy?"

"No."

Obviously he, too, could be blunt. "I see."

He grinned as they stopped next to the hedge that separated their lots. "It's the truth. Being Amish ain't easy, Lilly."

"I guess that's where we are, then, huh? We both want to do impossible things."

Surprising her, he shook his head.

"They're not impossible. God doesn't hand us impossible tasks. Just hard ones. And scary." With a faint wave, he walked through the hedge.

Back to his life.

As Lilly slowly started up her own driveway, she thought about his words. Caleb was exactly right. Just because the Lord handed her opportunities and choices, it didn't automatically mean that things were going to get easier. All it seemed to do was make her confused.

CHAPTER 10

Robert knew he shouldn't have kissed Lilly Allen in the corn maze. More to the point, he certainly shouldn't be still thinking about it.

After all, what they had done was wrong. *Wrong.* They weren't married. They weren't even courting.

They never could.

A future between the two of them was not a possibility. How could it be? Lilly was English. He was not. She was young — only nineteen years old. So why was Lilly the first person he thought of when he woke up every morning? How come her image couldn't ever seem to be erased from his mind?

How was it that no matter how hard he berated himself . . . he still wanted to see her? Be with her?

As Robert sat in the relative privacy of his buggy and continued to stare at the outside of the Sugarcreek Inn — again — he called himself ten times the fool. A smarter man would direct his horse right out of the parking lot and back to his store.

Instead, he slowly edged out of the black conveyance and planted his feet on the ground. Glanced at the row of cars near the restaurant's door. And looked at her car for what had to be the twentieth time.

Lilly was inside. Working. So he would, indeed, have a chance to talk with her. He nodded, as if nodding could convincingly erase her from his head.

But as sure as the vivid fall foliage would eventually fade to a dreary winter gray, Robert knew he couldn't prevent himself from walking forward. With a strong sense of inevitability, he started walking toward the door.

He'd almost reached the sidewalk that lined the front when a voice called out to him. "Robert, hello."

As patient as he could, he smiled weakly at Edith, Grace's grandmother. "Nice to see you, Edith."

"*Ach.* You used to call me *Grossmammi,* Robert."

He had — but after a time, it had felt too strange. After all, she'd been Grace's grandmother, not his. And Grace, of course, was gone. But instead of bringing any of that up, he stood politely as she carefully walked toward him down the sidewalk. "How are you?"

"I am as good as I can be, I suppose." Tapping her cane on the cement near her feet, she added, "If my gout would give me a rest, I would be a mite better."

He nodded his head politely. "I hope you feel better soon, *Grossmammi*."

She smiled. "You are a dear boy. What are you up to today? Taking some time off work?"

"Just for a short while. I thought I'd get a sandwich inside. Maybe a piece of pie."

Not fooled for a minute, she narrowed her eyes through her wire-rimmed spectacles. "Yes. I had heard you've been spending quite a bit of time at this particular spot, eating pie."

To his embarrassment, his cheeks heated. "I didn't realize I was the fodder for gossip."

"Oh, I think you did. It seems everyone has something to say about you driving that girl around in your buggy."

"Even you?"

Robert held himself still as her eyebrows snapped together and she inhaled sharply.

As long as he'd known her, Grace's grandmother had never been shy about handing out pointed barbs. He most likely deserved a lashing from her tongue, anyway. He had been cheeky, egging on the older woman.

But instead of scolding, she only looked him up and down. "Perhaps it's time to be honest with yourself."

"About . . ."

"About that girl in there, of course," she retorted. "Robert, if you like her, you might as well be bold about it, don'tcha think? People will talk no matter." Patting his arm, her voice became gentler. "There's no shame in moving on, son. Take it from me — we must all do it sometime or another. *Du Herr sie mit due,* Robert," she added before tottering away.

Before he had a chance to reply that he wished the Lord to be with her as well.

Stunned by her words, he stood motionless as he watched Grace's grandmother disappear into the quilt-and-craft shop.

Another buggy's arrival to the parking lot spurred Robert into motion. The last thing he needed was to have yet another conversation on the sidewalk about Lilly.

Pushing the rest of his doubts away, he opened the door to the restaurant and stepped inside.

As always, the welcoming scent of yeast

rolls, roast chicken, and coffee greeted him.

As did Lilly.

"Robert! Hi!" Lilly said with a smile. "I didn't expect to see you in today. It's Monday."

"What does that have to do with anything?"

"You've never been here on a Monday before. Usually, you stop by on Tuesdays for the Swiss Steak."

He hadn't been able to stay away until Tuesday.

But that, of course, couldn't be said. "I do like Swiss Steak. But I had a hunger for something else today," he murmured as he followed her to a table.

Wearing a pair of jeans, boots, and a burnt orange sweater, Robert thought she looked as pretty as ever.

"A different sort of hunger, hmm?" Her eyes sparkled. "I'm almost afraid to ask what you want."

As well she should!

When they were standing by his table, she leaned forward. Just a slight bit. "So . . . do you know what you want?"

He knew. Of course, he also knew that everything he was thinking couldn't be said out loud. "I'll need to see the menu."

She looked at her empty hands in surprise.

"I can't believe I forgot to grab one. I'll be right back."

When she turned and walked back to the hostess station, Robert sat down and watched her. She looked flustered — exactly the way he was feeling.

He needed to settle things about their relationship in his mind. No way could he continue to simply happen to "drop" by her restaurant. Something needed to be said.

She returned with a menu. "Here," she said, practically slapping it on the table. "I mean, why don't you take a look at the menu?"

He almost smiled. "All right." Oh, but she was so different than he. So young and impulsive.

They were different in the way that winter was different than summer. Or the way rain differed from snow.

But there was something holding them together, too. He'd known it since the first time he saw her. Had been certain of it since he'd held her in his arms. They were not destined to simply be friends.

She nibbled her bottom lip. "Would you like some coffee?"

"That would be good. And a slice of apple pie. And . . . do you have time to sit with me for a moment or two?"

"I'd like to." She turned toward the kitchen. "I'll go see if I can take my break a little early."

When she moved away, Robert closed his eyes in frustration. He didn't know what he was doing. He didn't know how he was supposed to act. All he did know was that he wanted to see her. Wanted to be with her, and he was willing to become a target of gossip in order to achieve his goals.

Less than five minutes later, Lilly approached, holding two slices of pie, two mugs of hot coffee, and a sheepish expression on her face. "Mrs. Kent said sitting with you was no problem, since there's no one else in here right now. I don't even have to use this as my break."

"I'm glad."

After placing the plates and mugs on the table, she perched in the chair across from him. "Me too."

The warm cup felt good in between his hands. And sipping the brew gave his mouth something to do, because he was all tongue-tied. But he had to say something. "How's the cat?"

"Midnight? She's good. Of course, she's a handful, too. Every time I turn around, she's gotten into something. Last night she was on the kitchen counter, happily shredding one of my mother's kitchen towels."

"Perhaps you should have named her Mischief."

She chuckled, brightening his spirits. "Maybe so. Or perhaps Lucky. At least once a day, my mother threatens to toss Midnight out the door. But then her little pink paws and green eyes take over, and she gets scooped up and cuddled again."

"She's a right beauty of a cat."

"And so full of fun. Just last night she was playing with my dad's newspaper when he was reading it. He was trying to act like he minded, but I know he didn't."

Lilly paused. "Things have been a little awkward at home, my mom being pregnant and all. She and I are doing okay . . . but it's still nice to have something easy to talk about."

"*Jah.* I mean, I imagine so," he muttered. Oh, but it was sometimes so hard to concentrate on just her words. While she talked, Lilly punctuated almost every word with her hands. Robert couldn't help but watch her slim fingers wave through the air, capturing his attention and imagination, too. They were small. Soft-looking. He wondered what they'd feel like, clasped securely between his own again.

She stilled. "Robert?"

Belatedly, he realized he'd been staring at her hands. "Oh, I'm sorry. Um . . . perhaps I could stop by one day soon and see the kitten?"

Her eyes widened. "Sure," she said slowly. "I mean of course. That . . . that would be great."

"I don't have to, if that would make you uncomfortable."

"That's not it at all." She looked right and left, then finally leaned forward a bit. "Robert, can I ask you something?"

"Anything."

"Is there . . . I mean . . . do you feel that there's something between us?"

As he struggled to answer, he found himself scanning her face. Noticing everything about her. The wayward curl caressing her cheek. Her softly parted lips. The fine lines of her neck. And the way her sweater's color made her cheeks seem brighter.

When she'd leaned forward, the edge of her sweater dipped a bit, revealing a few more inches of skin.

Robert looked away. Then felt completely embarrassed. It was only her shoulder. Why was he acting so spun up?

Because he knew how he was going to have to answer her. With the truth.

"For me, there is."

Her lips pursed, then relaxed. "I'm so glad you said that."

"So you feel the same way?" Too much was at stake for him to continue to talk in vague generalities. He knew he couldn't go back once he went forward.

"Oh, yes." A wrinkle formed between her eyes. "But what do you think that means?"

Robert pushed his plate away, then just as firmly, weaved his fingers together. If he wasn't careful, he was going to give in to temptation and reach out for her hand. Just to feel her skin. No, more than that. He wanted to kiss her. Right there in the middle of the Sugarcreek Inn.

"I'm not sure what it means," he finally said. "Though, I will tell you that it's taken me by surprise."

"Is this — what we're doing — even allowed?"

"In truth, we're not doing anything but eating pie."

As Lilly looked at their untouched plates and grinned, Robert found himself chuckling. No, they weren't fooling anyone.

Not even themselves. "All right. How about . . . we're not doing anything other than sharing coffee together?"

"There's nothing wrong with that." She

curved her fingers around the mug again, drawing his eyes back to her hands.

"So, may I stop by your home?"

"Of course." Brown eyes met his. "Tonight?"

"Yes. Perhaps seven or so?"

"I'll look forward to it. Would you like to join us for dinner?"

"No." He was not ready to share a meal with her parents.

"That's probably just as well. There's no telling what my parents would ask you."

Her worries amused him. He had his reservations about whether the two of them could ever overcome their differences. But it had been a long time since he'd worried about what a woman's parents thought of him.

The front door chimed as a group of six ladies in jeans and tennis shoes entered. Lilly scooted back her chair and stood up. "I better go tend to them."

"Yes. I should go back to work, too."

"So . . . do you know where I live?"

"I do. You're next to the Grabers'. I'll see you around seven."

She smiled again, then approached the women and pulled out a stack of menus. As they walked toward the back, to the window where the girls in the back kitchen were visible, Robert fished out a few dollars and set them on the table. By now he knew exactly how much a piece of pie and a cup of coffee were.

He left the usual amount. As he walked back out to the sidewalk, he realized that he probably should have taken that slice of pie for later.

Surely sometime that day, he'd feel like eating again.

CHAPTER 11

"I've got someone coming over tonight after dinner," Lilly told her mother as she opened a bag of chopped lettuce and poured it into a glass salad bowl.

Still stirring the pot of spaghetti sauce, her mom looked her way. "Who?"

"Robert Miller. He's the man I went to the farmer's market with."

"I remember. He's the man who bought you Midnight."

"Yes." Unscrewing the bottle of ranch dressing, Lilly paused, waiting for the inevitable.

As Midnight scrambled around their feet, playing with one of Ty's rubber balls, her mother groaned. "Perhaps he'll take this kitten back. She's the bane of my existence."

"Oh, Mom. You love her."

"I suppose I do." Her mom turned from the stove top. "So, I know you two are friends. Is that still all you are?"

"Maybe. Though, I think we might be sliding toward something closer."

"Lilly, what are you going to do if you and this man do decide you want more than friendship?"

"I don't know." Lilly turned away, on the off chance that her mom would be able to see the confusion written all over her face. And her dismay. Only a few hours ago, Lilly had asked the same exact question to Robert.

But her mother didn't even look up from the pot of spaghetti noodles she was boiling. "Well, I mean, you either have to stay just friends with him or convince him to leave his order. Right?"

There was one other option . . . "I'm not sure."

"Aren't you? Even I know that Robert can't risk ruining his reputation by continually calling on you. Something has to happen."

"Mom, stop. You're jumping to conclusions."

"I'm just being realistic. You might want to start thinking ahead, too."

"Everything's fine. Stop worrying so much."

"I can't help but worry. Last year was so

hard. I just don't want you to get hurt again."

The past year had been difficult. Everything in her life had changed because of one impulsive night with Alec. Ever since, she'd been struggling to keep her head above water.

Now, things were finally starting to feel right. She had no desire to keep discussing past decisions. "Mom, all I said was that Robert was stopping by."

Her mother drew in a breath, obviously ready to spout off a slew of opinions. But instead of criticizing, she simply murmured, "Well, I'll look forward to getting to know him. Since, you know, he might be around for a while."

"Don't say anything weird to him."

"I won't. Call your brother and dad, dear. We better eat so everything will be cleaned up by the time Robert comes over. What's his last name again?"

"Miller. His name is Robert Miller. And, he's a widower. His first wife, Grace, died of cancer."

Her mother paused. "So he's had his share of obstacles, too."

"Yes. Yes, he has."

"Lilly?"

Lilly paused. "Yes?"

"Honey, if this Robert Miller has caught your eye after everything you've been through, he must be a very special man."

"I think so."

"You're a wonderful girl, Lilly. And maybe it doesn't really matter if he's Amish or not. And though a year ago I never would have imagined saying this, I don't think the Amish are much different from us. I know I've really enjoyed getting to know Elsa."

Just thirty minutes later, Robert was in the house.

It felt strange to see him in the family room. Robert's steady presence seemed to take up a lot of space. And the stiff way he stood, hat in hand, made her realize that he, too, was feeling the awkwardness of the situation.

Standing by his side, Lilly smiled at him encouragingly as her parents asked him too many questions.

When he'd first arrived, Ty had bounded in, Midnight in his arms. Robert's expression had gentled as he'd carefully rubbed the kitten's neck. Then Ty left to go watch TV and her parents had begun their questions in earnest.

Lilly wasn't sure when her dad had been informed about Robert's visit, or about her intentions to keep seeing him, but like her mom, he was on good behavior.

Except that neither of them was content to leave them alone.

"You can make a living building furniture, Robert?"

"I don't just build furniture. Sometimes people hire me to make custom cabinets for their kitchen. Or to make a mantel for their fireplace."

"I didn't know there was a market for such things."

"It's not cheap. But the work is good," Robert said modestly.

"It is beautiful," Lilly said. "I've visited the shop and seen everything for myself."

"I'll have to stop by," her dad murmured. "Soon."

Her mother gestured to the pair of couches. "I feel funny, standing in the living room like this. Why don't we all sit down? I could get us some coffee."

Robert's eyes widened. Lilly took it on herself to save him. "Actually, we're going to go sit on the front porch."

Her father scoffed. "Lilly, it's forty degrees out there."

"I'll be fine. Robert, will you?"

He fingered his jacket. "Forty degrees isn't so cold."

Lilly pulled him out of the living room and guided him toward the front door.

"Lilly, Robert? Would you two like some hot chocolate?" her mother asked.

"That would be nice," he said, smiling her mother's way. "I know Lilly enjoys hot chocolate very much."

Just as they closed the door behind them, Lilly heard her father say, "How in the world does that guy know that?"

When they were finally alone, Lilly stood by Robert's side in the fading light. Few stars were out; clouds had descended on the area. Sleet and rain were expected overnight.

After a long moment, Robert grinned. "I have to say, I've never been so thankful for a front porch."

Lilly bypassed the two wicker chairs and sat on the stoop. Robert sat next to her. "I'm sorry," she said. "I never imagined that my parents would trap you in our family room like that."

"Asking questions is no problem. I had the answers, you know."

"You did, didn't you? I'm sorry. Sometimes I forget just how mature you are. I bet nothing gets you very rattled."

"Some things rattle me," he said softly, his eyes searching hers. "But you're right. Not much does make me uncomfortable. Is that a bad thing?"

"No. It's a very good thing. See, sometimes I forget that you don't need me standing by your side, trying to help you out."

"I liked it. You reminded me of a guard dog barking loud enough to scare off anyone who dared to disagree with you."

"I felt that way, I guess," Lilly said, chuckling. "I didn't want them to scare you away."

"It would take more than inquisitive parents to do that."

"I'm thankful for that." Looking for something to say, she gazed at the front yard, at the hedge that separated her family's property with the Grabers'. "Tell me about church. I saw all the buggies over there on Sunday."

"Church is church."

"Come on, Robert. What is it like?"

"It's a time for worship. But it's more than that, too. It's a time to visit and relax. We always share a meal together."

"And that's all?"

"More or less. It's a good time to catch up on news. You know how people like to talk."

"Did . . . did you hear any questions about us?"

"No. But . . . there really is no *us,* is there?"

Lilly wasn't sure how to answer that. But she ventured forward. "Maybe there is. That kiss —"

The door opened, startling them and stalling whatever response Robert had been about to make. To their surprise, it was Ty who came out, gingerly carrying mugs of hot chocolate in his hands. "Mom sent me out with these."

Lilly scrambled up to take them from him. "Tell her thank you."

Without replying, Ty trotted back in. There were mountains of whipped cream on each mug. Robert looked at the concoction and grinned. "Is this for my benefit, or yours?"

"Mine."

"I like your sweet tooth."

"Robert —"

He interrupted her. "I don't know what to say about that kiss except that I enjoyed it."

"Do you regret it?"

"I should."

"Oh." She felt like he was fishing for responses from her, but she wasn't sure whether she should grab hold of his line or keep her feelings in the shadows.

"But I don't."

"I don't, either." Lilly looked at him in wonder. What had they just admitted? Only that they shared a very personal attraction?

He sipped his drink. "However, I don't suppose we should kiss each other again. That is, anytime soon."

"No. Probably not."

Robert set his mug on the step next to him. Turned to her. Treated her to an incredibly slow, terribly attractive smile. "I want you to know . . . Fact is, you make me happy, Lilly. Today, right now, that's good enough for me. I haven't been all that happy over the last few years."

"I know what you mean."

"So, if you're in agreement, perhaps we could spend more time together."

"And not kiss."

He shook his head, like he couldn't believe her gall. Then, he laughed. "This is why I can't stay away from you, Lilly Allen. You make me laugh."

As the sky darkened, she relaxed beside Robert. "Would you like to hear about the crazy customer I waited on this afternoon?"

Reaching out, he grasped her hand. "Of course," he murmured.

Taking the lead, she did her best to entertain him, taking special care to exaggerate the woman's mannerisms just enough to make him grin.

One story led to another. And another . . . as the sky grew dark and their laughter echoed across the wide, open spaces. Their hands melding together. Perfectly matched. Everything was going to be okay.

Nothing about the future needed to be decided. And for right now, for this week, that was more than enough.

Never again would she take happiness for granted.

CHAPTER 12

His family seemed bigger when they were all gathered around the fireplace and sitting still.

When Caleb had mentioned to his parents that he had something very important to speak to them about, his mom turned to him in concern. "How important, Caleb?"

"Real important." Even though her eyes had widened with worry, Caleb hadn't tried to allay her fears. After all, what he wanted to discuss with his family was terribly important to him.

Probably the most important thing he ever had to speak of in his entire life.

"I see. Well, if things are that important, I will make sure all of us are here. Tim and Clara, too."

Even his cousin and his old schoolteacher? Well, perhaps that was the right choice. The more who heard his words, the less discussion there would be when everything was said and done.

"Will seven o'clock work for you?"

"Anytime is fine, Mamm."

"Seven will be best, then. It will be right after supper." Brushing her hands against each other, she murmured, "I'll go send Judith to the store to let Joshua and Gretta know. Carrie can walk over to Tim and Clara's now."

Caleb felt uncomfortable that everyone went to so much trouble for him.

But as he looked at everyone assembled — everyone he loved — Caleb knew he had made the right choice. And Lilly had given him the right advice as well. It was better to have secrets out in the open, especially secrets that would affect others.

His heart warmed as he surveyed the room: all six of his siblings were there. Even little Toby, all of three. Next up was Maggie, trying to be a big girl at five. Carrie, at seven. Anson and Judith and Joshua and his wife Gretta.

In two chairs next to the fireplace, Cousin Tim and Clara were sitting together, unabashedly holding hands. Since they'd been married, they only had eyes for each other. The whole family would have taken to teasing Tim except for the fact that they were all so happy for Clara and didn't want to embarrass her. She was terribly shy. And, love and affection was a new thing for her, too. Even Caleb knew she'd never imagined that she'd marry.

Just before his gaze moved past them, Caleb met Clara's knowing look. For a moment, he almost lost his nerve. Clara — being his former schoolteacher — had a way of peering right through all his layers, like she saw far more than anyone could have guessed. He would be hard-pressed to ever lie to her.

Sitting beside him, Judith and Joshua were snacking.

Somehow, Mamm had made time to bake up a batch of pumpkin bars — his older siblings' favorite.

"Caleb, are you ready?" his father murmured as he walked by with a steaming hot mug of coffee.

"I am."

With a look of understanding, Daed took his seat, a rocking chair on the other side of the fireplace. When he settled in, all eyes turned to him. "Perhaps we all ought to say a prayer," his father murmured.

Immediately, they all bowed their heads.

Caleb was used to silent prayers, as was the Amish way. But this time their father

176

spoke. "Dear Heavenly Father, please be with us as we all help Caleb. Please let him know our love for him, and our belief in his strength and abilities. In Your name we pray. Amen."

A chill ran up his arms as one by one, each person in the room raised their head and looked at him. Waiting.

It was time. Because he felt like he should, Caleb got to his feet. "I think I need to leave here for a time. As part of my *rumspringa*," he said bluntly. The moment the words were out of his mouth, Caleb braced himself for a slew of comments. Waited for Joshua to tell him he was acting stupid. For Cousin Tim to shake his head in disappointment.

But instead, everyone just looked like they were waiting for something more for him to say.

Now he felt even more on the spot. "This hasn't been an easy choice," he added slowly. "I've been restless." Looking out the window behind his father, Caleb thought about how the hills were beckoning him. Not to go out into the wilderness, but to venture beyond them. To other cities and places. Other places where he could start over with a clean slate.

At least, he thought that was what he wanted. "I need to see more of the world.

Other places beyond Sugarcreek. I want to try new things."

Joshua grunted. "What sort of things?"

"Nothing bad. Just stuff. I want to go to movies. To learn to drive a car. To talk on a cell phone . . ." His words drifted off as he realized how childish he was sounding.

"But Caleb, you already have been able to do some of that. Why do you need to go far away?"

"I didn't say I'd go far."

"If not far, then where would you go?" Carrie asked.

Of course Carrie would ask such a thing. She always went straight to the point, no matter what the topic. "I don't know. Maybe Cleveland."

Carrie wrinkled her nose. "What's there?"

Oh, he wished he had all the answers, but he didn't. "I don't know."

"Then why do you want to go?"

To Caleb's surprise, Joshua put his hand on Carrie's shoulder. "Enough, Carrie. Learn patience. Caleb is doing his best to explain."

"I'm trying, but it's more of a feeling, you see. I feel like it's something I've got to at least try. If that makes any sense."

His mother looked on the verge of tears, but to his surprise, she didn't look as shocked as he had thought she would be. "How long do you intend to go for? How long is 'a time'?"

"I don't know."

"You must have some thoughts. Forever? Do you think you'll leave forever?"

He swallowed hard. He knew what she was asking. Did he intend to leave and never return to Sugarcreek? To their way of life?

Such a question deserved an honest answer. "Maybe." He cleared his throat. "That is what I'm thinking about. I'm not just looking for new things to do . . . I'm thinking that maybe I don't want to join the church." There. He said it.

The tension in the room thickened as they all watched their father struggle to control his temper.

"Caleb," he bit out, "don't play games."

"I'm not." Feeling trapped, he began to talk faster. "I know what you all are thinking. And believe you me, I've been thinking the same things."

Judith blinked. "And what is that?"

"Oh, you know . . . that I shouldn't want to do anything else. That I should be happy with how things are. That after seeing everything on the outside, I should be happy staying where I'm at."

"Don't put words in my mouth, bruder,"

Joshua warned.

Caleb admired his older brother. In his eyes, Joshua was everything he should have been. So in some ways, his disappointment was hardest to bear. "I guess you think I'm an idiot."

Shaking her head, Judith stood up and slipped an arm around his shoulders, giving him support.

He looked at her in surprise.

"Oh, bruder," she murmured with a sad, small smile. "Don't you know your family any better? None of us is thinking you're an idiot."

He was almost afraid to follow her gaze. "No?"

"No. Caleb, you may be shocked to hear this, but I, for one, have suspected for some time that this announcement of yours was coming."

"You — you did?"

With a sad smile, Judith nodded. "It's been no secret that you've been dissatisfied with how things are. Plus, we know you've talked to Mrs. Miller, and she's helped other kids get away."

"These feelings have been brewing for a while, haven't they?" Joshua murmured.

There was no point in denying it. *"Jah."*

"Even I knew you were feeling lost,"

Gretta added.

"I haven't meant to be," Caleb said quickly. "I just have."

With a winsome look in Joshua's direction, Gretta murmured, "I know about feeling lost. Sometimes you can feel that way even though you know you have everything you need. But ya can't help it . . . right?"

"Right." Caleb felt at a loss for words. He felt so much love. So much support. All day he'd been mentally preparing himself to face a crowd of condemnation. Instead, his family was reaching out to him.

Maybe not in support, but definitely in concern.

"So, how were you planning to leave us? You weren't planning to sneak away, were ya?"

Well, there was the anger he'd expected to hear. "I don't want to do that, Mamm. That's why I asked to speak with you and Daed." He looked around at everyone with a mild annoyance. "You didn't have to call a family meeting."

"I'm glad I'm here," Anson announced. "I hate being left out."

Clara chuckled. "I have to agree with you there, Anson. I'm glad we're all here."

"When are you planning to leave us?" his father asked. "Do you have a date in mind?"

Just the thought of something so exact made his hands sweat. "Not exactly."

"Really?"

"Really. Daed, I don't want to make trouble, I just want to follow the direction that God is choosing for me. And I've felt Him give me the strength to talk to you all. I have been praying about it."

He rocked back and forth. "I see. Prayer is *gut,* of course."

Still looking to be the angriest person in the room, his mother cleared her throat. "So, son, you don't know where you're going, or when you're going to do anything . . . or what you're going to do?"

"I did mention how I was feeling to Lilly. She is the one who said that maybe I could just go somewhere for a little while. Just to see what I thought about living away."

"Did she have some place in mind?"

Feeling like he was betraying a confidence, he nodded. "She said maybe I could stay with some friends of hers back in Strongsville. I'm not sure, though. It was just an idea."

Caleb braced himself. Finally, here it would come. The reprimands.

"But nothing was decided?"

He shook his head slowly. "No. She said I should talk to you."

"If this is what you are truly wanting to do, I think you should go talk to Lilly again," Clara said, surprising them all.

Tim stared at her. "Why would you suggest that?"

"Just because we don't want something to happen, doesn't mean it won't. Plus, it's been my experience that being denied something only makes it seem more special."

His mom slowly nodded. "Yes. That is true. Perhaps you should go speak with Lilly again. I think maybe she might have an idea of what it's like, to start over and such. Perhaps she can give you some ideas to think about."

Slowly, his father nodded. "Caleb, this week, you will need to go visit with Lilly."

Caleb looked from his parents to his brother to his sister to everyone else that was assembled. "I never thought you all would be so agreeable."

His mother stood up. As she did so, her plum-colored dress settled around her hips, in the way it always did. His mother was the heart of the family, and it pained Caleb to see that he was hurting her. "Oh, I'm not feeling too agreeable, son, but I am resigned. All things considered, I'd rather let you live away from us for a bit in the hopes that

you'll come back instead of losing you forever."

"I love you all," he said, surprising himself.
Never before had he been all that good
about sharing his feelings.

In a rush, Judith hugged him. "We know
that."

Carrie hopped to her feet. "Are we finally
all done? Because I want to show Clara my
new picture."

Maggie reached for Clara's hand. "I
wanna see it, too."

"Yes, *dochder.* We are done." His mother
sighed. "For now, anyway."

Slowly everyone dispersed. Maggie and
Carrie chatted with Clara. Judith joined
their mother in the kitchen. Their father
walked Joshua and Gretta outside so they
could leave. Tim was looking at Anson's
newest cut on his finger.

Before he knew it, Caleb was alone in the
room. To his amazement, the solitude didn't
feel good. Instead, he felt at a loss. Almost
empty.

The fire that had burned in him for the
last year was settling to a low ebb. It was as
if now that everything had come out in the
open, and he was going to be able to do
what he wanted, that some of the drive had
deserted him.

How could that be? Had he only been wanting to cause trouble?

Then Anson peered into the room and broke the spell. "Here you are, I thought you were outside. Come on out to the barn, Caleb. We're all saying good night to Tim and Clara."

"I'll be right there."

"Better hurry."

"I will."

"Good." Anson turned, walked two steps, then looked his way again. "Caleb, are you leaving because of me?"

"Of course not. Why would you even ask such a thing?"

" 'Cause you've been mad at me, saying that I don't do enough chores."

"You don't do enough, Anson. You do your best to get out of chores, and Judith and I have to take up the slack. But, that's not why I want to leave. I just want to see something else. If even for a little while."

"Doubt anywhere will be as nice as Sugarcreek," Anson said. "It's the best place I know."

And that, Caleb realized with some surprise, was the crux of it all. Sugarcreek, Ohio, was the only place he knew. The only place on earth.

And now that he was sixteen, why, that didn't seem right.

CHAPTER 13

The last person Lilly expected to see at the Sugarcreek Inn was Josh. Ever since they had spoken harshly to each other at the market, they'd mutually decided to keep their distance. She'd missed him, but had been disappointed in his attitude more than anything.

"Gretta's not here," she said when he walked to the hostess station.

"I know."

"Oh. Well . . . would you like a table?" At his nod, she led the way through the near-empty dining room, completely aware of his presence behind her: his pace was slow. Plodding.

Finally, when they reached a table near the window, and he sat down, he looked at her directly. "Lilly, I, uh, I came to see you."

Looking at him more closely, she noticed his shoulders were stiff. Tension emanated from him like steam. "Oh my gosh — is something wrong with Gretta?"

"She's fine. When I left her, she was knitting a blanket and fussing about her swollen ankles." He stumbled over the next words like even talking about such things embarrassed him. "I don't know about that . . . she's been uncomfortable."

"Poor Gretta."

"We went to the English doctor when she wasn't feeling too well the other day. The doctor said her blood pressure was a bit high. And that Gretta's time might be within the week. She's supposed to stay off her feet and rest."

Still wondering why Josh was paying her a visit, Lilly ventured another guess. "Hey, can I drive you anywhere? Do you need some help? Is she staying at your parents'?" When he still hesitated, she blurted, "I could bring over some books or ice cream . . ."

After she stood in front of him for a moment, he said, "Lilly, do you have time to talk? Though I wouldn't mind something to eat, I actually came here to speak with you about something. Something important."

And it had to be a concern of great importance for him to leave the store. Worried again, Lilly looked at her watch. "I have a break coming up. I'll go ask Mrs. Kent if I could take it now."

Quickly, she went to the kitchen, asked Miriam for a cinnamon roll, then checked in with her boss who was in her office. "Can I take ten minutes now? A friend's here."

Looking away from her computer screen, Mrs. Kent smiled. "Is your girlfriend from home visiting again?"

"No. It's Joshua Graber, Gretta's husband."

"Is everything all right?"

"With Gretta, I think so. But there's something else I think. It's not like Josh to come in here just to visit."

"No, I wouldn't imagine so." Mrs. Kent stood up. "Go ahead, then. I'll waitress for a bit, my neck was getting a cramp from working on the computer all morning."

Moments later, Lilly brought Josh his roll and a cup of coffee for each of them. After taking a seat across from him, she murmured, "What's up?"

"Two things. One is about Caleb."

She blinked. "What about him?"

"He called a family meeting the other night." With a shake of his head, he added, "It was quite an event. The thing of it is, Caleb wants to get out of here, Lilly."

"Here?"

"I mean, Sugarcreek. Caleb wants to go

to the city. He wants to go to Cleveland."

Lilly was glad he was taking a big bite of his roll because she needed a moment to gather her thoughts. She was pleased that Caleb had taken her advice and talked to his family. But now that everything was out in the open, Lilly found herself torn. She wanted to be helpful to Josh, and wanted to give him support and her friendship, but she didn't want to completely disregard Caleb's confidences, either. In a lot of ways, she'd sympathized with Caleb. Sometimes things at home weren't great. And when a person was fifteen or sixteen, there was nothing to do about that.

Piercing blue eyes met hers. "He said he's talked to you about this. He has, hasn't he?"

"Yes." Though she felt a little like she was tattling, she said, "Caleb's told me that he wishes he had more choices. That he was envious of Charlie."

"He told us some things like that when we all got together. I'm worried about him, Lilly. And I know the rest of us are even more so."

His eyes looked so sad, his expression so defeated, Lilly knew that he was taking the news hard. In many ways, Josh was the go-to person in the Graber family. His parents depended on him. And his younger brothers and sisters looked to him for guidance. "What did your parents say?"

"Not all that much. As a matter of fact, they took it better than the kids. Better than I would've ever imagined. Much better than I think Caleb imagined, too. Though my mother looked upset, I don't think she was terribly surprised."

Lilly was relieved. Though Caleb had confided in her some, and she'd done her best to just listen, she knew it was unlikely that his parents would have the same responses.

"Actually, my parents said that Caleb should talk to you about Cleveland. They know you have ties there. And that, perhaps, you've been through enough to guide him better than, say, me."

"Josh, I don't know what you think, but I haven't been trying to guide him to do anything in particular; I'm just trying to be a friend. I like Caleb a lot, but I would never start pushing him to leave all of you."

"I believe you. And I don't think it would make a bit of difference if you had, or had not. He says his mind is made up. He says he wants to leave. But I'm not so sure."

"What do you want me to do when he comes to talk to me?"

"You need to do what you think best . . .

but my parents and I were hoping that maybe you could help him find a place to stay in the city. We would all rest better then."

She started to talk, but he held up a hand. "Lilly, I know it's a lot to ask. And I know Caleb's problems and our family's problems are none of your concern. But I, for one, am afraid that he's going to get hurt if he doesn't have someone looking out for him."

He did need a net. "Things outside of this little town are far different. Even English kids would have a difficult time adjusting, I think. For someone who grew up Amish?" She winced. "It's going to be a real shock for him."

"Thank you for any help you can provide." He pushed his half-eaten sweet roll away.

Lilly was just about to escape when Joshua spoke again.

"Now, about you and Robert —"

"Yes?" There was nowhere to run.

His voice was strained. "Lilly, he's a good man, that Robert Miller is."

"I'm sure he is. I mean, he seems to be. I think he's great."

If anything, her statement seemed to make him even more uncomfortable. "He's a good man. But . . . Robert Miller is Amish, Lilly." Josh picked up an unused spoon and twirled it between his fingers. "His situation is not like mine before I married Gretta. He's joined the church. He's taken vows. Those are sacred, serious things."

"I know that."

"He's not going to change," he warned. "Robert is not going to jump the fence. Not even for you. Not even if he wanted to. His vows are too sacred."

Each word Josh spoke was punctuated with certainty. Each word was said with such force, she felt chastised. Reprimanded. "I would never ask him to leave his faith."

Josh's cheeks flushed. "What I'm trying to say, is that I don't think your relationship with him can be like our friendship."

"Oh? How so?"

"I'm afraid he thinks of you differently." He cracked two knuckles as he struggled on. "You know what I mean. He looks at you in a courting way. But, Lilly, I don't want to see him get hurt."

Did Josh not even care how she was feeling? How she was putting her heart on the line, too? "I won't corrupt him, Josh," she said, not even trying to hide the hurt in her voice.

"Lilly, I didn't say —"

"You said enough," she interrupted. "You sound so . . . What in the world do you think is happening between us? What do you think we've done?"

"You've gone for a buggy ride . . ."

"So? Miriam's told me what some kids are doing at singings. She's told me how a whole lot more happens there besides carrying tunes."

To her amusement, he blushed. "That's not your concern."

She was so fired up, she continued. "Besides, we're not even talking about silly kids. Robert is a grown man!"

"I know. But he's in a tough spot emotionally."

"Guess what? I am, too."

"I didn't say you weren't. I'm only trying to help you. And him, too."

"Josh, I like Robert. And I'm very aware he's Amish. And guess what? I'm still interested in him. In a serious relationship." She waited a moment to let that sink in. "Do you get what I'm saying?"

Mute, he shook his head.

"I'm seriously thinking about becoming more deeply involved with him."

"But he can't leave the order, Lilly."

She was so frustrated with him, she blurted words she'd barely even had come to understand herself. "Then maybe I'll become Amish."

"You?"

"Yes, me." He looked so incredulous, she felt her face burn. "Come on, Josh. That wouldn't be a bad thing."

But instead of him looking joyous for her, instead of offering her support, Josh shook his head softly. "Lilly, this . . . what you're talking about . . . it would be a huge mistake."

"Why?"

"Lilly . . . you truly have a desire to follow the *Ordnung*? The laws of our church are strict and all encompassing."

"Maybe."

"That's not good enough. You have to be sure."

"I realize that. But I also realize that I don't have to know today."

"Lilly. You really would choose to live simply? To give up your car . . ."

His tone amplified every doubt that was nestled deep inside her. "I . . . I could try."

"Trying isn't good enough." A hint of wariness filled his eyes as he continued. "And, there's another reason that I don't think you'd suit."

Folding her arms over her chest, she glared. "What else could there possibly be?"

"It's your past."

She was taken completely off guard. As

long as they'd been friends, Josh had never acted like she wasn't good enough for him. In fact, he'd done just the opposite. He'd made her think that she was good enough for anyone. Even good enough for God.

"You had a baby," he mumbled.

"I had a miscarriage."

"But you had relations outside of marriage."

"That isn't news, Josh. I told you and your family all about it months ago."

"I know. But it's different now. Robert's family will find fault with that, for sure."

"Josh, I can't believe no Amish girl ever became pregnant outside of marriage. Lots of kids make mistakes."

"They make mistakes but then they get married. You did not. Please don't think too much more about Robert. He won't be able to marry you. Not if he wants to keep his standing in our community."

"And no one would ever accept me in the Amish community, either?"

Pursing his lips, he shook his head. "I'm not sayin' you're not a good woman, Lilly. It's just that for you to become Amish, why, it would be like trying to put a square peg into a round hole. It isn't going to work."

Tears flooded her eyes so quickly, she ducked her head as he stood up. She felt him stand by her side for a moment, like he was waiting for her to look at him.

But she couldn't.

Finally, he tossed a ten-dollar bill on the table and walked outside. Seconds later, the front door chimed again.

"Lilly?" Mrs. Kent called out. "Are you done with your break?"

"I am," she murmured. Then, with a furious swipe of her eyes, she lifted her head, stood up, and greeted the newcomers. Yes, she was upset with Josh — upset with herself, for getting so caught up with Alec that she had made a mistake . . . and upset that she was still somehow paying for it now. But that didn't mean she didn't have a job to do.

"Welcome to the Sugarcreek Inn," she said with a watery smile. "A table for four?"

CHAPTER 14

Caleb knew he should be grateful that his family was being so open-minded about him venturing to Cleveland. But somehow obtaining his parents' permission made him feel like he was still a child.

If he was so sure about his need to leave, shouldn't he be able to leave on his own? Wasn't it time for him to accept the burdens of his responsibilities all by himself?

It seemed wrong that the most important event in his life was now being managed by so many others.

When he walked through the hedge that separated his family's land from the Allens', he couldn't help but remember the first time he'd seen the family. It had been late November. Just days after Anson had broken his arm. He'd spied Lilly arguing with her brother on their driveway.

Now Caleb knew that she and Charlie had been arguing about her pregnancy and their abrupt move to Sugarcreek. That day, though, all he'd seen was a pair of teenagers having more freedoms than he'd ever imagined. From that point on, he'd ached to be just like them.

"Hey, you," Lilly called out when he stepped onto their driveway. "Come up to the front. I'm sitting on the porch."

When he walked up the two steps to meet her, Caleb saw that she had two mugs of hot cider. "Want some?"

"Sure." Sitting down in the rocking chair next to her, Caleb felt completely nervous. "Thanks for meeting with me."

She grinned. "I didn't have much choice. Your parents asked me to."

"Oh."

Her smile vanished. "Hey, forget I said that. I'm sorry. Don't mind me. I'm a little grumpy. A certain somebody at the restaurant put me in a bad mood."

Caleb figured a bad customer there was like any he'd had at the store, and he had no need to think about them. As a few seconds passed, and she said nothing more, he said, "Lilly, I don't know what to say."

"Well, you better think of something! You've got your whole family in a dither."

Remembering how calm they'd all been, he shook his head. "Not really."

"They might be all smiles to you, but underneath, I promise, they're really worried."

"I don't know what to do now. Part of me feels like I should have never said anything."

"Caleb, you didn't have a choice. Not really. Things would have been worse if you had just left in the middle of the night."

It was like she'd read his mind. "Perhaps."

"You know, I've been where you are."

Caleb doubted it. "You've wanted to stop being Amish and move away?" he asked sarcastically.

"I've had to tell my parents things they didn't want to hear. First when I told them I was pregnant, and then when I told them I wanted to keep the baby and not put it up for adoption. Telling difficult news isn't easy."

Leaning against his chair, he looked beyond Lilly, to the neatly mowed grass in the front of Lilly's house. To the small garden that was in dire need of tilling — the Allens really were terrible gardeners.

As her words sank in, he relaxed. "It hasn't been easy at all."

After sipping from her mug, she murmured, "Caleb, do you still want me to call my friend?"

Here it was. He could either accept her

offer and move forward . . . or he could back away and stay in Sugarcreek. Where it was safe. "Yes."

"All right, then. I'll give her a call and see if we can drive over to Strongsville tomorrow."

"So soon?"

"I have the day off. And, well, it's what you want, right?"

"Sure." He hoped Lilly didn't notice that he wasn't really as excited about the visit as he'd wanted to be.

"Now, don't get your hopes up. My friend Cassidy might not be able to help us too much. But at least you'll get to start thinking about options." She gave him a sideways look. "If you still want to leave."

"Going on Sunday is fine."

"Okay. Great. How about we leave at nine? Is that too early?"

"I guess not."

"What's wrong with you? I thought you'd be excited."

He didn't know what was wrong, other than that everything was suddenly happening too quickly. "It's just that this Sunday is church. My folks won't like me missing." Actually, that was an understatement.

His parents wouldn't like it one bit. The whole family would be up at dawn, especially since church was at Tim and Clara's new home. Because they were newly married, their entire family would be expected to go over early and help set up.

"Does missing church matter to you?"

"Maybe."

Her expression turned serious. "Caleb . . . you can't have it both ways, you know. You either want to stay where you are and abide by all the rules . . . or it's time to make changes. You can't just complain to everyone who will listen. You shouldn't make plans without intending to follow through."

She was right. This was his chance to seriously move forward. To prepare to leave. "I'll be ready at nine."

"Come over, then."

For the first time, true fear about what he was doing settled inside of him. It was one thing to have a dream. It was quite another to put it into action.

As he thought of the few English kids he'd hung around with in Sugarcreek, Caleb began to worry. They'd all teased him some about his funny way of speaking. About his longish hair. With them, he hadn't really cared . . . but he'd feel different if he was living with the English. "Do you think your friend will think I'm too different?"

Eyes serious, Lilly shrugged. "I don't

know. I'm not going to lie to you — you do look different than most sixteen-year-old boys, but with a haircut and different clothes, you could fit in. Eventually."

"So it's just the clothes, right?" The uneasiness dissipated. That, he could deal with. He knew he wouldn't be dressing Amish anyway.

"Maybe it's just the clothes . . . or maybe not. It's a whole way of looking at the world around you."

"Everyone looks at their surroundings one way or another."

Lilly pulled up her knees and rested her chin on them. "I guess that's true. But I don't know. I used to think people could change, and could put their past behind them, but maybe I was wrong. Maybe we all carry our pasts with us like marks on our arms . . . for better or worse."

Caleb had a feeling she was talking about how very "English" she was . . . and how it had to do with Robert Miller. To his way of thinking, she would have an even harder time becoming Amish than he would becoming English.

Caleb lifted his chin. For a moment, he yearned to tell her that everything was going to work out for the best. That she shouldn't worry about the future because

God was with them. That there surely had to be a reason that he was thinking about turning English at the same time that she was considering a future with an Amish man.

But it wasn't the right time. She was still keeping secrets . . . and he was starting to think that he didn't know any right answers.

Mouth dry, he stood up. "I'm going to go on back now."

"Yes, I suppose you should. Bye, Caleb. See you tomorrow."

After crossing through the hedge, he walked back into his family's barn. The dusty, dank smell in the darkened area was completely familiar. Almost comforting. As Jim whickered a greeting, he let his eyes adjust to the light, then wandered over to give the horse some attention. "Hey, buddy," he murmured, scratching the horse around his ears the way he loved.

Looking more closely at the horse's coat, irritation coursed through him. Flecks of mud and dirt spotted Jim's broad side; far more decorated his white stockings.

Once again, Anson hadn't done what he was supposed to. "That brother of mine. Will he ever learn to do his chores?"

In response, Jim's ears darted forward and

Caleb immediately felt remorseful. The horse could sense anger or nervousness quicker than a snap. "It's okay, horse. I'm just griping. Ready for some brushing?" he murmured.

He turned just in time to see Anson dragging his feet behind Judith. "Look who I found playing by the side of the road," she said. "Our long-lost bruder."

Anson pulled out his bottom lip. "I wasn't lost. And I wasn't doing anything wrong, neither."

Judith rolled her eyes. "Oh, no. Not at all!" she said mockingly. "You were just causing everyone around you to be scared to death."

"What was he doing?"

"He and Ty were hopping along the road side by side, not paying a bit of attention to the vehicles flying by. I, myself, saw a car have to swerve out of the way in order to avoid them."

"Anson, you should know better."

"Don't start up disciplining me too, Caleb," Anson snapped. "You weren't even there."

Anson's tone was filled with more than a touch of indignation and pride. Sharing an exasperated look with his sister, Caleb suddenly felt sorrier than ever for his parents. How were they able to keep their calm so often? With seven children, no less? At the moment, he was sorely tempted to shake some sense into his brother's head.

Crossing her arms over her chest, Judith tapped her feet. "I had to go find Anson because when I came in here earlier, I saw he hadn't done all his chores. I'm supposed to be at the store, helping Joshua."

Tilting his head up, Anson glared. "I don't know why you're being so mean. I just forgot."

"Oh, no, you didn't," Caleb said. "I've been ten, too. I know exactly what you were thinking. You didn't forget. You just didn't want to muck out the stalls and brush Jim, and thought if you weren't around someone else would do the work. Like me."

"I fed him."

"That's not good enough," Judith said. "Anson, Caleb and I are tired of doing your chores."

When Caleb watched his brother roll his eyes, his temper snapped. "We were tired months ago. If Mamm and Daed aren't going to make you do your part, I sure intend to. This lazing about isn't good for you, and it isn't fair to the rest of us."

"I don't know why you even care, Caleb. All you want to do is leave me." Bright red spots licked Anson's cheeks as he clumsily

206

corrected himself. "I mean, *leave us.* So we're going to have to do all of your chores soon anyway."

Guilt flooded him. "That's not the same."

"Sure it is. I listened to everything you and Mamm and Daed said the other night. All you care about is yourself."

There were a thousand things Caleb was tempted to say to that. He knew that Anson was grasping at any straw to get his way, and had become extremely good at doing so during his various accidents and recuperations.

But a small part of him knew that his little brother had a point. He hadn't been thinking about how his absence would affect the workload for the rest of the family. He truly was selfish in that regard.

"Come get a brush and start working on Jim," he muttered. "And don't be too rough, neither. That horse has done nothing to deserve that."

With a mutinous expression, Anson strode over to the horse.

Shaking her head, Judith turned to go just as Caleb walked over to her. "I'm going to go inside and tell Mamm."

Usually Caleb wouldn't have encouraged Judith to start tattling, but he, for one, was tired of their parents looking away when

Anson goofed off. Maybe Judith telling on their little brother would do some good. "Good luck."

"I'm just glad I saw him playing on the side of the road." She shook her head. "I don't know what's gotten into him."

"I think he's used to everyone fussing over him. We sure did fuss quite a bit after he and Ty were lost in the river."

"I guess you're right." She turned, then looked his way again. "Hey . . . Caleb . . . about what Anson said, don't let it get to you."

"He's probably right. I am talking about leaving you."

"No, he wasn't, Caleb. No one was shocked about you being dissatisfied. I, for one, think it's a *gut* thing that you want to leave her for a little while, just to see what the outside world is like. I just hope you'll want to come back. And not because of the chores, either."

"Promise?" He knew it took a lot for her to say what she did. Of them all, Judith seemed to be the most settled and content with their way of life. He had thought she would have given him the hardest time about wanting a change.

"I promise."

"I'm going to visit Lilly's friends tomorrow."

"Really? Already?"

He nodded. "Lilly says it's the only time she can get away." He paused, considering his next words. "I'm kind of nervous about going," he admitted.

"I bet. Though, you're only sixteen, Caleb." Reaching out, she squeezed his shoulder. "I promise, nothing has to be decided now."

"I'm starting to realize that," he mumbled and watched her slowly walk into the house before he turned back to Anson. "You being careful with Jim?"

"I am," Anson replied sharply.

Caleb narrowed his eyes, but luckily saw that his brother was brushing Jim slowly and carefully, just the way the horse enjoyed.

Without a word, he passed by Anson, walked over to the chicken pen and started work on that. One of the roosters glared at him in disdain.

Caleb glared right back until the bird turned away.

These were things he knew to do. He knew just how to gather eggs and fix broken chicken wire. He knew how to bale hay and how to drive a buggy. And just how Jim liked to be brushed with the curry comb.

None of that knowledge would be any good among the *Englischers,* however.

Somewhat desperately, he wondered what would.

CHAPTER 15

On one particularly bad morning-after spending the previous night tossing and turning without hardly more than a few minutes of sleep at a stretch — Robert had timed how long it took him to get ready for his day.

Nineteen minutes.

Yes, it had taken nineteen minutes to shower, get dressed, make his bed, and brew two cups of coffee. Nineteen minutes, and he hadn't even been hurrying.

That was worrisome.

Usually, he didn't eat breakfast — there wasn't much of a point to sit at the table by himself. But that morning, he'd decided to eat after all. After whisking an egg with a bit of water, then adding some chopped-up ham from his leftover dinner, he cooked his eggs. A thick slice of bread, toasted in his oven's broiler, went on the plate, too.

All of that took ten minutes.

It took another five eating it, and four minutes to wash his plate and set it neatly on the wooden rack next to the sink.

All told, from the moment he'd opened his eyes to the time he walked out the door, he'd been up for thirty-nine minutes.

That was all.

The difference between his mornings now and the way things had been with Grace was very great, indeed. During their first year of marriage, he'd taken to lazing a bit, because she would fuss over him. Every so often, he'd pull her into bed beside him and kiss her, just because he could.

Breakfast had been a time to discuss their day's plans, and with Grace, everything had importance. He'd used to silently pray for patience as she'd talk to him about her plans to spring clean or to bake cobbler or ponder over the color choices for one of the many quilts she was piecing.

Whenever he finally left the house, it was with the taste of her kisses still on his lips, and the promise that she'd be waiting for him when he'd returned.

Robert figured he'd walked through their first year of marriage with a permanent smile on his face. Yes, things between them had been pleasing.

Now, of course, it all was gone. Now he

usually rushed through his morning routine
— such that it was — because it hurt too
much to compare it to how things used to
be.

Perhaps some men could have made
adjustments or would have begun to welcome the sheer ease of living alone. But so
far, that hadn't been him.

When she'd gotten sick, things had
changed, of course. During her last few
weeks, the kitchen had been constantly dirty
— he'd had no time to rinse off plates or
glasses. His parents had come over often.
Many nights, his father stayed by his side.
Other relatives silently sat in his front room
and prayed. Ladies came, delivered soups
and casseroles, and then stayed to clean and
tidy the mess.

But he'd hardly done more than acknowledge their presence with a cursory nod.
He'd hardly been aware of anything but her
weakened state.

After her funeral, more people had
stopped over until he'd finally had enough.
As gently as he could, he had asked everyone
to leave. In exchange, he'd promised to
reach out to them again when he was ready.
Just as soon as he'd gotten some much
needed time and space.

That had been three years ago.

Now he had more time and space than he ever wanted. The home was dark and too quiet. Some rooms were never used. Robert couldn't recall the last time he'd walked into Grace's sewing room. The room that he'd built for their *kinner*.

Ever since Grace had passed on, it felt like he was living in someone else's house.

Yes, Grace and the love they'd shared had made their house a home.

For the most part, he had come to terms with things. No longer was he claimed by sudden onslaughts of tears that stung his eyes and clogged his throat. No longer did he see her old sewing machine and ache to see her working in front of it.

Or strain to listen for her humming while she mopped the kitchen floor or kneaded bread. Grace, she did so like to hum. And she had never met a tune that she wasn't able to ruin by twisting it out of sorts.

But this early morning, this Sunday, he felt her loss more than ever. He missed her. Almost just as much, he was growing tired of being alone.

Which, of course, brought his mind back to Lilly Allen. If he sat still long enough, Robert could still recall how she'd felt in his arms. Soft and womanly, and responsive. She'd been full of laughter and happiness, and he'd instinctively known that she'd enjoyed his kisses just as much as he had enjoyed hers.

He supposed a stronger man wouldn't dwell on such things. A better Christian would only concentrate on their ease of conversation. On the way she made him feel whole again.

But he'd never claimed to be a strong man. No, he was weak and missed the comfort of a woman's arms. At twenty-four, his brain told him that he wasn't a terrible person. After all, his married friends often smiled in a way that said that they still enjoyed private times with their wives very much.

Yes, living a life as humbly as possible didn't offer that much happiness. Not really. There was no comfort in eyeing a future completely alone.

Desperate to get out of his melancholy mood, Robert pulled out his Bible and opened it randomly. Chapter three of Philippians fell open. He thought that was probably fitting. After all, sometimes he did feel like Paul, writing letters to others while imprisoned in a place not of his own choosing. Of course, Paul still had found reason for happiness and joy.

Robert wished he had a little more of the

apostle's heavenly spirit.

He'd just read another two chapters in the Book when Abe and his father appeared at his door. "Robert, we're glad to find you home!" his father said, all smiles.

"Good morning," he said as they wandered in and pulled off their overcoats. "I didn't expect you two to stop by before church. To what do I owe this visit?"

Abe looked at his father warily. "We just happened to have started out a little early for Tim and Clara's home and thought to pay you a call."

Happened to be early? That was not likely.

Pay him a call? His father didn't pay calls. No, something was on their minds. No matter what they said, their visit was especially out of the ordinary. "I see."

His father cleared his throat. "Nothing wrong with taking time to visit with my son, is there?"

"Of course not. I am always glad for your company."

"So, you're alone?"

"Jah." Sensing the undercurrent of suspicion, he cast a glance his father's way. "Who else would be here?"

When his father just looked guilty, Abe jumped in. "No one that we know of. I mean, of course, you wouldn't have a guest here. Most especially not a woman."

A woman?

And that's when Robert felt the full reason for their visit. They were worried about Lilly Allen.

They'd come over to lecture. And condemn.

Both the words and the airy way he spoke proved to all three of them that Abe was telling a lie. The fact that his cousin was still dancing around subterfuge grated on Robert's nerves.

Surely they were all beyond making up such things?

But instead of bringing up the obvious — that he knew Abe and his father had paid a call on him for a much different reason than social chatting — Robert went to the kitchen and turned on the faucet. "I'll make us some fresh coffee."

"That would be nice. The air is still damp from last night's rain. Hot coffee would set me to rights. That is, if making it is no trouble," Daed said.

"Of course it isn't." Carefully Robert cleaned out the percolator and added fresh coffee grounds. Within four minutes, fresh dark coffee would begin trickling out.

To his shame, Robert had once timed that, too.

Abe leaned against the counter and watched him with a look of mild interest. "I never have learned how to work one of those things."

Robert was just irritated enough with his cousin to snap at him. "That's most likely because Mary is alive and healthy."

The skin around Abe's mouth turned white. "You shouldn't say such things."

"Why? It's the truth," Robert retorted, sick and tired of Abe pretending that nothing had changed when Grace had died.

The simple fact was that *everything* had changed when Grace died, and there was no circling around the cold, hard facts. When she'd gotten sick, he'd had to get used to doing everything. He'd gotten used to caring for her, and for doing her chores.

Abe still liked to think that a few casseroles and encouraging words had made his life easier.

But nothing was ever that simple — especially not his life without Grace. "I never learned to make coffee until Grace got sick," he said quietly. "It was only then that I learned to make coffee and cook."

While Abe shifted uneasily, obviously at a loss for the perfect trite saying to make everything all better, his father took control. "Come sit down, Robert. And look to see what I brought you." He pushed a sack toward Robert.

As soon as he unfolded the top of the paper sack, the unmistakable scent of fresh bread greeted him. He sniffed appreciatively. "Mom's been baking, I see."

"All day and night."

Robert knew his mother didn't sleep when she was worried. "Is everything all right at home?"

"It is not," Abe said quickly. Helping himself at the cabinets, he pulled out three mugs and poured the brewed coffee into each of them. When he joined them at the table, his voice sounded even more judgmental. "She told me herself that she couldn't sleep from worrying so much about you."

Robert sighed.

"Word's gotten around the whole community about you and that *Englischer*."

Robert loved his cousin, but he'd had just about enough of his high-handed attitude. Abe had no idea what it was like to lose a wife and to have to keep on living. He'd also had enough of Abe's girlish penchant for gossip.

"Word's gotten around, has it? Hmm. I wonder who has been talking?"

"More folks than you might imagine."

"There's only one man I'm imagining who has been talking."

With a sideways look at Abe, his *daed* murmured, "Robert, we just don't want you to hurt yourself. To hurt your heart."

"Thank you for your concern, but my heart's already been broken. My wife is gone."

His father winced at Robert's bitter tone of voice. "I know you've been through a rough time, with Grace's illness and all. But there's got to be someone nearby who's a better fit."

Though the reasonable part of him agreed, Robert was just peeved enough to push his father's buttons. "Lilly's pretty nearby, Daed."

"You know what we're talking about." The chair scooted and creaked as Abe shifted restlessly. "I'm telling you, cousin, if you'd just give us a chance, we could introduce you to all kinds of women . . ."

"I'm not interested."

"You should be. That girl is not for you."

Robert flinched at both his cousin's tone and choice of words. "She's not exactly a girl."

"She's close enough," Abe proclaimed. "And in addition, she's got other issues to think about." He waited a full three seconds before dropping his next bombshell. "Word is out that Lilly Allen is taking Caleb Graber to the city today. She's going to help him leave. And she's doing this on a church day, too."

Robert was shocked by the statement. But he was almost just as shocked by his cousin's need to make sure Robert knew every bad thing about Lilly.

Warily, he looked at Abe, opposite him at the table, sitting so full of himself with his arms crossed and his expression smug. Was that the kind of man his cousin had become? The type of person to look on others' misfortunes with glee?

Slowly, he turned to his father. "Daed? Have you been listening to this gossip, too?"

"I can't help but listen," he murmured grudgingly. Though it was obvious that his father, too, was a bit startled by Abe's enthusiasm, he also looked resigned to see the conversation through. "Frank Graber told me about Caleb's trip himself."

"Caleb is Frank's son. And Lilly Allen is their friend and neighbor. Surely what they all are doing is their concern, not ours."

"I agree with that," Abe said. "But you are our concern, Robert. And because of that, we need to keep you under our watch."

"I'm a grown man. I don't need to be

under anyone's watch."

Sipping his coffee, Robert's father glanced over toward Abe. "What Abe is trying to say, is that Lilly Allen, while very beautiful, is not the woman for you. You're never going to be able to change her."

"Perhaps she'll want to change herself?" he added rashly. "Who knows? Perhaps she'll even consider becoming Plain."

Abe rolled his eyes. "I seriously doubt that. No *Englischer* would want to start living with no electricity."

"Some have done it. Why, there's a woman in the next county who's a fine Amish wife and she grew up English." But even as he said the words, Robert felt full of misgivings. Lilly prided herself on her independence.

"This girl is different, and you know it."

"Perhaps you could go on a vacation or something, Robert?" his father suggested. "Go on a bus trip out west. Or down to Florida, maybe."

"You think what I need is a change of scenery?" Robert felt so out of sorts, he thought that his temper was going to burst. "Taking a trip to the beach is not what I need. What I need is . . ." His voice trailed off as he struggled to put into words all of his wishes and dreams. All of his struggles and hopes.

He wondered how he could ever admit, to the two men who were the closest to him in the world, that what he needed was companionship. A partner. He wanted a relationship . . . a woman's smile. The feel of her in his arms when he went to sleep at night and when he awoke in the morning.

He wanted marriage. A marriage with a feel and an identity of its own — not just a mere copy of what he and Grace once had.

And none of the Amish women in his community held his attention like Lilly did.

He knew what he wanted. What he ached for.

As the silence across the three feet of table lengthened and pulled a tension into the air so thick that it could almost be seen, his father leaned forward. "What do you need, son?"

"I need to be happy," Robert finally said. "I want to be happy again. And I'm willing to do whatever it takes in order to feel that way."

Abe stood up. "You're making a mistake," he said bluntly. "And you'll rue your impulsive ways when you realize it, too."

Robert got to his feet as well. "It's my mistake to make. Abe, I hope you and Mary have a long and prosperous life together. I hope the two of you enjoy each other's company and find comfort for many years to come." He sighed, for a moment debating whether to say what was on his mind or to hold his tongue. "But if something does happen to Mary, I promise that I will be by your side. I promise I'll be there for you . . . even when I don't always agree with your decisions. It would have been nice if you could have made such a promise to me."

Abe's eyebrows snapped together. "Now, wait a minute. I have been there for you —"

"You've been by my side to make sure I stay on the 'right' path. You've been here to tell me how our people are judging my behavior," Robert said softly. "But what you don't realize is that no matter what happens in the future . . . I will never, ever forget the past."

Chapter 16

"What's she like, this Cassidy friend of yours?"

Lilly looked at Caleb and tried to describe her old friend in just a few words. It was difficult. Almost as hard as her phone call to Cassidy had been.

To put it mildly, Cassidy had been surprised that the first time Lilly had reached out to her was because she wanted Cassidy and her brother Eric to spend their Sunday afternoon with a sixteen-year-old Amish kid.

"She's got brown hair and brown eyes."

"And?"

Lilly thought some more. "She loves to go shopping." She paused. "Let's see. Cassidy is honest. And she's funny." She glanced his way again, unsure if she was giving him the information he wanted.

Caleb still stared at her. "But what is she *like?*"

"Hmm." Lilly tried to think of a story that

would illustrate what her friend from home was like. "Well, one time during our freshman year, a couple of girls we're really into finally being in high school and we're kind of putting on airs. It was ridiculous, really. They went to the mall and bought all kinds of expensive clothes and told everyone how much money they were spending."

"And people respected that?"

"People respected that they had spent all that money," she corrected with a hint of foreboding. That was the kind of thing Caleb was going to have trouble with. Not the spending money, but the unspoken nuances that reigned supreme in an English teen's life. Things were "in" or "out." And a teenager's knowledge of that determined whether they would be included in groups or not.

Realizing her mind had been wandering, Lilly lightened her tone. "Anyway, part of their acting all grown up was to completely ignore Cassidy and me. As retaliation, Cassidy started a rumor that they'd bought all their clothes from a resale shop."

"What's that?"

"It's a place where people sell their old clothes and get money for it, and others can buy them. You can get good deals there if you go to some of the best stores. Anyway, everyone believed that rumor. So whenever the girls continued to brag about their expensive things, people just snickered."

Caleb looked impressed. "So Cassidy's a mean sort of girl."

"No, not really. She's just fair, I think. She was tired of being looked down on by girls who were trying to be something they weren't. Anyway, there's more to the story than that. About a week later, Cassidy went out of her way to befriend the girls. She felt really guilty for what she'd done." She glanced Caleb's way. "That's what I'm trying to get at. She's impulsive yet friendly. She's got a sense of what's right and wrong, but she struggles with it, too. She's not all sweet and perfect. She's just, well . . . Cassidy. You'll like her, Caleb."

As she sped along 90 toward Cleveland, keeping in the middle lane, Caleb looked like he was weighing that story over and over in his head. Finally he spoke. "Do you think she's going to like me?"

"She's going to like you fine. And she should anyway. You're great."

Caleb didn't say anything. Lilly wasn't sure if her words embarrassed him, or if it was all just too much to take in. They hit traffic closer to the city, so she had to stop thinking about Caleb's worries and concentrate on the traffic.

But he was doing enough sightseeing to keep them both occupied. "What's that?"

"It's a steel mill. There're still a few around. Not like there used to be, though. More than a dozen factories around here have closed since our parents were our age."

"The factories are very big."

"They are. I've never been in one, but people have told me they're like a small city. Real mazes in there."

As traffic picked up, they saw some of the skyscrapers in the distances, and the wide expanse of Lake Erie to the north. "It looks like the ocean," Caleb said. "I mean the ocean that I've seen in pictures at school."

Glancing at the wide expanse of water, with the silky blue waves rushing the shore, and the whitecaps decorating them, Lilly smiled. "No, you're right. It looks a lot like the ocean. I love to look at the water." It was one of the reasons she'd driven a little farther north than she needed to. "Every once in a while, I meet someone who talks as if the Great Lakes aren't really all that big — like they're just overgrown lakes. They have no idea how much they look like the ocean."

She started south on 71 toward Strongsville. "We're only about thirty minutes away now."

Beside her, Caleb kept quiet. Lilly could practically feel him tense up as she exited the freeway.

The silence remained as she headed into the heart of the suburb — toward the only place she'd ever really known until they'd moved to Sugarcreek.

To her surprise, Lilly hardly had to even look at the streets. Even after all this time, it felt like she'd just taken that exit a week ago.

But what was surprising was that she wasn't feeling as nostalgic as she thought she would. Maybe it was the nervousness she felt about seeing Cassidy again. Maybe it was her second-guesses about taking Caleb. She didn't want Caleb to be made fun of.

But she couldn't protect him. He was desperate for a change, and she knew enough about that to want to help him in any way that she could.

"Hey, Caleb, just to let you know . . . Cassidy doesn't know I was pregnant."

He looked at her in surprise. "Why not?"

"My mom and dad didn't want anyone to know," she blurted, then amended her words. "No, that's not completely true. I didn't want anyone to know, either."

"Because you'd be shunned."

"Shunned? Yeah, in a way I was worried about that."

Shunning.

The word caught her off guard. It was such an antiquated word. Such an Amish word. Yet, that was what she'd feared the most, wasn't it?

She'd been afraid that she'd be made fun of. Left behind while everyone else went on with their lives . . .

All this time, she'd acted like it had been her parents who'd been so afraid of what others thought. She'd been so self-righteous, lashing out at them. Blaming them for so much.

Perhaps, even secretly blaming them for her miscarriage. It had been so much easier to put the bad feelings on their shoulders. To resent them for everything. So much easier to blame her parents, like a spoiled child.

Instead of accepting responsibility like the grown-up she'd been trying too hard to be.

The realization wasn't a good one. In fact, it was bitter and embarrassing. For a moment, her hands tightened on the steering wheel and everything around them blurred.

"Lilly!"

She jerked back to the present. "What?"

Caleb's hands flew in the air. Obviously he was dying to place his hands on the steering wheel, but didn't dare. "The car!"

Only then did she realize that her Civic had started to drift to the left. With a jerk, she righted the car. "Sorry," she bit out. Then, realizing that her weak apology did nothing to soothe the moment, Lilly breathed deeply. "I'm sorry," she said again. "When you mentioned shunning, it brought forth a lot of memories and thoughts I've been trying hard to ignore."

Still looking alarmed, Caleb faced forward. "S'okay."

"Um, back to what you said . . . yes, I think I was worried about being shunned by my friends. I had a great group of both guy and girlfriends. Though I let my parents be the driving force for the move, I know now that I was grateful for it."

"They really wouldn't have accepted you with a baby?"

"I don't know. Maybe they would have. Maybe not." She reflected some more. "I think I was more worried about their opinion of me than anything else. I didn't want it to change."

"Because they thought so highly of you?"

"Yes. No, that doesn't sound quite right.

It was more like they thought I was a perfect fit in their group. If I was different, I wouldn't fit in so well, you know?"

The moment she said the words, Lilly regretted them. Caleb had his own problems. He didn't need hers to shoulder as well. "Guess what?" She pointed to a red brick house with black shutters. "We're here."

"What if I don't get along with them? I'll be out of choices."

"I've started to realize that God provides more choices than we can ever imagine. If this isn't the answer for you, then something else will come along. It's just that simple."

"You make it sound so easy."

"I know it's not." She was mature enough to admit that she didn't know all the answers. And that it would be wrong to even try. "I don't know. I guess I just decided to start hoping and praying for solutions. That counts for something, right?"

He leaned his head back against the seat's headrest, his wheat-colored hair mixing with the beige upholstery fabric. "It does. I didn't think I would be so *naerfich*. So nervous."

"I think it means you care," she said softly. "So that's a good thing. Now, let's go in. Mrs. Leonard is probably looking out her living room window at us, wondering why we are still sitting in the car." Before he could stall, she opened her car door and grabbed her purse.

But she still took the time to say a quick, silent prayer for guidance.

Cassidy opened the door before they were even halfway up the walk. "Hi! You made it."

"We did. We're not late, are we?"

"No, I was just looking for you." She eyed Caleb up and down. "Hi. I'm Cassidy."

"Caleb."

She stepped backward to allow them entrance, then closed the door behind her. "My mom is so excited to see you two. She's in the living room, waiting."

As they followed Cassidy, Caleb looked around, stunned.

Lilly didn't blame him. Walking into the Leonards' home was like walking into another world, one that was a little bit more colorful and unusual than his own.

She didn't know anyone else whose house looked like theirs, though a few other neighbors and friends had tried. Belatedly, Lilly realized she probably should have mentioned something to Caleb about it. It wasn't all that big, but it was beautifully decorated inside — like something out of a magazine, but with a huge batch of whimsy, too.

She and her other girlfriends used to love having sleepovers at Cassidy's because staying at the home was like staying in a museum, or at least a really kitschy gift shop. Back when they were small, she'd at first been afraid she'd accidentally break something and Cassidy's mom would get mad. But she never did.

Funny how all those good memories had been carefully pushed away. Had she really been so afraid to look back at her past?

Lilly watched Caleb. He was staring at his heavy-soled work boots, which appeared glaringly harsh against the array of fancy furnishings . . . and she wondered what such a home looked like to Caleb . . . what he was thinking.

CHAPTER 17

Caleb tried not to feel completely conspicuous as he followed Lilly into the fanciest room he'd ever seen.

He tried to think of something his father always said. Everyone's the same in God's eyes. Caleb had always taken that to be true.

Mrs. Leonard was a small woman — shorter than his sister Judith, with fine features and an interested, almost birdlike expression on her face. She was dressed in a faded pair of jeans, cowboy boots, and a bright turquoise sweater. Matching stones hung from her ears.

Yes, she looked very modern and unique. But her voice and mannerisms were as comforting as his own grandmother's hug. "We're so glad you came for a visit, Caleb."

"I . . . I am, too."

"I'm so looking forward to getting to know you."

Catching his eye, Lilly gave him a quick

smile. That surely signaled for him to not be worried. Too much.

"Hey." A guy a bit older than Caleb sauntered in. "I'm Eric."

"Caleb."

Eric held up a half-eaten apple. "You hungry?"

Eating an apple felt better than sitting there like a lump on a log. "Sure."

"Come on in the kitchen, then. Mom, we'll be right back." Eric's voice was respectful, but the look on his face was full of humor. "I don't know how your mother is, but mine loves to tell me the same thing, over and over."

"I've gotten that treatment before."

"I can promise you, if we'd sat in there for an hour, my mom wouldn't have moved from her spot on the couch — she's been so anxious to catch up with Lilly."

Once in the kitchen, Eric pulled open the refrigerator's produce drawer and extracted another juicy red apple. After Caleb took it, Eric leaned on the counter. "So why do you want to leave your family?"

"It's not my family I want to leave. It's farming." Even as he said the words, Caleb second-guessed himself. Was it just farming that he wanted to leave? He could have sworn it was far more.

"But I thought you guys owned a store?"

"We do, and farm a bit, too. But I don't want to work there, either."

"And you're done with school?"

"Yes. We, um, stop formal schooling after the eighth grade."

Chewing on another bite, Eric shrugged. "Wow. I think it would be cool to not have to stress your whole junior and senior year about getting into college. That seems to be all I ever do."

Eric's words confused him. The boys he'd met in Sugarcreek hadn't ever talked about college — they'd been more intent on having fun. "Is that all you do with your time? Study?"

"No. I do pretty much what most high school kids do, I guess. I play basketball. I hang out with my friends. Do homework. Oh, and then there's my youth group."

He hadn't heard of that term before. "What's that?"

"It's a bunch of high school kids in my church."

Caleb had been so fixated on leaving the Amish faith he'd neglected to think about how other kids his age practiced their religion. "You go to church?"

"Well, yeah. Because you were coming, we went early this morning. If you live with us, you can go if you want. There's a ton of kids who go to the high school Sunday-school classes. And we do other stuff together. Last summer we went on a mission trip to West Virginia."

"Eric . . ." Mrs. Leonard was calling from the living room. "If you're going to go, you better leave now. Or bring Caleb back in here."

"All right." To Caleb, he said, "I told my mom I'd take you out for a drive, if you wanted to go. Want to?"

"Sure."

"Don't forget to watch the time, Eric!" reminded his mother.

Eric shook his head at her warning. After throwing his apple core in the trash, he glanced Caleb's way again. "If you live here, get ready to be told what to do."

"I'm used to that," Caleb murmured. "Very used to that."

An hour later, they were back in the fancy living room. Eric had shown Caleb his school and a basketball court where he and his friends hung out. They'd met a few of his friends, but before too much time had passed, Eric mumbled that they'd better get back home.

And Mrs. Leonard — as Eric had predicted — was still sitting on the couch across from Lilly and Cassidy.

After refusing her offer of making Caleb something to eat, she looked at him directly. "Now, I know you've probably already told all this to Eric, but I want to hear it from you. What has made you decide that you want to live here, in Strongsville?"

The direct question, combined with her searching gaze, made him feel like an animal with a target on its back. To his embarrassment, he started to sweat. "I . . . I . . ."

"He's kind of trying to figure out what to do with the rest of his life," Lilly interjected.

"But why do you need to figure that out now?" Cassidy asked. "You're only sixteen."

He wondered how he was ever going to be able to describe his situation to people who were so different from him. Slowly, he said, "In my order, it's normal for kids my age to have a *rumspringa,* a running-around time. It's during this time that we investigate life outside. I have been doing things with *Englischers* in Sugarcreek, but it hasn't felt enough. Soon, I'll need to make a decision about whether I become Amish or not."

"You really don't know what you want to do?" Eric asked slowly.

"I'm conflicted. I love my family. We own a store and we have a small farm, too. Both of those jobs would be good options for my future. But neither appeals to me. At least, not in the way that I'd hoped."

"Perhaps you simply need more time?"

"I'm not sure."

Eric leaned forward. "Do your parents know you came out here?"

"Yes."

"Aren't they mad at you?"

Mrs. Leonard shook her head in exasperation. "Eric!"

"Well, wouldn't you be? Besides, it's just a question."

"It's all right," Caleb said, realizing that questions of this sort were indeed all right.

They weren't anything he hadn't asked himself already. What was even harder, though, was that he wasn't quite sure how to answer. Caleb began to wonder if he was the only sixteen-year-old in the world who felt so confused about who he was. Most other Amish teens he knew pretty much already had their future in mind. They were merely using their running-around time as a way to take a break from constant chores.

Or there were some who had already planned to not join their order. They planned to become Mennonite, or to live with non-Amish relatives and go to high school.

It seemed like only he had no idea what he wanted. Nothing sounded right. Not farming . . . and maybe not even moving to Strongsville. "No, they weren't mad. But I thought they were going to be." When the others leaned forward, obviously waiting for him to tell more, Caleb tried to answer. "It's not that I don't like being Amish; I'm just not sure if it is who I want to be forever." He paused. "I had always thought there were no choices for my life, how I lived. That I was either destined to farm or work at our family's store or leave the order. But maybe there are choices I haven't been able to imagine."

"And if you don't explore options, you're going to regret it," Eric responded.

"I think that's true."

"Already I think you'll fit right in with us, Caleb," Mrs. Leonard said. "Don't make a decision now. If you want to stay with us for a few months, we'd be happy to have you."

"I think you need a break," Cassidy said. "I mean, how can you know who you want to be *forever?* You're not supposed to."

"It's different for Amish teenagers," Lilly interjected gently. "There's a lot of rules to being Amish. They give up a lot of things."

"Do you have to?" Cassidy asked.

"Yes," Caleb said.

"But for a while they don't," Lilly said in a rush. "During their *rumspringa* — their running-around time — they get a chance to see new things for a time."

Cassidy leaned forward, obviously struggling to understand. "So you haven't gotten to do that?"

"My *rumspringa* started . . . but lately it hasn't felt like enough," Caleb explained.

"Then what will be?"

"I don't know." Feeling a little deflated, Caleb sank back deeper into the down-filled cushions. "I thought I knew, but now I'm not so sure."

Mrs. Leonard took control. "I'm sorry. Some hosts we are. All we've done since you've gotten here is pester you with questions." Turning to her left, she smiled in Lilly's direction. "For the last hour, all Cassidy and I have been doing is filling you in on all of your friends. Why don't you fill us in on everything that's been going on with you since you've moved."

"Oh. Well. I got a job."

"Cassidy told me that. You're a waitress, right?"

"Yes."

"I thought you were going to go to college? You were such a good student, Lilly. What happened?"

Caleb watched his neighbor turn pale. Though he ached to help her out, he knew that this was a time for her to explain herself — just like he had done.

"Oh, well . . ."

She was going to lie. He felt it. Caleb squished back into the cushions and prepared to keep his expression as neutral as possible while she lied to them.

Mrs. Leonard chuckled. "Come on, Lilly. Now you've got me really intrigued. Don't keep us in suspense!"

"Well, I was pregnant, but I lost the baby. I miscarried it."

"What?" Cassidy shouted.

Even Mrs. Leonard looked startled.

"We moved because I was pregnant."

"With Alec's baby?" asked Cassidy.

"Yep. He wasn't interested in being a father. Which was okay. We weren't a match made in heaven, you know?"

"I can't believe you never told me."

"My parents didn't want anyone to know . . ."

"But that's no reason to not tell me," insisted Cassidy.

"Okay. How about I didn't want to see you look at me the way you are right now? Is that good enough?"

Caleb's stomach fluttered as Cassidy's

eyes filled with tears.

"And how is that?" protested Cassidy.

"Like there's something wrong with me."

"There is. You're a liar."

"Cassidy —"

"Lilly, I can't believe you. When I think about all the stuff I told you, all the secrets I told you . . . you always said we were close. But maybe we really weren't."

"Don't say that."

"Lilly, you left Strongsville without telling me a thing."

"It was too hard to talk about."

"I could have helped."

"Look, a lot of things that happened were out of my control," Lilly said. "Alec broke up with me, and then my parents insisted we move. Then, they kept saying that if I just kept moving forward, in less than a year, I could go to college and no one would know what happened."

"And you believed them?"

"I wanted to. But then it all got confused. And then I lost the baby. And then I didn't know how to tell you everything."

"Except now. When you want something."

"Wow," Lilly murmured. "I knew we'd drifted apart, but I guess I didn't realize just how much."

Caleb looked at his hands. This was the

worst visit ever. Now all three of the Leonards looked like they'd rather be doing anything but have him and Lilly there.

At the moment, Caleb felt the same way.

CHAPTER 18

It took an hour for Robert to drive his courting buggy to get to Lilly's home. Fifteen minutes to get his horse settled and summon the nerve to walk to her front door.

But only one second to learn that she wasn't home.

"She's actually in Cleveland today. She decided to visit some friends," her mother said when she answered the door. As she looked him over, Mrs. Allen didn't even try to conceal her curiosity. "I don't expect her to be back until after dark."

"I see."

"But I'll tell her you stopped by. I'm sure she'll be happy you did."

Well, now he felt silly and conspicuous, standing there at her front door like he'd been invited. Like he knew her well enough to come over without notice.

And even more at a loss when he suddenly recalled Abe's rant about Lilly taking Caleb to the *Englischers.* He should have remembered that.

"I . . . uh, thank you." Because there was little else to say, he turned and started down the steps.

"Wait." When he paused, she stepped out onto the porch. "Would you like to come in for a few minutes?"

He wasn't sure what the right thing to do was. "Well . . . I."

She looked him over, making him feel even more conspicuous. But then, to his surprise, she smiled and held out her hands. "I promise I won't grill you like we did the other night."

"Well . . ." He'd never been good at these English social customs. He shook her hand quickly, taking care not to clasp her hand too hard.

She craned her neck behind him, like she noticed his buggy and horse for the first time. "How about you come in just to get something to drink?"

Now he felt flustered. Mrs. Allen looked like she was wanting something, but he just wasn't sure what it was. "No. I mean, *Danke.* I mean. No, thank you. I'll be fine."

Again, she stilled him with her chatty conversation. "You know, I've ridden in our neighbor's buggy once. It's a long journey to get out here." She crossed her arms over her chest. Surveying him with something that almost looked like amusement. "Perhaps your horse might like a break?"

"He would. If you're sure it's all right . . ."

Her eyes lit up. "It's more than all right. I'm delighted." Before he could attempt to say anything else, she turned and bustled inside.

Hastily, he stepped in and carefully closed the door behind him.

When he'd visited before, he'd been so aware of Lilly, and so inundated with questions, he hadn't taken the time to really look at the home.

Now that he had the opportunity, he was surprised to find the house to his liking. It wasn't terribly fancy like other English homes he'd been in. Some had so much stuff around that he worried about turning around.

Here, though, the furniture was solid oak and not too frilly. Some of it he recognized as Amish craftsmanship, too. That made him feel more at ease, though he didn't know why.

As he looked around, he was drawn to the many photographs decorating every surface.

His feet slowed as he looked closer and closer. Lots were of Lilly. Happy pictures of her and her brothers. He couldn't help but smile at one with her wearing thick glasses.

Though he'd never been one to gaze at photographs all that much — his people didn't subscribe to picture taking, of course — Robert found himself unable to look away from the images of Lilly.

In each one, he tried to study the nuances in her expression.

"Robert? I'm back here," Mrs. Allen called out from the kitchen.

He hurried in to meet her.

"Take a stool and I'll pour you some iced tea."

Just as he was about to sit, Midnight appeared from around a corner, meowing a merry hello.

He picked her up and held her at eye level. Like a dancer, she balanced in his large palm and gazed right back at him. Then, just as suddenly, she arched her back a bit and swiped a tiny pink paw across his thumb.

Robert chuckled. "Ach, but you are a fierce one, ain't ya? Don't worry none. I mean you no harm."

The little cat meowed again and squirmed. Amused, Robert set her down and watched the kitten scamper after a band of light shining in through the window.

Next to him, Mrs. Allen watched the cat pounce and spring, and she laughed. "I'm not sure what we did before Midnight came into our life. Since she's arrived, I've laughed more than I can remember."

"Laughter is always welcome. I take it Lilly is enjoying the kitten? Midnight?"

"Oh, yes. Actually, we all are." She grinned as the kitten jumped on the beam of light and then scampered away . . . with one of Ty's socks in her mouth. "That cat. She takes all kinds of little odds and ends. Half the time, I don't even know where she stashes them! She's as dark as midnight, so I guess it's a fitting name. You know, Robert, I should really be giving you a talking-to about giving my daughter gifts."

"You don't like me doing things for her?"

"It's not that . . . you've made her very happy." She placed a tall glass of iced tea in front of him. "However, as her mother, I worry about her staying happy."

"Staying?"

"Robert, Lilly has already been in a relationship once that wasn't suitable. I don't know if what you two have can go anywhere." She stretched a bit, revealing a belly that was starting to swell. The unmistakable look of pregnancy. Remembering just how upset Lilly had been when she'd stopped in his parking lot, he looked away.

She noticed. "I seem to be getting bigger by the day," she said sheepishly. "I don't remember growing so huge with my others, but I guess I did."

There was only one thing to say. "Babies are truly God's miracles."

"You are exactly right about that," she said with a smile.

"I've always enjoyed children. My wife and I were never blessed."

"Lilly told me you are a widower. I am sorry for your loss."

"Thank you," he said simply.

"But now you're interested in my daughter?"

His heart felt like it leapt up and took a hold of his throat. Having his relatives give them their opinions about things was one thing. But it was quite another for Mrs. Allen to pass on her opinion.

To Robert's way of thinking, she had every right to speak her mind.

And he had no reason to evade the truth. "I am interested in her."

Over the rim of her glass, she eyed him. "Thank you for not telling me to mind my own business."

"She's your daughter."

"She's been through a lot, you know."

"I know."

"But I suppose you have, too . . ."

"Yes." Thinking about Grace and her death while sitting with Lilly's mother felt awkward. Not because he couldn't reconcile the two in his mind, but because he wasn't sure how to express his strong emotions for Lilly without making it seem that his feelings for Grace had been diminished.

Of course, that had been the way it was when he'd talked to Abe about Lilly. Robert often felt that when he said anything positive about Lilly, it meant he was finding fault with Grace.

While he was still debating how to describe his feelings, Mrs. Allen spoke again. "Robert, Lilly doesn't tell me too much. Where do you see the two of you heading?"

"I'm not sure what you mean."

"I mean, are you just friends? Is there something more? Do you hope to get married one day? And if so, would you live as you do now, as the Amish?" Drumming her fingers on the counter, she fired off another question. "And how would all of that happen?" Robert ached to stand up and walk right out of Mrs. Allen's kitchen. The things she was asking were personal, and needed to be decided between himself and Lilly. "I don't have all your answers yet," he said simply.

"I'm sure you don't. But don't you have any idea?"

"I am hoping Lilly will become Amish, of course." He spoke bluntly, his patience at an end from her quick-fire questioning.

A moment passed as he watched her process his words.

Robert half waited for her to tell him everything that was wrong with his statement. Yet, she surprised him by not flying off the handle. "I didn't think becoming Amish was easy."

"It's not."

"But not impossible?"

"No."

"What about for you to leave your church. Can you do that?"

Robert considered her question carefully. Truthfully, even the thought of leaving his order made him feel ill. Being a part of the Amish faith wasn't just his relationship with God — it was his way of life.

But would he ever leave it? He wasn't sure. He didn't want to . . . but he also was enough of a man to realize that his faith wasn't all who he was. He had a strong desire to love and to be loved. If he was lucky enough to find love again, he just didn't know if he could refuse it.

"It's rarely done," he said quietly. "I've already spoken my vows to the church, you see."

"But it has been done before?"

"Yes." Even to his own ears, his spoken affirmative sounded hollow and desolate.

She fumbled for the words. "Perhaps you could become Mennonite? I've been doing some reading. That seems like a compromise."

"It doesn't work like that, Mrs. Allen. At least, not for me. Religions aren't interchangeable. Either I'm Amish or I'm not. And I'm afraid, for Lilly's sake, that I'm Amish."

Before she could pepper him with questions again, he spoke. Though caution told him to hold his tongue, his heart had something different in mind.

And because the woman sitting across from him loved Lilly, too, he tried his best to explain all the feelings bursting inside of him. "I am intrigued by Lilly. She makes me interested in life again. She makes me want to be married again. But I'm not in a rush. I'm willing to let her think about this. To let her make up her mind in her own time."

Her whole body relaxed. "It's so nice to

hear you say that. See . . . I used to want to control everything she did. But now I realize that I can't do that. I've decided that the Lord is really working through us these days. He's given Scott and me a baby when we thought those days were over. And now he's brought you into Lilly's life when I know she hadn't intended to love again."

Robert couldn't help the surge of happiness that ran through him at her words. He wanted Lilly to be as happy as possible.

"If you're the reason she's been smiling again . . . I just want you to know that we're grateful. And we'll support whatever she wants to do."

"Does she know of your support?"

"She should know, but I'm not sure if she believes it. Lilly doesn't always listen to what I say."

He had to chuckle at that. That did sound like the Lilly he knew . . . the girl who wanted so much and wasn't afraid to reach for it.

But who was still afraid to be rejected.

"I thank you for the tea," he said as he stood up.

"You're welcome. I'll tell her you stopped by."

He hoped she would. And once more, he

hoped he'd know better what to say when they met again.

CHAPTER 19

Robert was just sanding the edges of some shelves in his workshop when Lilly came in. After taking a moment to admire how pretty her hair looked, pinned back from her face, he pulled off his gloves and approached. "Good morning, Lilly. What brings you here this Monday morning?"

A small smile played on her lips. "Your visit to my house yesterday."

"Ah."

"Ah? That's all you have to say?" As if Lilly couldn't help herself, she placed her hand on his arm. "Robert, my mom said she invited you in to have tea."

Her voice sounded musical — so happy and full of whimsy.

"She did," he said lightly, enjoying the humor he spied in her eyes . . . and liking how he was responsible for putting it there. "And I accepted her invitation."

"That was sweet of you."

Liking the way her hand felt on his arm, he covered it with his palm. "Not so much. Your mother was very . . . cordial."

"I hope she didn't drive you crazy. Did she ask you a bunch of questions about us?"

"She did."

"I'm sorry. She likes to get a little too involved."

"It was nothing I couldn't handle." He was so happy that she came to see him, happy that she'd reached out to him, that he couldn't help but take her other hand and hold it as well.

"I'm sorry I missed you."

"You had good reason, yes? I heard you took Caleb Graber to Cleveland."

"You heard about that? I guess news travels fast."

"It always does. So, how was your trip? Were you glad to be back?" Part of him wondered if she was thinking about moving back there now. Returning to some place familiar could make a person long for it more.

"It was interesting. I don't know if either of us got what we were expecting, though."

"What were you expecting?"

"Reassurance. I wanted to go back and feel right about my decision not to return to Strongsville. I think Caleb wanted to be

258

sure that he would be okay in the English world." Her voice lowered. Became more halting.

"What do you mean?"

"I've kind of turned my back on my hometown and most of my friends. I hadn't thought that I could go back and be the same person."

"Were you wrong?"

She shook her head slowly. "No. I'm not the person I used to be. I feel so much older than Cassidy. Like I've aged five years instead of just one. I'm not interested in college courses or music or fashion. Not like I used to be, at least."

"What are you interested in?"

"Sugarcreek." Her cheeks heated as she slowly lifted her eyes to his. "You."

Her gaze was so earnest, her lips slightly parted, for a moment he considered lowering his mouth and kissing her again.

With effort, he forced himself to focus on her words. "I'm terribly glad to hear that."

"That's funny. Because I am terribly glad to hear you say that, too."

The way Lilly was looking up at him, like he was everything she'd ever hoped he would be, like they had a chance together, tore down all the barriers he'd put up to keep himself from harm.

Now it felt completely right to wrap his arms around her. And to finally give in to his greatest desire. He leaned down and kissed her.

For just a moment, he wanted to forget their many differences. To push aside a conversation about a future. For just a moment, he wanted to simply feel Lilly in his arms. Responding to him.

For just a few moments, he wanted to have hope.

Later that day, long after Lilly had left his workshop and he'd put in hours of work, Robert forced himself to attend to something that had been troubling him for some time. It was time to visit with Abe.

As his horse made its slow way up the path to his cousin's white clapboard house, Robert braced himself for the inevitable argument that was sure to come. He also couldn't help but think as he approached Abe's white house with its faded yellow chimney, of how much this ride contrasted with the one he made soon after he and Grace had decided to marry. He'd been joyous then; bursting at the seams. And Abe enthusiastically hugged him and congratulated him when they arrived.

A couple of men had even kindly told him

that they were jealous of his good fortune. Grace was a lovely woman and had boasted a genuinely sweet nature. Robert had had no doubt that the two of them were going to have a long, happy life together.

Of course, all those dreams had fallen apart.

Robert parked the buggy and spied Abe picking up rocks with his seven-year-old in a field. It was a common chore, rock picking, so as to prepare a garden with soil that was ready to be worked. He picked up a bucket and wandered out to meet him.

"Care for some help?" he called out.

"Of course," Abe said with a smile. "I was just telling young John here that picking rocks is a mighty important task. But that it can be daunting, too."

"Some you have to dig out," John said.

"I know." Robert followed them, walking down the row, picking up a pebble or small rock and adding it to his bucket.

"Any special reason you came out today?"

"I wanted to talk."

"In private?"

"Perhaps that would be best."

Abe looked to his son. "John, you may take a break now."

When John rushed away eagerly, Robert took a deep breath and plunged in. There was no easy way to say what he was about to say. Especially since the topic meant so much to him. "Abe, I've come to talk to you about Lilly Allen."

A hint of apprehension appeared in Abe's eyes. "Yes?"

"I know you don't approve of my relationship with her, but I came here to ask you for your support."

"Support in what way?"

"I like her, Abe. I like her a lot. Lilly's made me feel things I never thought I'd feel again. Even if you don't agree with me, I'm hoping you will at least try to understand my feelings."

After studying Robert for a moment, Abe bent down and picked up a rock. "You don't think it's a passing fancy?"

"Nee." Robert waited, half expecting Abe to berate him for being so foolish. Or to bring up Grace — to remind Robert of what a wonderful-*gut* woman she was. To tell him that he should never want someone so different.

After what felt like an hour, Abe sighed. "I don't want to be your enemy, Robert. I don't want to make your days miserable. Though I don't understand your feelings for the English girl, I promise I will try to support you." He picked up another two rocks. "As best I can."

"Danke."

"What are you going to do now? Court her? Persuade Lilly to become Amish?"

"I don't know. At the moment, I just want to keep seeing her."

"Perhaps not looking at the future so much is the right thing to do," suggested Abe.

"Perhaps, yes . . . or maybe, no. Fact is, I don't know if I'm doing the right thing or doing everything wrong."

"But you know you have to try?"

"But I know I have to try. It can't be helped, Abe. She's in my heart."

After a pause, Abe enfolded Robert into a quick, rough hug. "If she's in your heart, I suppose I best make a bit of room for her in my heart as well. We only want what's best for you, you know."

"I think Lilly might be what's best."

"Who am I to tell you no, then? There has to be a reason God has brought the two of you together."

"When I find out the reason, you'll be one of the first to know."

Abe bent down and picked up another rock. "From the looks of things, when you find out, I'll still be here, picking rocks."

For the first time all day, Robert relaxed. Everything was going to be just fine.

CHAPTER 20

"Robert! It's so good to see you." Rushing around the back table, Lilly immediately sat down next to him by the window. In his usual place. "I didn't know you were here."

Something like amusement lit his eyes as he curved his fingers around a coffee mug. "Mrs. Kent said you were helping out in the back, so I told her not to bother you. What were you doing today?"

"Slicing and peeling apples. With Gretta on maternity leave, Miriam is really busy."

"Is she alone back there?"

"No, but the two other people who come in aren't very good, if you want to know the truth. One lady is only part-time and works really slow. The other girl is just fifteen and still makes a lot of mistakes." Unsure whether to be embarrassed or not, she said, "Actually, I asked Mrs. Kent and Miriam if I could start doing more in the back of the restaurant. I kind of like it back there. And

I'm learning to become a good cook, which is nice."

"You don't know how to cook now?"

He looked so surprised, she sank down in her chair. "Not so much. Well, not so much beyond mac and cheese. What about you?"

"I can cook more than I used to . . ." His voice drifted off, like he was imagining another time.

Lilly knew he was thinking about his wife and how much he missed her. *Of course,* he missed her. Robert picked up his mug again, but seeing as the coffee was all gone, he placed it back on the table.

Lilly hopped up. "I'm sorry. I didn't even think to ask you about what you wanted . . . more coffee? Pie?"

"You," he blurted. Low but sweet.

And without a bit of doubt in his voice.

Mesmerized, she sat back down.

His cheeks colored. "I'm not good at explaining myself, Lilly. Not like you are, or like most of the men you probably know."

"Actually, you seem to be doing a pretty good job."

"Can you leave work, Lilly? Even just for a little while?"

Alarm coursed through her, along with a hint of happiness. Something was going on with him. "I'll go clock out and get my things. Maybe we could go for a walk?"

"That would be fine."

She put her things in her car while he waited. Then Robert fell into step beside her as they took a turn down the sidewalk.

Around them, cars were speeding by on the street and inn customers were standing in the parking lot, talking and laughing. In the distance, a flock of geese squawked as they continued their journey south for the winter.

Lilly stuffed her hands in her pockets as they walked along. When they reached an area where no one was in hearing distance, Robert paused.

"Have you ever loved someone completely?" Robert asked. "Loved with your whole heart? So much so that it wasn't likely that there'd be room for anything else?"

Lilly thought about her relationship with Alec. For a time, she'd thought she'd loved him. She wouldn't have slept with him if she hadn't.

And they'd certainly had a lot of good times together. She'd enjoyed being his girlfriend and having everyone comment about how great they were together. When they'd first started to date, she'd gotten all tingly whenever he'd smiled her way. But those feelings of excitement had faded and in its place different emotions had replaced them.

Doubts and fears and restlessness had replaced infatuation. And the cold reality of rejection quickly dispelled any thoughts of love she'd imagined.

And it all happened in less than a year.

"No," she finally said. "No, I never have loved like that. Is that how you felt with Grace?"

"It was." As they strolled down the sidewalk together, their footsteps matched. The sun was out just enough for their bodies to cast shadows. Lilly couldn't help but glance at them. Hers was so much smaller than Robert's.

Every so often, the light would catch them just right and their shadows would blend together. They'd become one. As they walked, Lilly found herself staring at their shadows. Catching her breath as their fuzzy shadows blended and melded together. Though it was a fanciful thing, she wondered if one day their lives could become like that. Two separate beings combining easily into one.

"My love for Grace was more than I thought it could be. And when she left me, I didn't know if I could ever recover."

Reaching out, he touched her hand. For a moment, Lilly thought he would thread his fingers through her own.

But just as quickly, he dropped his hand.

"Lilly, I'm afraid I'm not speaking too well. What I'm trying to say is that I've been blessed to know what love is. And . . . what I feel for you is love."

"Are you sure?"

"I know what love is, Lilly."

So, there it was. "I might not have been in love before," admitted Lilly, "but you've helped me discover it."

Beside her, she felt his satisfaction like a tangible thing. What she said pleased him. She was glad of it, but still had no idea what their feelings meant. "So where does that lead us?"

"Marriage one day?"

She swallowed. In her dreams, she'd imagined being someone's wife. Robert's wife. But were they too different? What if he was disappointed? "Everything you've ever told me about Grace makes me think she was a wonderful woman. I don't think I can replicate her."

"I don't want you to. I loved Grace; she was perfect for me then. But her passing left me changed. Different." With a sigh, he started walking again. Lilly fell into step beside him. "If another woman who tried to be a copy of Grace appeared in my life, I don't think she would interest me."

That, she could understand. "Because you've changed."

"Yes. I'm not the same man who fell in love with her. Before, I yearned for the beauty of love; the simple pleasure of being in someone's company. Before Grace got sick, I only knew this beauty and happiness. So much in my life had gone the way it was supposed to. I had few struggles."

"But things are different now?"

"Oh, yes."

The sidewalk was still crowded, but the side streets far less so. After a moment's pause, Robert guided Lilly to the right and down toward a secluded cul-de-sac filled with oak trees. Rich, vibrant reds and golds covered all the branches. A few leaves had already made their way to the ground, speckling the black pavement with dots of color.

Right off the quiet street was a gravel path. Robert led Lilly there. Soon, they were surrounded by thick branches on one side and corn stalks on another.

The thick covering muffled the noise from the rest of the world. And as they walked along, Lilly felt like they were the only two people out for miles. And because of that, the conversation seemed more intimate.

Just when she was going to ask where he was taking her, Robert stopped next to a bench. "Lilly, I remember the first time I saw you. I was grief stricken and mighty irritated with my cousin Abe. He had just stopped by my shop and shooed me out the door. I went to your restaurant in a terrible mood. I was going to sit there for exactly ten minutes, and then go back to work."

Though she'd been in a cloud that day, Lilly found that she, too, remembered that day just like it had been hours before. "I remember you had a horrible scowl," she said, sitting down on the bench. Robert took a seat beside her, reached for her hands, and she continued. "My mom and Mrs. Graber were whispering about you, too. I thought it was because you were so grumpy. Later I found out it was because they were worried about you."

"I felt so on display. I had been doing myself a disservice by keeping to myself so much. The longer I refused to step into society again, the more speculation there was about my doing so."

She knew what a great step that admission was. He was a private person, and distrustful of gossip.

"What you might not recall is what you were wearing."

"You remember?"

"I could never forget. You had on jeans and a sweater and your hair was curly around your face." His lips twitched. "And you were out of patience with my sour disposition."

"You were so tight-lipped; it seemed like you were getting charged for each word you spoke. But I still waited on you."

"Yes, you did. And I was glad. Because there was something about you that made me look twice. A sadness that seemed to surround your being."

"I wasn't feeling well," she recalled. "And things weren't going well at home, either." Though she'd come to an agreement of sorts with her parents about the baby, there was still enough tension between them all to make being home a less than comfortable experience.

"You were the reason I was able to take breaks from work. Some days, you were the only motivation I had to leave the shop for a few minutes." Squeezing her hands, he stared hard at them. "When I heard you were pregnant, I'm ashamed to say that I was almost relieved."

"Why?"

"Because I was sure the baby's father would come back to you. That you'd be with him and move on."

"And live happily ever after?" Unable to stop herself, a vision of her and Alec pushing a stroller popped in her mind.

"Maybe."

"I guess I hoped things would end up happily-ever-after with me, too. But they didn't. Alec and I were over for good . . . and, well, then everything happened with the baby."

Amazing how saying the word *miscarriage* still hurt so much.

Another look, one of empathy, entered his eyes — and their clear, sky blue hue deepened to the color of the sea after a storm.

Lilly realized she'd begun to rely on looking into his face to read his thoughts. Robert Miller was reticent, but his expressions were anything but. And if she looked hard enough, she could practically read his mind.

His eyes flicked away, then centered on their entwined fingers. "I know what it's like to feel pain. To grieve for a loss. I hope you don't think I was making light of it."

"I don't think that."

"I guess what I'm struggling to tell you is that as much as you intrigued me, I knew a relationship between us would be a difficult thing. I found myself looking for ways to turn away."

"I can understand that. I've had some of the same thoughts."

"Whenever I thought about all the ways we wouldn't be suited to each other, I was relieved. Because then I would become convinced that you were not the person for me. But the opposite happened. Instead of wanting to see less of you, my thoughts were filled with you. I hated thinking of you being alone. Or of you suffering." Robert was fighting off the inevitable, but he muttered, "The truth is, all the time you were home recuperating, I thought about you night and day. I prayed for you and worried."

Her mouth went dry. The idea that he'd cared so much about her humbled her. And gave her hope. Tightening her fingers on his, she whispered, "Robert, I had no idea."

"Of course you didn't. I wouldn't have expected you to even think about me. But I'm just telling you all of this so you know that what I'm about to say is not a sudden, impulsive thing. It's been a feeling that has been brewing inside of me for months."

He took a fortifying breath. "Lilly, I've fallen completely in love with you. You hold my heart."

Studying his face, she waited to feel

stunned.

But she didn't. Little by little, love had edged its way into her heart, too. Without her even knowing, her heart had healed from its many hurts. From Alec's rejection. From the loss of the baby. From her parents' disappointment in her. From the feeling that she was alone in the world.

In place of the emptiness, loss, and grief had come a warmth and a comfort. The confidence that she'd been feeling in herself was in direct response to Robert's attentions, and the way he made her feel whenever they were together.

Slowly his hand released hers. Without his warm clasp, her own fell to her lap. Though they were only sitting inches apart, she felt the separation clearly. All of a sudden, she felt half the person she was, without his connection.

Just as she was forming a response . . . just as she was about to let him know that she, too, had fallen in love, Robert spoke again in a rush.

"It's okay if you don't feel the same."

"No! I —"

"See, perhaps it's better that you don't share my same feelings . . . yet. It will give you time to prepare yourself."

She couldn't continue to let him fumble.

Reaching out, she cupped her palm along his jaw. The short beard in her hands felt soft; the jaw, firm and perfect . . . and her eyes drifted to the columns of taut tendons at his neck, so strong-looking.

With a start she realized that there was so much about Robert Miller that she already knew and treasured. "I don't need time to prepare."

"You might when you hear what else has been on my mind." Almost sheepishly, he tilted his head into her hand, so her palm slipped up above his jawline. Soon, her palm was cupping his cheek, holding him. Above his rough beard, the smooth, warm skin of his cheek caressed her hand. All at once, she felt vulnerable, yet powerful, too. Without words, he was literally putting himself in the palm of her hand. Trusting her touch.

Then — just as if she'd imagined it — Robert was sitting straight again. Their bodies a respectful distance apart. His gaze shuttered.

The only thing that gave way to what had just happened was his nervous swallow. "Lilly, there's no other way to say this, but I hope you'll not be scared."

Of course, she was scared now. A man didn't preface anything kind with a statement like that. "Just say it, Robert."

He took a deep breath. "Fact is, I want to marry you."

"Marry?"

He nodded but looked so solemn, he could have been on his way to a funeral. Then he reached for her left hand, curved both of his around it. "Lilly Allen, I love you and I want you to be my wife."

His wife.

Suddenly, she felt like she was free-falling. Free-falling into a pit of nothingness.

Marriage? To Robert?

Suddenly, it all felt too much. Her dreams were coming true. He loved her. He wanted to marry her.

With a jerk, she pulled her hands from his.

CHAPTER 21

Breathe!

Robert forced himself to exhale and then inhale again as Lilly stared at him. Her brown eyes, which he could describe in his sleep, were filled with wonder. Her lips were slightly parted.

As the moments passed, a thick band of doubt gripped his chest and squeezed. Once again, he guided himself through the motions of taking air into his lungs. Then he couldn't take it anymore. "Is there a full moon out tonight?" he joked. "Maybe we could just pretend the last two minutes never happened."

She shook her head. "Why would I want to do that? You've just made me so very happy."

Little by little, hope edged out doubt. He scanned her face again. There was happiness and something akin to amusement in her eyes. Lilly's cheeks were flushed.

But he still wasn't precisely sure what she was thinking. "You're happy?"

"Yes. Of course."

Oh, but she was driving him crazy! "Then will you please answer my question?" he prodded impatiently. "A man needs to hear the words, you know."

She laughed again — a joyous, free sound. "Yes."

He was so afraid to hope. And, that Lilly — she so loved to tease. He never knew when she was really serious. "Yes, you'll answer?"

"Yes, I'll answer you." Before he could take another breath, she curved her hands around his neck. "You're so silly. Yes, Robert, I will marry you."

Wrapping his arms around her, he hugged her close. How did he get so lucky? "I'm so pleased."

She laughed again. "Did you really think I'd say no?"

He shifted, then reached for her, pulling her close. Before Lilly knew it, she was half sitting on his lap like a golden retriever puppy. All arms and legs and energy. "I wasn't sure what you would say," he admitted. "Marriage to me will bring a great many changes to you — your life. It might be difficult."

A shadow crossed her face before she shook it away. "Let's not talk about problems. Not right this minute."

"You're right. I'm being foolish, bringing up worries all the time."

"You're not being foolish. I just want to thank my lucky stars right now. I want us to count our blessings. Oh, Robert, falling in love has been so easy. Just about the easiest thing I've done in months."

Her words sounded so perfect, it was impossible not to agree. Loving Lilly *had* been easy. And freeing. A feeling of foreboding slithered into his senses. Was it supposed to be like this? He almost felt as if they were living in a child's fairy tale — not in the real world.

Her head tucked into his shoulder, she snuggled a little closer. "I love you."

When she raised her head and looked into his eyes, Robert brushed his knuckle against her cheek — marveling at how soft her skin was. And, of course, he couldn't resist her any longer. Leaning his head toward hers, he brushed his lips against hers, kissing her lightly.

When she responded, he deepened the kiss and traced a path down her spine with his fingers. Felt the fine bones of her ribs under her sweater. And let himself get caught up in the moment again. Once again.

It was Lilly who pulled away. "We better stop before we get carried away," she murmured, her cheeks deliciously flushed.

He was just vain enough to be pleased with her comment. He wanted Lilly to yearn for him. He wanted her to think about him the same way he thought of her.

But of course, there was also a need for restraint. "I'm tempted to sit here with you all night, but perhaps we should go back to your home. There's a lot to do."

"Like what?"

"We need to tell your parents, of course."

She tensed. Looked away. "Let's wait a bit."

"Why?" Suddenly, he was worried about their future again. "Have you changed your mind already?"

"Of course not. I'm just not ready to share our news. It feels so special. Special and private. I don't want to ruin the moment. Tomorrow's soon enough."

He cautioned himself to not fret over her words. Just because she wanted to wait didn't mean she didn't want a future with him. And she was probably right. There was no reason they had to tell the whole world. "You're right. Tomorrow is soon enough. We can wait, if that's what you want."

"It's exactly what I want."

"All right, then." Getting to his feet, he knew it was time to walk her back to the restaurant. Lilly was quiet beside him, quieter than he could ever remember her being.

But that was no bother. Around them, the air smelled sweeter and the stars seemed brighter. Everything felt better and exaggerated and like new. Perhaps because he was so ready to begin a new life, too?

Later, as his horse clip-clopped on the dark road, and no lights except for his kerosene lamp could be seen for miles and miles, he again was struck by what a wonderful sense of peace he felt.

Lilly loved him. Loved him so much that she was willing to change her life in order to live by his side. As his wife.

It was only later, after he'd heated soup for dinner and was eating it in the quiet of his kitchen . . . that he realized that Lilly had not actually agreed to become Amish.

Only professed her love for him.

It was awkward to see Josh at the counter of the store and have no desire to speak with him. Especially since the store was relatively empty and he wanted to talk.

"Lilly, where are ya going in such a hurry,

anyway?" he asked, resting his elbows on the counter.

"To see your wife."

His eyes lit up. "That's good of you." Straightening, he walked around the counter. "I'll go get her and bring her down. Then the three of us can have a chat."

She edged toward the stairs. "Oh, I don't want to make her come all the way down. I'll just go on up."

"She won't mind. The exercise will do her good."

"Josh, I came over to speak with Gretta. Alone."

"Oh." A wealth of emotions crossed his features. Curiosity and . . . disappointment?

Lilly wasn't surprised. She'd been friends with Josh first. Actually, she and Gretta had gotten off to a rocky start, since at first Gretta thought Josh might have been interested in her.

But that was in the past. Ever since they started working together, their friendship had really grown. And now, well, she needed information only an Amish girl could give her.

Not that she was in a hurry to tell Josh any of that. "I'll see you later," she said in a rush as she darted up the stairs and quickly knocked on the apartment door.

As soon as Gretta opened the door, she beamed. "Lilly, how *gut* to see you! Did you come over to shop?"

"No . . . I actually came to talk to you. Do you have time?"

Gretta raised a brow. "Of course, I have time. Come in."

The moment she closed the door, she grabbed Lilly's hand. "Now, tell me what is new and don't say *nothing.* Your eyes are shining."

Gretta didn't have to worry about that. Lilly was so anxious to share her news, she could hardly stand it. "Robert Miller asked me to marry him."

"Oh my word! What did you say?"

"I said yes." Feeling her cheeks heat. "I . . . I love him."

"I know you do." All smiles, she pulled Lilly into a hug. "Oh, wouldn't it be something? After everything that you've been through, if you became Plain?"

"It would be something," Lilly agreed, feeling a bit stunned. It was hard enough to imagine being married. Thinking about changing her whole life was hard to even contemplate. "Gretta, right now, I can't even imagine it."

As practical as ever, Gretta nodded sagely. "Of course you can't, standing here in front of me in your jeans and sneakers. With your hair all around your face." Narrowing her eyes, she looked to be making a sudden decision. "Follow me."

Lilly walked past the tiny kitchen and sitting area, past the bathroom, and into Gretta and Josh's bedroom. The room, painted a pale blue, was barely big enough for the quilt-covered bed, one side table, and a chest of drawers. On one wall was a wooden bar with hooks on it. Two dresses and a pair of Josh's pants hung on them.

Making a decision, Gretta picked a dark blue dress off the hook and handed it to Lilly. "Try it on."

Playing dress-up in Amish clothes felt wrong. "I couldn't."

"Sure you could." Hugging her stomach, she smiled. "It's not like I'm about to put this dress on, anyway. I'm far too big! Go on into the bathroom and put it on."

Though she'd seen the dress on Gretta a dozen times, it felt strange in her hands. "There's no buttons."

"I've got pins, Lilly. Let's just see how you look. *Jah?*"

"All right. Sure."

She went into the bathroom and removed her jeans and T-shirt, then slipped on the dress. When Gretta wasn't pregnant, she and Lilly seemed to be almost the same size. Lilly was easily able to hold the front together. She opened the door. "You better come pin me up."

Gretta chuckled as she easily fastened the dress together. Lilly couldn't do much except stare at her reflection. Already, she looked different. Almost like a stranger.

Beside her, Gretta examined Lilly's reflection. After a moment, she frowned.

"What's wrong?" Lilly asked.

"You need a *kapp.* I'll be right back."

Hastily, Lilly dug in the pocket of her jeans that were lying on the floor and pulled out an elastic. Quickly, she pulled her hair back, fastening a ponytail at her neck. Gretta clucked a bit when she returned. After handing the *kapp* to Lilly, she smoothed Lilly's hair back and then tucked the bottom of Lilly's ponytail under, making a bun.

Then, she stepped back. "This is my *kapp* for *gmay,* for church. Slip it on."

"Are you sure?"

"In for a penny, in for a pound, yes?"

"I suppose so." Taking a deep breath, she carefully slipped the white *kapp* on her head, smoothing out the ties over her shoulders.

Then she looked in the mirror again.

"Oh, my!" Gretta said, her voice filled with wonder. "Look at you."

Lilly couldn't seem to do anything but look at herself. "I look Amish," she whispered.

"Almost. All you have to do is take off your makeup." Gretta tilted her head to one side. "The kapp suits you, I think."

It felt funny, wearing something on her head. It felt strange wearing the loose dress. But as she examined her reflection, she said, "This is what I would look like, being Robert's wife."

Next to her, Gretta stiffened a bit. "*Nee,* Lilly," she murmured. "This is what you would look like when you *join our church.* When you *become Amish.*"

Lilly's mouth went dry. Gretta was right. She wasn't just going to be Robert Miller's wife. She would be leaving behind everything she'd ever known . . . and adopting a new way of life.

Before making her vows to Robert, she would have to take vows to Robert's community. To be baptized. To hold their way of life close to her heart. She would be making promises to God.

Could she even do that?

Slowly, she pulled off the *kapp* and handed it back to Gretta. "Thank you for letting me try this on. I think I'll change back to my jeans now."

"Yes. Perhaps that would be best."

As Gretta closed the door behind her, Lilly felt a disturbing, awkward knot settle in her stomach.

She tried not to notice that she didn't dare look at herself in the mirror again.

Not until she was back in her jeans and T-shirt.

CHAPTER 22

Caleb was ringing up Miriam's sale and preparing to lock up the store for the evening when Joshua bounded down the stairs from his apartment in a panic. "It's happening!"

"What is?" Caleb asked. Lately, every single thing Gretta did was cause for his brother to panic. In addition, when he wasn't climbing stairs to check on his wife, he was distracted and moony. He sometimes forgot to do tasks. Other times, he spent double the time needed to do the most basic of chores.

Everyone had noticed Joshua's new, terribly unfamiliar distracted nature; and it had become a great source of amusement for their parents.

Not so much for Judith and Caleb. They had to deal with the bulk of the work their brother now never completed. Between Joshua's forgetfulness and Anson's lazy ways, Caleb and Judith were fostering their own frustrations.

Then, of course, were the looming worries about what the family was going to do when Caleb left. If Joshua didn't get his head back on straight, their father was going to have to ask Tim to start working at the store, which would be a disaster. Tim was a farmer, not a merchant.

"Gretta," Joshua sputtered, bringing Caleb back to the present. "Her baby's on the way!"

"Are you sure?"

"Oh, yes." A line of moisture formed on his brow. "She's got pains. And her water broke."

Miriam clasped her hands together. "Oh, my! This is exciting!"

Now it was Caleb who felt the hard clench of panic deep inside his belly. Daring to look up at the ceiling, he was almost afraid to see Gretta standing there looking down at them. "What do you need?"

"Her sister Margaret is with her now, but she wants to go to the hospital."

There had been some talk of Gretta delivering at home with just a midwife in attendance, but because she was especially big — and her blood pressure elevated — everyone had been in agreement that the labor-and-delivery center was the best choice.

As Caleb stared at his brother like a dunce, Miriam took charge. "Who have you asked to drive you, Joshua?"

"The Allens said they would." Running a hand through his hair, he muttered, "But I'm not sure who is home." He looked at all of them wide-eyed. "What . . . what do you think we should do?"

Finally Caleb was able to start functioning again. "We need to call them, don'tcha think?"

"Joshua?" Gretta called out from up above. "Josh!"

All three looked at the stairs. Joshua paled. Caleb's stomach knotted.

Only Miriam seemed to still be able to think. "Come now, boys. Let's get busy," she said, clapping her hands to bring them out of their stunned silence. "What do you need done?"

Caleb spun into action. "I'll go to the back room and use the business phone to call the Allens," he pronounced, thankful once again that they were allowed this convenience for emergencies. "Josh, you go back up to Gretta and help her get ready to go to the hospital. Miriam, would you shoo the last of the customers out of here for me?"

"I'd be happy to," she said.

Less than twenty minutes later, Caleb was standing at Miriam's side, waving off Lilly Allen, his mother, Joshua and Gretta, and Margaret. As Lilly's car rolled out of sight, he murmured, "Have you ever seen Joshua more out of sorts?"

Miriam chuckled. "Never. Gretta looked calm as a cucumber, though." With a superior look, she said, "Girls always can be counted on in a crisis."

"Hardly. When I called the Allens, my mother was in their kitchen having coffee. By the time we got off the phone, she sounded as flustered as a turkey in November."

Miriam grinned at his comparison. "I guess you have a point. It is terribly exciting, though. Imagine, a new baby in your family in just a few hours!" She looked behind her at the quiet building. "Caleb, the store is empty and locked up. Do you need any more help?"

"*Nee, danke.* When I talked to Judith, she said she was going to go home and gather everyone. I'm going to do some chores around the farm then go up to the hospital later with Tim and Clara."

"I'm going to go tell everyone at the inn about Gretta. I'm sure Mrs. Kent will be so excited; she might end up going to the hospital with me." With a look of delight, she added, "I have a feeling we'll all be going to the hospital as soon as we hear the joyful news."

Caleb wasn't surprised to hear her statement. Joining together wasn't an unusual occurrence for them. It was simply what they did. Community was everything.

Though, things were changing. One day, it might not be his community.

That knowledge dampened his spirits. Shouldn't he be resenting all these obligations? Shouldn't he be wishing he was free? What was wrong with him?

"See you later, then," he murmured.

All smiles, Miriam reached for his hands. "Bless you, Caleb. Best of luck to your brother and his wife. I'll spread the word that there's a need for praying, and soon."

"Danke."

He watched her walk away, and was just about to go to the stables and hook up Jim to the rig when a Jeep pulled up.

"Hey! Hey, Caleb!" the driver called out. "Look at you, all dressed Plain. What's up?"

Caleb approached the trio. Jeremy, his buddy Blake, and Jeremy's girlfriend Paige were *Englischer* teens from the local high school. He'd joined them a time or two at a few kids' houses for parties. As the three of them gaped at him from the inside of the vehicle, he felt completely conspicuous.

Though Jeremy and his friends knew he was Amish, he'd taken care not to let any of them see him in his usual clothes. It had felt too different, and he desperately just wanted to fit in with them.

A part of him waited for them to tease his way of dressing as he approached. But, instead, they were looking at him like they always did, with easy acceptance.

"Hey. I was just closing up the store. My brother left for the hospital a couple of minutes ago. He and his wife are about to have a baby."

"Your brother's already going to be a dad?" Blake frowned. "How old is he?"

"Twenty."

"That's just two years older than I am." Jeremy grimaced. "There's no way I'd want to have a baby right now."

Caleb was in no hurry to point out any more differences between his family's life and theirs. "What are you guys doing?"

"Driving around. Hey, are you free? A bunch of us are going over to Callie's. She's got some of her parents' beer."

He knew Callie, too. Though she might be a little wild by his sister Judith's standards, she was really nice. And she'd flirted with him a time or two as well.

But he knew he shouldn't be going anywhere but home and to his chores.

"Say you'll join us," Paige said. "Callie thinks you're cute."

Jeremy waved off her comment. "She thinks every guy is cute. But, hey, you're welcome to come along. There's room in the car. Come on."

The pull to join them was strong. Though he'd never really enjoyed their company all that much, the three of them symbolized everything he'd been searching for. It was a chance to stop doing everything that was expected of him and have some fun.

To be normal.

But if he decided to stay with Cassidy and Eric, he was going to be in Cleveland in just a few weeks. It would be best if he stuck to his obligations.

"I better not . . . I really should go home and later to the hospital with everyone."

Blake looked at him like he was crazy. "Why? All you're going to be doing is sitting around."

Paige chimed in. "My cousin Katrina had a baby last month. She was in labor for ten hours."

"Yeah. No one will care if you show up in

two hours or four. No one's even going to be looking for you, anyway."

What they said made sense. "I don't have any other clothes with me."

"I think you look fine. Kind of handsome, in a weird, old-fashioned way," Paige said. "I'm sure Callie will think so, too. Come on."

"Yeah. It's not like your brother's going to care whether you're standing around or not. Come with us and I'll drop you off at the hospital later."

Everything they said had a point. Plus, if having a baby took as long as they said, he could see his friends for a while, then go to the hospital just like he'd planned. "Move over, Paige. I'm coming with ya," he said.

Jeremy smiled. "We knew you would. After all, even though you dress funny, you're just like us, right?"

"Right," he replied as he jumped in the car. Jeremy gunned the accelerator and they sped through the traffic light.

As the store and Jim and his family's buggy faded into the distance, Caleb forced himself not to think about what he was leaving behind.

And what his parents were going to say when they realized that he hadn't come right home.

CHAPTER 23

From the moment Caleb had called her house and delivered the news about Gretta going into labor, Lilly felt like everything around her was spinning out of control. Elsa and her mom had been in a panic, and Judith flashed between giddy and a nervous wreck.

It had been up to Lilly to get things organized. "Mom, I'll drive them; you stay here and wait for Ty. Elsa, I'll pick you and Toby up in ten minutes. Go tell Judith to wait for Maggie, Anson, and Carrie. Caleb should be back soon. When everyone gets home, either my dad or my mom can take the rest of your family to the hospital."

Unbelievably, neither woman had questioned a thing; had just hugged and parted within seconds.

After slipping on a sweater and boots, she drove over, picked Elsa up, and then drove as fast as she could to the Grabers' store.

Ten minutes after that, her car was filled with Elsa, Margaret, a panicked Josh, and a very big Gretta.

The forty-minute trip to the hospital had felt surreal. Hardly any of them talked. Instead, all eyes and ears were focused on Gretta's every move. By the time they got to the hospital, Lilly had been sweating. She'd felt like the whole car had experienced each one of Gretta's contractions together.

After dropping off Josh and Gretta, she parked the car and walked into the lobby with Margaret and Elsa by her side. Margaret's nerves had led her to speak only in Pennsylvania Dutch, but Lilly didn't mind. The pleasant sounds of the unfamiliar language soothed her nerves.

As did the knowledge that one day she would be speaking the same words, too. Perhaps she would even be making this trip with Robert, but for reasons of their own.

The idea made her feel all shimmery and warm.

But as she wondered who she would call to drive them to the hospital, that same familiar lump of dread appeared in her stomach again.

Three hours later, the waiting room was crowded with Grabers, Lilly's parents,

Gretta's sister Margaret and her folks. They all looked up expectantly when Josh appeared in the doorway.

"It's going to be a while longer," he said. "Gretta's doing fine, but the doctor said the baby is going to take its time. Maybe you all want to leave for a while?"

"Not a chance," Mr. Graber said. "We'll be here until the baby comes."

"But it might be hours."

He held up a crisp *Budget.* "I've got a paper and I'm comfortable. Don't fret now, son. Believe it or not, I've waited for babes to arrive a time or two."

Everyone chuckled as Josh turned beet red. "I guess you have. I'm going to get back to Gretta now."

"I'm sure she's looking for you, dear," Elsa said over a pair of knitting needles. "Don't you worry about us."

Josh was just about to leave when he turned to them all in surprise. "Hey, where's Caleb?"

"Not here," Anson said.

"Where is he? At the store?"

"I don't think so," Lilly said. "I bet he's just goofing off. Don't worry."

Her mother saved the day. "Lilly's right. Teenage boys don't have the patience for hospital waiting rooms."

"Yes. It's fine, son," Mr. Graber murmured. "Don't you worry. Go back to Gretta, now. I'm sure she's lookin' for ya."

When he was out of sight, Elsa looked at Lilly. "Where do you think he is?"

"I honestly have no idea," she murmured.

Four hours later, Josh came out, beaming with pride. "We have a son!"

Everyone stood up. Running to his side, Elsa kissed his cheek. "That's wonderful-*gut!* And he's okay? Gretta's fine, too?"

"Oh, sure. She is just fine. I can't believe I was so worried. Gretta delivering a baby is no trouble at all."

He only looked puzzled when laughter greeted his statement.

Walking next to Mr. and Mrs. Graber as they left the hospital, Lilly found herself smiling as they fielded questions from Carrie and Anson about Gretta and Josh and the adorable, tiny baby — William.

"Yes, Carrie," Mrs. Graber said. "I promise, they will be coming home tomorrow."

"What time?"

"I don't know."

Moments later, it was Anson's turn to quiz his parents, and it was Frank Graber's turn to do the careful answering. "I don't know why Gretta needs that needle in her arm, but the doctor seems to think she does."

"Does it hurt?"

"I don't think so."

Even little Maggie chimed in. "I love William."

That earned their youngest girl a swing up into her father's arms. "I love him, too."

Lilly smiled as she watched Maggie whisper into her father's ear and heard his touching reply.

"Yes, William is a *verra* fine *bobbli,* and sure to have wonderful-*gut* parents, indeed."

When everyone stopped in front of Lilly's car, Anson threw out another question. "Can we get ice cream?"

"Please?" Maggie and Carrie called out.

Mrs. Graber turned a put-upon expression to Lilly. "Why is it that *kinner* think that every special occasion should be celebrated with a sweet treat?"

Lilly winked Anson's way. "I don't know, but I might be the wrong person to ask. I love ice cream."

Mr. Graber chuckled. "Just down the road is an ice cream shop. Lilly, would you have time to drive us?"

"Definitely."

Fifteen minutes later, Mr. and Mrs. Graber, Anson, Maggie, Carrie, and Toby and Lilly were all licking ice cream cones.

The kids scrambled into their own booth while Lilly scooted into another one across from Mr. and Mrs. Graber. "Mr. Graber, I would never have guessed you would have an ice cream, too."

Elsa looked at her husband and grinned. "I doubt he would ever pass up such a treat. My Frank has always had a sweet tooth, Lilly."

He looked shame-faced. "I suppose that's true."

Lilly noticed they were attracting more than a few stares from other patrons around them. The hospital was in Mansfield, not Sugarcreek, so the Amish weren't as familiar a sight. The stares and the thoughts made her realize that she might one day be classified as *different* — if she became Amish.

"Lilly, this is nice, getting a change to sit here like this," Mr. Graber said, claiming her attention once again. "Tell us what you've been up to — besides driving Caleb around Cleveland," Mr. Graber said.

Though she knew she could just talk about work and her mother's own pregnancy, Lilly decided to trust them with something more personal. There was something about this pair that had always inspired a real trust. Back when she'd been pregnant, she'd found it easier to tell them about her hopes of keeping the baby than her parents.

"Well, I've been spending time with Robert Miller," she said haltingly.

"I knew that," Mrs. Graber murmured. "I also know that he's right fond of you."

"I, um, know he is. Actually, I'm fond of him, too." Suddenly, her words couldn't be stopped. "Actually I've fallen in love with Robert Miller."

Mrs. Graber looked at her husband. "Well, what do you know!"

Frank's expression turned gentle. "And how did you fall *in lieb,* Lilly?"

"In love? I'm not really sure." She tried to remember when she'd begun to view Robert's actions in a different way. Was it months ago when he used to sit at the same table at the restaurant just to speak with her? Had it been when he'd bought her a kitten?

Or was it something much smaller, such as when he'd simply stop what he was doing whenever she showed up at his workshop . . . making her feel that she was very important to him? "All I know is that from, practically, the first real conversation we had, something clicked between us."

"Love is like that, yes?" Frank swiped a wayward chocolate trickle from the side of his mouth. "Sometimes it just sneaks up on ya."

Elsa clucked and handed him another two napkins. "Have you told your parents your feelings, Lilly?"

"Not in so many words. For some reason, I always feel more comfortable telling you two how I really feel."

Mr. and Mrs. Graber exchanged glances. "We're not your parents, yes? It's always easier to tell other people difficult things."

"I agree." She thought for a moment, considering just why she hadn't shared all her feelings with her mom. "The truth is, I've been afraid to hear what they thought." Because that admission bothered her, she raised her chin. "But it doesn't really matter what they think, anyway. This is between me and Robert."

"Yes. Everyone grows up sooner or later, don't they?" Elsa carefully wiped the corner of her lip with a napkin. "Well, I for one, can see how you and Robert Miller found each other. You two are a good match, I think."

Though most of the kids were busy with their ice cream, Anson approached just in time to hear the end of their conversation. "Are you and Robert going to get married? Are ya going to become one of us?"

She loved how he said that. *One of us.* That was how she felt. Like she was just a few months away from fitting in again. "I hope so. But I'm not sure how to start."

Anson worried his bottom lip. "I've never met anyone who wanted to be one of us. Only people who want to leave."

His mother glared. "Anson. You watch your tongue."

"Why? It's true."

"Still, this is not your conversation. Hush, now."

Anson glared but sat silent as Mr. Graber carefully finished off the rest of his cone. "The way I see it, Lilly, I think you already have started."

She looked at the obvious. At her jeans and sweatshirt. Together, they looked as far from living Plain as anything could be. "Do you really think so?"

Fine lines appeared around the corners of his eyes. "It's not the clothes that matter, child. Not really." Pressing a hand to his chest, he murmured, "It's what's in our hearts that matters, *jah?*"

"Yes."

"Say *jah,* not *yes!*" Anson chirped.

"Anson . . ." Mrs. Graber warned.

"Jah," Lilly said, surprising herself with the word. All she'd really wanted to do was

make peace. But hearing the Pennsylvania-Dutch word come from her mouth jarred her senses.

Frank blinked, then slowly smiled. "Well, now. Perhaps you will be one of us before we know it. After all, you have what is most important, don'tcha think?"

"What is that?"

"You have a sincere want."

His words had been spoken as a statement. Not a question. But she answered all the same.

Erasing any lingering doubts that had played at the edges of her mind. "I sincerely love Robert very much."

But instead of bringing more smiles of satisfaction, Lilly noticed Elsa frowning at her husband. "What did I say wrong?" Lilly asked.

Anson scooted out of his chair to talk with Judith. With a bit more privacy, Elsa murmured, "Lilly, you must be sure about what I'm about to ask. This sincere want of yours . . . are you certain it is not *just* for Robert Miller?"

She was confused. "I'm not confused about Robert. I have fallen in love with him."

"We understand that," Frank murmured. "He is a fine man, and would make any

woman a wonderful-*gut* husband. But . . .
he needs an Amish wife."

"Can that be you, Lilly?" Elsa asked. "Do
you truly desire our way of life? Being
Amish isn't something you can do with a
light heart."

All of a sudden, Lilly felt as if she was
back in high school, with great dreams and
hopes and no idea about how she was going
to achieve them. Had that been what she'd
been doing with Robert? Fantasizing about
a simple, idealistic life . . . without truly
thinking about the difficult day-to-day
changes she would have to deal with. "I
guess I didn't think about that, not really,"
she said slowly. "Perhaps I should."

Frank spoke up. "I think you should pray
on it, Lilly. Prayerfully consider all you are
reaching for . . . and all you would be giving up."

"Giving up?"

"For example, we've certainly appreciated
all the times you've been our driver. But if
you were Amish, you would have to give up
your car, which means some of your independence. You'd have to get used to waiting
to go to the city for your needs, or planning
to be gone for most of a day if you go by
buggy."

"You'd have to depend on others . . . and

you're a terribly independent woman, Lilly."

Surprised, Lilly realized Elsa's words were true. "I guess I have become independent."

Elsa nodded sagely. "This . . . this jumping into love with Robert isn't a bad thing, Lilly. It shows you've got a wondrous heart."

Slumping against her seat, Lilly felt more confused than ever. It was amazing how her impressions had changed just during one candid conversation.

How could that be? If she was as in love with Robert as she thought she was, would she really have let her mind change so quickly?

And their talk about independence was especially true. She liked relying on herself, and she needed to be able to do that. She was a woman of her times. She was used to cell phones and laptops and her car. Just as importantly, she was used to using those tools as a means to get her places quickly. To provide for herself.

Now, could she give it all away?

She just wasn't sure.

Just as she was about to try to redirect the conversation, her cell phone rang. Seeing that it was a local number, she picked it up. And then felt as frozen as the custard in her cup had once been. "Caleb? Caleb, where are you?"

Across from her, Elsa and Frank's postures stilled.

She felt just as alarmed when she heard his next words. "I'm in trouble."

Trading glances with Caleb's parents, she slowly said, "What's wrong?"

"Everything . . . Lilly, I need your help." He paused, then continued, his words coming out in a rush. "I'm at the police station."

"The police station? What in the world have you been doing? We looked for you at the hospital. Your parents are sitting right here —"

"Lilly, stop! Stop and listen. I can only use this phone for a few minutes more. Can you come to the police station now?"

"Of course."

"Good. Now, the first thing you need to do is —"

This time she was the interrupting one. "Caleb, hold on a sec. I'm actually sitting here with your parents. Now, start from the beginning. What happened?"

"Too much."

Tears pricked her eyes, he sounded so dejected. "I know it's hard, but we need to be prepared. What have you been doing? You know, we wondered why you never showed up at the hospital."

"I got in some trouble with some English kids."

"Eric and his friends?" That didn't make sense. Had they come all the way in town from Strongsville?

"Oh, no. These are just local kids I've hung around with."

"And?"

"And, I've been feeling so confused that, when they asked me to go to Callie's house to drink beer, I accepted."

Lilly closed her eyes in frustration. "So you went to Callie's house to drink beer . . ." she prodded.

Elsa gasped. Frank's face became thunderous.

"But then we got bored, so we started driving around." He choked on a sob. "Later, Blake ran the Jeep into a tree, and the police came. When they found alcohol on our breath, they brought us all here." After a moment, he added, "It's been horrible."

Lilly knew there would be time to get more information when they saw him. "Is anyone hurt?"

"No. Well, Blake's kind of bruised from the air bag going off, but other than that he's okay. I'm just really ready to get out of here." The phone jiggled for a moment, then he got back on the line. "I have to get off the phone now. Lilly, will you come get me? Soon?"

"Of course. We'll be right there, Caleb."

She heard his heartfelt sigh of relief through the phone. "Thanks. Hey, and Lilly?"

"Yes?"

"I'm so glad you had your cell phone. I've been freaking out. If you hadn't answered, I don't know what I would have done."

Because his words were so true . . . because at the moment she felt like thanking the Lord for providing her with the means to talk to Caleb, Lilly couldn't help but agree. Feeling hollow, she nodded, though she knew, of course, that he couldn't see her. "Don't worry. We'll be there as soon as we can."

When she disconnected, she reached out and curved her left hand over Elsa's clasped ones. "Caleb was out drinking with some English kids."

"And he's at the police station?" Frank asked.

"Yes. The boy who was driving lost control of his car and hit a tree. When the police arrived, they found three drunk boys, so they took them there to settle down."

"Is this a normal chain of events?"

"I don't know. If the boy who got in the accident was drinking, he would be in big trouble." She shrugged. "I don't know what will happen to the other kids in the car."

"I, for one, am plenty scared," Elsa said. "Frank, I just don't know what we're going to do with that boy of ours. More and more, I think we're losing touch with him."

Frank opened his mouth, then looking Lilly's way, shut it just as quickly. "I'll gather the *kinner*," he mumbled as he turned away.

"Lilly, we'd be *verra* grateful if you could take us to the police station as soon as possible. Do you know where to go?"

"I'm not sure, but I can find out," she murmured. "I promise, I'll get us there as soon as I can."

As she followed the Grabers out to her car, she called information and got the address and directions to the courthouse. By the time everyone was buckled in, she was able to look at Caleb's parents with more than a bit of assurance. "I know where to go," she said with a weak smile.

"Thank the good Lord for you," Elsa said, her voice thick with gratitude. "I just don't know what we'd do without you."

As Lilly exited the parking lot and made her way to the highway, she silently gave praise to their Maker. He'd just given her a sign.

It was going to be up to her to follow his wishes and plans, even if her heart was going to break one more time.

CHAPTER 24

Blake and Jeremy's parents arrived before Caleb had even gotten off the phone with Lilly. When the officer came to the cell and removed them, the boys left without so much as a backward glance in Caleb's direction.

When the iron door slammed shut again, enclosing him in the bare, cold room, Caleb wondered if he'd ever felt so low.

He had truly made a huge mistake.

He hadn't known the boys very well, and what little he did know of them, he hadn't liked that much. What was worse was that they seemed to instinctively know that and used his feelings to their benefit.

Their seemingly good-natured teasing about his clothes and long hair had been expected. But then, when they gave him a beer . . . and then a shot of whiskey . . . and then another shot . . . and then expected him to give them money for it all, Caleb knew he was in a very bad situation, indeed.

He'd given them ten dollars in one-dollar bills he'd earned in tips working at the store last Saturday. His parents didn't like him accepting tip money for carrying groceries and such to *Englischers'* cars, but Caleb hadn't thought there'd been any great harm in taking the money.

Most of the people's wallets had been full of paper money and Caleb believed they wouldn't feel the loss much. While he, on the other hand, appreciated having some spending money of his own.

Of course, now it was all gone.

The door leading into the main part of the police station opened again and the same man who had escorted Blake and Jeremy approached.

Caleb stood up.

To his surprise, the man almost smiled. "Hey. Are you okay?"

"Yes."

"I heard you threw up."

Oh, he had. Right in the back of Blake's car when they'd crashed. Blake had sworn at him, but Caleb had been too green around the gills to care. "I'm better now."

The officer — his name was Ferguson — shook his head. "Drinking and joyriding isn't a good way to spend your extra time, son."

"I know that."

"Now."

Caleb nodded, thoroughly miserable. "Yes. Now."

"Blake Reamy, he's been here before. He's got a wild streak about a mile wide. You two friends now?"

Caleb wasn't sure where the conversation was going, but he was so afraid of sitting in the room all alone, he didn't care. Anything was better than being alone with just his regrets. "No."

"Want to tell me what happened?"

"I made a mistake."

"Uh-hum?"

Because the officer sounded so sympathetic, Caleb spoke a little more. "See, I've been wondering what to do with my life. I've thought that maybe I should become English. Leave my family. Leave Sugarcreek."

"I know some Amish kids do that."

"A friend took me to Cleveland to meet some of her English friends. They were real nice. But they're far away. I started thinking maybe I could get along with some English kids here."

"Ah."

"That's not the whole truth. Part of me just wanted to rebel a little."

"You did that. Do you have a taste for it?"

"Not at all." Because Officer Ferguson didn't look like he'd mind, Caleb took his seat again back on the hard plastic mattress on the cot. "Now I just want to go home."

The man looked at him thoughtfully. "I don't know if this helps, but I will tell you that you're sure not the first person to ever try walking on the wild side and regretting it. We've all done it."

"Even you?"

"Even me." He grinned, showing perfect white teeth. "Now, that doesn't mean what I did was right, because it wasn't. I learned that I like being where it's comfortable. And being around people who know and love me."

A hard rap on the door behind them made the officer turn. "Yes?"

A lady with short red hair poked her head down the hall. "The boy's parents are here. A Mr. and Mrs. Graber."

"Good. I think Caleb's ready to see them. Give them the paperwork, Janice. We'll be right out." Reaching into a pocket, he pulled out his keys. "Ready to get out of here?"

"Yeah. How mad do you think my folks are going to be?"

"On a scale of one to ten? I'd say an eleven or twelve. Parents don't like fishing their kids out of jail, Caleb."

"I guess you're right."

Officer Ferguson placed a hand on Caleb's shoulder. "I have a feeling you're going to be okay, though. You seem like a nice kid, and the nice ones always come from nice parents."

Officer Ferguson was tall. Caleb tilted his head up to meet his gaze. "This sounds weird, but thanks for coming back here and talking to me."

He winked. "This sounds weird, but I'm kind of glad you came in today. We don't get too many kids like you."

"Amish?"

"Good kids. You're going to be just fine, Caleb Graber. But — and I mean this in the best way — I hope I never see you again."

Feeling like each foot weighed a hundred pounds, Caleb slowly followed Officer Ferguson down the dim hallway. He braced himself for a torrent of tears from his mother and a litany of retorts from his father when the officer opened the door and directed Caleb to step out into the bright lobby.

He couldn't remember ever feeling more

embarrassed than when he forced himself to face his family. His head pounded when, one by one, each of his four siblings, his parents, and Lilly turned and looked at him, each one more agitated than the last.

"I'm sorry," he said. Knowing how insignificant his apology sounded.

After a long moment, his father stepped forward. "Oh, Caleb," he murmured, then hugged him close. Right there in front of everyone.

Caleb closed his eyes and gave thanks. Gave thanks for everything. Even the bad stuff.

CHAPTER 25

Robert's mind was spinning. There was so much to plan. He needed to see if Lilly wanted to live with an Amish family, and perhaps if Mary would be able to help teach her Pennsylvania Dutch.

Antsy, he got to his feet and paced the length of his home. He'd need to help Lilly learn how to do laundry. He imagined some of the neighbor ladies would need to show her how to can and care for the house.

But as he turned a corner, he looked around again, and tried to imagine the rooms from Lilly's point of view. Suddenly, the cozy rooms and clean lines didn't look as perfect as he liked.

And perhaps they were dirtier than she was used to as well. He made a mental note to try and mop the floors.

Most likely, she'd never lived in a home as plain and simple as this one. To a foreign eye, the simple two-story house might seem small and bare.

What if she didn't care for it?

When a car pulled into his driveway, he looked through the window and at first saw that it needed some cleaning. Then, with a start, he realized Lilly had come.

Seeing him through the window, she gave a little wave. Feeling like a lovesick fool, he waved right back. Then hurried to the door and opened it.

Dressed in black slacks and a vibrant blue sweater, he thought she looked beautiful. Lilly's coloring of dark blond curls and deep brown eyes seemed to offer the perfect palate to anything she wore.

Of course, he was so taken by her, Robert was sure that almost anything she wore would look pretty to him. Already, he was imagining her dressed Plain. Even a gray dress wouldn't diminish the glow she seemed to exude.

Hesitantly, she stopped just a few steps away.

Which in turn made his fanciful thoughts break into a thousand pieces. Something was new with her. Something different, and it didn't look to be treating her well, either.

"Lilly, I'm glad you came to visit. But it's a surprise, to be sure."

"Is it a bad time?"

"Of course not. But did you need something? What are you doing here?"

"I thought we needed to talk," she murmured as she stepped closer. Close enough for him to smell the scented shampoo she seemed to like so much.

And close enough to see that her eyes were a little puffy around the edges, as if she'd been crying.

"I went by your shop, but it was closed. So I took a chance that you might still be here."

Oh, what a blessing her presence was. "I'm glad you found me. What did you want to discuss?"

"Can we sit somewhere? Do you have time?"

"I have time." Belatedly, Robert noticed that her expression wasn't especially carefree. No, she looked like she carried the weight of the world on her shoulders. Before he could offer a chair, she sat on his front stoop.

Cautiously, he sat beside her. "Is everything all right?"

"I don't know." A wayward curl sprung out of her ponytail and caressed her face. With an impatient tug, she pushed it behind her ear. "Gretta had her baby."

"Did something go wrong?" He'd heard she'd delivered, but hadn't asked for any details. It wasn't a man's way to ask, anyway.

"Oh, no. She's fine. And the baby is, too. It's a boy."

"Well, then. That's a blessing."

"It is. Elsa and Frank are so excited, too. All of the Grabers are. His name is William."

Robert sat quietly as he waited for her to let him know what else was on her mind.

His patience was rewarded when she licked her bottom lip and spoke again. "Caleb wasn't at the hospital, though. Did you hear about what happened to him?"

"Nee."

"He, um, he went off with some kids and got in a car accident." Tilting her head toward his, she looked at him worriedly. "He's okay, though. But he was taken to the police station. We had to pick him up there."

"We?"

"I was having ice cream with the Grabers and they needed someone to drive them."

"Ah." Robert didn't know what she was expecting from him. He wasn't shocked that a teenager was drinking, or that an Amish teen had been in the company of some English ones.

"Frank and Elsa were really upset with him."

"I would imagine so." When she sent him another meaningful look, he shrugged his shoulders. "I don't know what you're wanting to hear from me, Lilly," he said honestly. "I feel sorry for Caleb and his parents, but I'm not all that surprised. Teenagers do all kinds of things they're not supposed to."

"I sure know that."

There was bitterness in her voice. Ah, was that what all of this was about? She was troubled by her past again? Or worse, worried that he was troubled? "Everyone makes mistakes, Lilly. The Lord doesn't expect perfection." He swallowed. "I . . . I don't expect it, either."

"Robert, I'm trying so hard to tell you something, but I don't know how."

"All you have to do is say the words." Though he was trying his best to be as calm as she needed him to be — inside, his nerves were awhirl. Did she not love him anymore?

"I love you."

He couldn't help but smile. "I'm glad."

"But I don't know if I can marry you." She held up a hand before he could speak a word. "This sounds so trite, but it's not you. It's me."

He didn't understand what trite meant.

He also didn't understand what she was talking about. "What does that mean?" He tried to reach for her hand, but she moved it from his reach. "Lilly? If we marry, there won't be just you and me. It will be the two of us. Together." Her gaze softened just as the brown eyes he adored so much filled with tears.

"You are so sweet."

"Don't make falling in love difficult," said Robert. "We'll get through everything."

"It's not falling in love that I'm worried about. It's being Amish."

"Ah." He felt like a fool for not addressing her concerns immediately. "I've already got that worked out, Lilly. I think you should move in with the Grabers. They live right next door to you, and I'm sure they wouldn't mind."

"I don't think —"

"I promise, they'll be patient with you. And I would never expect you to learn our ways immediately. And I'll help you with the language, too. And I bet my sister-in-law Mary could help, too. She's a wonderful-*gut* teacher."

"But I don't think I can —"

"And I'd never expect you to do everything yourself. I'll help you with the housework and things." He smiled. "After all, I've been doing things here for years now. I just want you to be in my life, Lilly. All I know is that I can't lose you."

Two tears slipped from her cheeks as more filled her eyes. "Robert, everything you have said is great. And I thought I could do all that. But when I was talking with Elsa and Frank, I realized I just can't. I'm not going to be able to become Amish."

Confused, he was doing his best to understand her train of thought. "Elsa and Frank talked you out of our plans?"

Her eyes widened. "No. I mean, not in the way you're thinking." She shrugged. "It's just, well . . . they know me well."

"Not that well . . ."

"Well enough for them to encourage me to question my motives. To question my goals."

"And what are those?" She flinched, and he hated himself for making her wary, but he couldn't help himself. Lilly was about to fall through his fingers. Was about to slip out of his life, and he couldn't bear it. Not now.

Not when he'd already lost so much.

Not when he'd already fought so hard for her.

"My goals to be true to myself," Lilly said quietly. "Robert, I know you don't like me to talk about Alec and my pregnancy, but I have to tell you that it was an extremely difficult time. Not just the pregnancy and miscarriage . . . but my relationship with my parents and brothers and even my friends. In a lot of ways, I lost everyone."

Had that been the problem? He was confused. "I never said I didn't want you to talk of those things. Of course, I know all that was hard for you."

"I don't think you do."

"I lost a wife, Lilly. I sat by her side until she took her last dying breath. I know what pain and loss is about."

"But you had the rest of the community by your side. I had none of that. I was alone. And because I was alone, I began to cherish some things about myself. Especially my independence."

He felt like they were talking in circles. "So you don't want to marry?"

"Robert, I don't want to lose my car. Or my phone." She rolled her eyes, as if she was utterly frustrated with her weaknesses. "Or my computer."

None of that meant anything to him. "But those are just things."

"To you, maybe so. To me, they allow me to accomplish things without relying on others."

"But God is the only one we should rely on."

"If that's true, then I think He's already given me permission to have those things." Looking sadder than ever, she murmured, "Robert, even the thought of going without my car — of having to ask someone to take me places, of not being able to call up a friend or not being able to have email or information right away — it frightens me."

"You could get used to it," he said firmly. He would help her, too. She just had to believe in them enough —

"But I'm not ready to do that. Robert, I love you, and I love the Lord, but I can't become Amish. I can't give up everything that I am. Not even for you."

Finally, he saw her. Not through the haze of dreams he'd been holding close. He finally saw her. Lilly Allen. And the truth became terribly clear. No, she couldn't give up everything she felt comfortable with for him.

He could see that now.

Part of what made her so vibrant was her zest for life. Her spark of independence. Her ability to do something without asking a half dozen people what they thought about it first. It was that fire inside of her that had led her to say yes to their outing to the farmer's market. It was that burst of self-reliance that allowed her to talk with everyone and anyone.

And it was her maturity that had spurred her to kiss him in the cornfield.

No, she wasn't a moldable girl, ready to rely on him to help her through things. She was strong. And she wanted what she wanted.

And she didn't want him. At least not enough. Slowly getting to his feet, he adjusted the brim of his straw hat so it would shield his eyes.

She was too bright for him now. It hurt to look at her. "Goodbye, Lilly Allen."

"But, wait! Robert!" She scrambled to her feet. "I want to talk to you about this."

"I think we have talked, *jah?*" A feeling of despair washed over him as he realized none of his plans were going to come to pass. He'd completely misjudged her.

And, perhaps, he'd completely misjudged himself.

"Not enough. Not about what to do."

He stepped closer to the door. Closer to the confines of his house, where there was safety and everything was the same as it ever was. "Lilly, there's nothing more to do or say. You've made a good point. I see now that it would be foolish for you to adopt our ways."

Though he tried not to, he adjusted his hat brim so that he could again see her face. She was crying unabashedly now. Tears fell from her cheeks and splashed to her sweater. Her shoulders shook.

And because she needed him to do one more thing, he did. Because he would do almost anything for her. "Goodbye, Lilly," he said again. And then, before he could stop himself, he turned and walked into his house.

Away from the vibrant fall colors. Away from the sun. Away from Lilly's light and cheer.

Behind him, the door shut.

He almost welcomed the darkness that surrounded him.

CHAPTER 26

His parents hadn't been afraid to describe every feeling they'd been grappling with during the last twelve hours. They hadn't been afraid to yell, or to bring him to tears.

Or, he thought glumly, to assign his punishment.

Caleb scooped up another shovel of soiled hay from the horse's stalls and added it to the overflowing wheelbarrow. For the next week, he had to do all of his siblings' chores, in addition to his own.

That meant he had to do Anson's stall cleaning, Carrie's jobs in the chicken coop, and to help wash dishes — Judith's usual area.

He had to dust for Maggie and even pick up things around the family room — little Toby's job.

The only reprieve he'd gotten was the laundry. He was exempt from that chore — but only because his mother was afraid he'd mess it all up.

Caleb scooped up more hay and tossed it in the wheelbarrow, then turned toward the compost area. As he walked, a rank smell floated upward . . . reminding Caleb of just how much he hated mucking out horse stalls.

Behind him, Jim nickered from his stall. It sounded high pitched enough that Caleb imagined the horse was snickering at him. He supposed he couldn't blame the horse. Spending an hour every morning ankle deep in soiled straw was no way to begin a day.

"Enjoy yourself all you want, Jim," he muttered. "I'll be laughing at you this winter when you're leading the buggy in the snow."

"Talking to the animals, Caleb?" his father said when Caleb slowly pushed the wheelbarrow out of the barn.

Caleb felt a blush come on but hoped his father didn't notice. Here he was, trying so hard to say he was old . . . and still couldn't help but talk to animals. "Only to Jim."

Instead of looking irritated, his father surprised him by smiling. "That horse. He's a *gut* listener, ain't so? If he could talk, he'd have hours of secrets to share, I think. I know; I've told him lots."

"I never knew you did such a thing."

"Sometimes I can't help it," he said as he

fell into step beside Caleb. As they continued walking along the well-worn path out to the compost pile, his father murmured, "It's a hard and lonely life, working all day in the fields with only a horse for company. But you know that, of course."

Lifting up the handles a bit, Caleb guided the barrow up another hill, then over the last ten yards to the compost area.

He didn't know what to say to his father. Never before had he imagined that his dad didn't always enjoy his work on the farm.

But perhaps his comment had much to do with their current activity. Usually, by this time of day, his father was at the store or busily working on some project that was needed to be done around the farm. Never did he take time off to walk along with Caleb.

Frank Graber was the most industrious man he'd ever met.

With some surprise, Caleb realized that his father was also a terribly good man. An honest one. A man who was devout and caring.

Could he ever measure up to standards like that? Joshua had, but Caleb knew he was made of different stuff. Was it even worth it to try?

After Caleb dumped the soiled hay and

turned around, his father spoke again. "I've been thinking a lot about you, Caleb."

"I bet you have," he said drily. "I bet you wish I'd just go away."

"No, I do not," he said forcibly. When Caleb stared at him in surprise, his father visibly gained control of himself. "I mean, I haven't ever wished you would leave, son. Not ever."

"Daed, I know you're upset with me. I know I've been nothing but trouble lately, what with my family meeting about wanting to leave and my phone call from the police station."

"Those have kept me up at night, I'll not lie about that. But we all make mistakes, Caleb."

"Not like me." He looked down at his boots, unable to look his father in the eye. Already, he could feel the bands of disapproval wafting from him. Seeing that in his eyes would only be harder to bear.

"I'm afraid that you are mistaken, Caleb."

Almost against his will, his head popped up. "What?"

"We all make mistakes. The Lord gives us options, but each of us must make our own way. And that is a difficult thing, I think. It is a hard path, trying to figure out what to do."

Caleb gazed into the fields. "For the last year, I thought what I wanted most was to go live among the English. All I did at night was worry how you and the rest of the family would take the news."

"I thought we did all right."

His father's hopeful tone teased a smile from him. "I think so, too."

"But now you aren't so sure you want to go?"

Miserably, he shook his head. "It's confusing me, too, Daed. See, I thought I was ready to grow up. But this episode with Blake and Jeremy scared me."

"I spoke with Scott Allen about those boys. He told me that even *Englischer* kids give them a wide berth. They seem to be magnets for trouble for everyone."

But instead of making him feel better, Caleb only felt worse. "Then how come I didn't know any better? How come I wasn't smart enough to figure it out?" In frustration, Caleb released the wheelbarrow. The sudden movement brought it to the hard ground with a bang, then the jarring set it on its side.

Stunned, Caleb watched one of the back wheels spin as his father only stood silent.

Without warning, tears pricked his eyes. "I'm sorry, Daed."

"It's merely knocked over, son. The barrow is fine." Before Caleb could stop him, his father picked up the wheelbarrow and set it to rights. "See now? It's as good as new."

"Danke."

"You are welcome, son. It's a father's duty sometimes to pick things up and set them to rights, anyway."

Caleb understood the analogy. "I'll try to be better."

"Perhaps you should just try to be yourself, *jah?* I don't need a perfect son."

Without warning, he felt the sting of his father's words. Never was he going to live up to his expectations. "You don't need me to be perfect because you have Joshua."

"Stop that, now," his father retorted sharply. "We both know he is not that . . . and he doesn't need to be, either. All he needs to be is who our God wants him to be. And that, I think, is good enough."

The statement washed over Caleb, healing old resentments that he always held close to his chest. Now that the air felt more clear, Caleb turned to his father. "Daed, I'm so confused. I thought I wanted to be English, but now I'm not so sure. And if I'm not sure, I want to know why. All I've been thinking and planning for the last year is how I could get away from here. But now that I'm getting the chance, I'm afraid."

"What are you afraid of?"

The question was so gently asked, Caleb shuddered a breath and thought hard. "I'm afraid I won't feel any better in the outside world," he said finally. "I'm afraid that everything I've been looking for isn't what my heart truly wants. It isn't what God wants. But, no matter how hard I listen, I can't seem to hear what He wants me to do."

To Caleb's surprise, his father laughed. "Caleb, you don't know how many times I, too, have ached to hear God's advice. Loud and clear. But He always seems to be working on his own time, yes?"

Thankful to be understood, Caleb nodded . . . and looked at his *daed* again, with fresh eyes.

Beside him, his father looked so strong and sturdy. Of course, he always had. Years of hard work and happiness had formed his body. He was tall and thick, and now had a layer of fat that his mother teased him about. His beard had touches of gray and the lines around his eyes were deeper than they used to be.

To his surprise, Caleb realized he wasn't looking for flaws in his father anymore.

Instead, he was looking for the things that gave him comfort and guidance.

Joshua had always been a replica of his father's personality. Steady. Assured. He looked so like him, that everyone always drew comparisons. Caleb, on the other hand, had felt so different. And that difference had been both a blessing and a curse. No one compared him to his father.

Which made him wonder if he should ever walk in his footsteps.

Looking at his boots, his father finally spoke. "Did you know when my grandfather opened the store, he faced a lot of opposition?"

"Yes." The stories surrounding the opening of the store were well known to everyone in the family. "But someone had to make a change, and there was a need for a store in Sugarcreek."

"Yes, that is all true. But there was also a different need, I'm thinking," he said quietly. "I think he wanted to find a place for himself where he could be successful."

"What do you mean?"

"I mean that for a time, I've thought you were much like my *daed,* Caleb. He was the restless sort." With a wry shake of his head, he added, "He weren't much of a farmer. Not ever. Everyone knew it."

"But we're all so proud of him."

"Ach, *jah.* We certainly are," agreed his father. "And I am grateful for the store. It's been a mighty good way to support a large family such as ours. But in some ways, I'm a more simple man that my *daed,* I think. There's nothing wrong with that, I don't think. It's just how it is."

The words reverberated through Caleb. Giving him a freedom he didn't previously think was in his grasp. Could it actually be that easy? That a man was simply who God made him?

That the Lord hadn't meant for him to leave the church, but perhaps just go his own way? As the questions rattled around in his brain and he struggled for answers, Caleb felt years older, like a veil had been lifted from his eyes and the dizzying barriers that had plagued him for the past year no longer mattered.

He was free to be himself. Even if it wasn't who he had thought everyone had wanted him to be.

But it was as the Lord had intended all along.

Looking toward the barn, his dad added, "See, I don't mind talkin' with the horses. I don't mind being ankle deep in mud come spring, or letting the Lord's will determine my plantings. There's a certain beauty that surrounds my life that way, I think. It gives me great peace. But it isn't for everyone."

"I don't want to farm."

"I know you don't. And I know dealing with the store isn't your place, either. That's just as well, I'm thinkin', because Joshua has always taken to it like a duck in water. But . . . maybe there's someplace else for you. A place for you to grow and thrive . . . in the Amish community."

"Like what?"

"Maybe you'd like working in the brick-yard. There's a prosperous business there. Many a man have worked in the brick factory for years. And have been happy about it."

Caleb had never thought of that. "You wouldn't mind?"

"Nee." With a grunt, his father bent down and picked up the wheelbarrow.

When Caleb offered to push instead, his father said, "Caleb, it's time we all decided that what we want for you needs to come second to *your* wants and needs. Every man has to take his place in the world when he grows up."

"Maybe I'll stop by the brickyards and take a look."

"Yes. I think you should. Just to take a

look-see, you know."

"I might not be able to work there until I'm eighteen."

"Even if that was the case, you'd know where you were headed, yes? That is, if you decide to stay here in Sugarcreek. And if you decided that you still want to be Amish."

Caleb stopped again. "How come I've had such a hard time growing up? How come I haven't known what to do? Who to be?"

"You'll have to ask Jesus when you get to heaven, I suppose. Just like poor Paul said from prison, 'I can do all things through Christ, because he gives me strength.' "

"Those are *gut* words to remember," Caleb said.

They had made it to the barn. Jim whinnied a hello. The floor still needed to be swept and the chicken coop cleaned. His father wrinkled his nose. "There's a lot of work still to be done here, I think."

There was so much to do. "Do you think I still need to do everyone's chores?"

His father laughed, the noise coming deep from within him and echoing through the barn's interior. "Without a doubt you still need to do everyone's chores, Caleb. You're still in trouble. But, perhaps, I should take some time and remind Anson of his duties around here. He hasn't been doing things as he should."

Though Caleb was tempted to blab about Anson never doing things as he should, he didn't. Anson could earn and receive his own lectures — he didn't need Caleb adding to them.

And, Caleb knew he should concentrate on himself and his goals instead of focusing on what was lacking.

Impulsively, Caleb stepped forward. Reached out to his father. *"Danke."*

Instead of replying, his father pulled him into a hug. When Caleb's hat fell to the ground, his *daed* pressed his lips to Caleb's head.

And then, without another word, he turned and left.

Jim whinnied again.

With a grin, Caleb walked to the horse and rubbed his neck. "Yes, horse. I agree. Things are going to be just fine." Wrinkling his nose, he added, "Well, they will be, as soon as I get that chicken coop cleaned."

CHAPTER 27

Gretta's words were sharp and to the point. "I think you're making a terrible mistake, Lilly Allen."

"You do, hmm?" Lilly looked up from the table she was washing. "What exactly, have I done wrong?"

"You know." Gretta's expression hardened, even though she was holding a sleeping Will. "You've fairly broke Robert Miller's heart."

Just seeing how tiny little Will was made Lilly's heart melt. He was a beautiful baby, but even his cherubic cheeks couldn't replace the cold mixture of feelings that Gretta's blame was producing. "Robert's broken heart, or otherwise, is not my responsibility."

Gretta helped herself to a chair, carefully shifting the baby in her arms as she did so. "I think otherwise."

Lilly had enough on her mind without

Gretta's guilt. "Shouldn't you be home in bed? It's only been a week, Gretta."

"The doctor said I could move around a bit as I see fit. And Will likes being out for a bit. We'll go home after you and I talk."

Lilly set her washrag down. "Did you actually come here to talk? Because it sure doesn't feel like that. I'm getting the impression that you marched over here to yell."

"I don't yell."

"Okay. Snip and nag. Look. Why don't you say your piece?"

Gretta's cheeks bloomed as she opened her mouth, then shut it again quickly. After a moment, she sputtered, "I think you made a poor decision. You've hurt Robert terribly. And he's been through so much."

"I know."

"And Elsa was ready to take you in. We would have all gladly helped you become Amish, you know. It would have been easy."

"No, it wouldn't," Lilly finally said. "It wouldn't be easy. It would be hard and difficult and frustrating. I don't think I can do it."

"I didn't think you were afraid of hard work."

"It's not the hard work. It's me. It's losing me, Gretta. I would simply be trying to fit in. And I can't do that."

"It's the woman's role to make things work."

"Then it's going to have to be someone else's role. Gretta, I wanted to do this. I wanted to fall in love with Robert and accept everything he is. I wanted to be a part of his life. And I'm willing to make sacrifices. But we're not simply talking about giving up a car. Or wanting to start wearing a *kapp.* We're talking about me adopting a new religion and all the rules that come with it."

Though she felt like she was doing an incredibly poor job of explaining herself, she continued. "I want to give my heart to Robert. But I can't give up my whole being, too. I'm sorry."

Trying to explain herself to Gretta was almost harder than broaching the subject with Robert. Never would she have imagined that not becoming Amish would be a problem. "If I thought I could change who I was — change who I am — I would have. But I just don't think I can. It might not mean too much to you, but I promise, I really did consider it."

"But his heart, Lilly. It's breaking."

Lilly was a little put out. After all, her heart was breaking, too. She loved Robert. His appearance in her life had pulled her out of a deep depression and given her hope. Knowing that he was gone forever was devastating. But nobody seemed to be thinking about that.

"Gretta, I don't want to discuss this with you. It's none of your business, anyway."

"It is. I care. I care about you both."

"Perhaps," she allowed. But it didn't feel that way. It felt like she was being judged and found wanting. Yet again.

Slowly, Gretta stood up. With the complete concentration that only a new mother can have, she carefully wrapped William back in his quilt and settled him in his buggy.

Only after arranging the quilt again did Gretta face Lilly. "I better get on home."

"Will you ever be able to forgive me?" Understanding and forgiveness were two different things.

"Of course. But I'm sad, too. This is a difficult thing. I suppose I was hoping for a perfect ending, but everything doesn't always work out that way, does it?"

"No. Rarely does everything turn out perfect."

Gretta's lips trembled. "I'm exhausted. I'd best get on home now."

"Do you need help? I could sit with him while you nap."

"*Nee.* I, too, can be independent."

Lilly watched her friend leave with a feeling of sadness. A barrier had just formed between the two of them. Perhaps it was just the knowledge that they would never actually be as close as sisters.

Their lives were too different for that.

With a feeling of regret, Lilly continued to watch Gretta walk away, the last of the falling leaves swirling around her skirts as she guided the stroller down the sidewalk.

When she disappeared from view, Lilly stepped closer to the window pane, and looked out beyond the buildings across the way. She looked out toward the hills and fields beyond.

The fields were dark and the majority of the trees stood bare. Their leaves had fallen and now things would lay still and barren until spring.

As she eyed the dark outline of trees against the dreary gray skies, Lilly wondered if her world would ever be bright again.

Going back to the shop was a difficult thing. Robert's mind kept straying and his heart wasn't in it. Even his hands felt awkward. He mismeasured and ruined a perfectly good piece of cherry with his ineptitude.

Halfheartedly, he worked for a few hours on the hope chest for Judith Graber. He did the best he could, then hopped in his buggy and headed home.

Thank goodness, the streets were practically deserted. He had no desire to see anyone he knew or to dodge vehicles. Everything felt like too much trouble. Like too much to think about.

When he finally got home, he thought his house looked even more dark and empty than ever. It looked so alone. Unkempt. Perhaps he would put on a fresh coat of white paint come spring.

With practiced hands, he unhooked the buggy and walked Star into the barn. It only took fifteen minutes to unharness him, give him a good brushing. Feeding him some oats and hay took no time, either.

Walking out of the barn, he stared at the house again. *The house.* Indeed, that's all it was to him now — only a place to give him shelter.

With Grace, it had been a home. When they'd married, she'd taken great pride in her flower and vegetable garden.

She'd been a stickler for a schedule, too. If it was noon, chances were great that she'd have lunch on the table. Six o'clock brought dinner. And dinner always consisted of a meat and two vegetables.

And laughter.

Grace had been his love, his light. He'd loved her so much, and she'd been everything to him. Everything.

And then, when he'd sat by her side and watched her fade away, he'd watched part of himself leave this earth, too.

He'd never gotten angry about her death. Perhaps because Grace had never shaken her fist and cried about it. Oh, he knew she was sad to leave him. And her pain had been terribly fierce at times, but she had looked forward to going to heaven the way some people looked forward to spring flowers or ice cream.

She'd just been that way.

Robert believed with all his heart that the Lord had a plan for him. He believed it with all his being and was in complete agreement with it.

He certainly wanted to follow God's plan.

But he felt so heavy inside, he didn't know how to look up again. He just didn't understand what the Lord had wanted him to do about Lilly.

He couldn't bear to go in the house. Though the temperature had dropped, he sat on the gravel outside the barn and leaned up against the outside. Closed his eyes. And prayed.

Lord, I don't know what you want of me, he

began. Swallowing hard, he continued.

I've tried to be everything I am. I've tried to become the man you want me to be.

But I don't understand why you brought Lilly Allen into my life. Was it just to tempt me? So I would know better than to look for things I shouldn't?

Was that what was in your plan?

Robert rested the back of his head against the wooden wall. Felt the rough wood against his neck. Felt the cool breeze sting his cheeks.

And did his best to listen. To feel. To try to know what was right.

But when he opened his eyes, all he felt was the same painful loss.

And noticed that the sky had darkened.

CHAPTER 28

Three weeks had passed since Caleb had ironed everything out with his father. Three weeks since he'd realized that he was destined to join the church and take his place in the family. Three weeks since the Lord had led him to a new understanding.

Ever since the decision had been made, a new tranquility had descended on his family. Instead of being torn that he didn't want to follow in either his father's or his brother Joshua's footsteps, the opposite had happened. Now jokes were made about Caleb being "his grandfather's son." The new title felt good.

For all the conversations and decisions that had been made, much of his life stayed the same. He finished up his punishment chores, and gladly gave Anson back his duties — much to his brother's dismay. He still worked at the store a few days a week. But this time he resented it less because he knew it wasn't his destiny.

Every now and then, Caleb also took some time for himself. One of his favorite places was still Mrs. Miller's home. He'd gotten lucky one afternoon when he'd stopped by; she'd greeted him with a fresh-made batch of pumpkin cookies.

"Here you go, Caleb," she said as she placed a plate in front of them. "They're still so warm, the cream cheese icing is practically dripping off of them. I got you a nice mug of hot chocolate, too."

From other ladies, he might have struggled with feeling like he was being babied. From Mrs. Miller, though, he always enjoyed her fussing.

"They smell wonderful. *Danke.*" After a brief — very brief — prayer of thanks, he took a hearty bite.

Closing his eyes in pleasure, he was happy to realize that they were, indeed, as good as they looked. "You make the best cookies."

"I like to bake, that's all," she said modestly. But even her humble words couldn't hide her glow of happiness at receiving his compliment. "Now, I've heard about how you're not going to go live with the English family. And, how you aren't all that anxious to hang out with those English boys around town, either. What are you planning to do?"

Even the small reminder of his scary afternoon at the police station made Caleb shudder. "I visited the brickyard. Though they can't promise me anything, the manager said there was a good chance I could work for him as soon as I turn eighteen."

"Are you all right with that? Eighteen is still two years away."

"I think I am." He shrugged. "Now that I don't feel like I'm being pushed into a future not of my choosing, I seem to be able to breathe easier."

"That's always a *gut* feeling, I think. And friends?"

"I have some. Enough."

"I've often found that it's the quality of friends that count, far more than the quantity," she mused.

"I'm finding that to be true." Lately, he had been leaning toward "quality" friends, friends who he knew were likely to be there for him through thick or thin. He'd been writing to Eric Leonard, and he had promised to visit one day soon. He'd also renewed ties with some of his childhood friends from the Amish school.

They'd accepted him after minor misgivings and were proving to be extremely close. Those boys all had the same background as he did. They also felt the same as he about their faith. He'd been such a fool to push them all away when he'd been so sure he belonged among the English.

He'd been so centered on only his wants and needs that he'd neglected to realize that so many of the other boys his age were going through the same things that he was.

"I'm happy for you. And relieved." Mrs. Miller set a cookie on the napkin in front of her. "I would have been happy to help you with whatever you wanted to do, but honestly, some of the paths you were researching were scary ones. I've heard that even adults have a difficult time if they leave the order and move away."

"I'm happy I'm not fighting with my parents as much anymore, too." Actually, he didn't think he could put into words how relieved he was to be able to have regular conversations with them. The constant thread of tension had been exhausting.

Eyes brightening, Mrs. Miller murmured, "And Anson? How's he doing?"

In spite of himself, Caleb grinned. His brother was a favorite of most everybody's. "Anson? Oh, he's the same. He's still a pain, but Judith and I finally talked to Mamm and Daed about how we felt about Anson and Carrie not picking up enough slack. Once we started giving examples, they

354

believed us and came round to our way of thinking. So he and Carrie are doing lots more."

He'd just taken a sip from the hot chocolate when the back door opened and a girl scampered in.

"Mrs. Miller, I'm so sorry I'm late. I ended up having to help carry some vegetables to my parents' stand, and you know how that goes."

Mrs. Miller stood up. "That's quite all right, Rebecca." She looked Caleb's way. "Heavens! I didn't mean to be rude. Do you two know each other?"

Slowly the girl turned around. Just as Caleb got to his feet, and gaped. "Rebecca Yoder?"

A dimple appeared as she smiled hesitantly. "Hi, Caleb."

Mrs. Miller clasped her hands together. "Oh, so you two do know each other!"

"A little bit," Rebecca allowed.

Unable to look away from that smile, he murmured, "You moved, didn't you?"

She nodded. "Two years ago." Turning to Mrs. Miller, she explained. "We moved to the other side of Sugarcreek when my father inherited his parents' farm."

"It's good to see you again," he said weakly. Then flushed. How could he sound so dumb?

Rebecca played with a fold in her apron. "Why don't you come to any of the singings?"

"I . . . I was thinking I just might start."

Her golden eyes sparkled. "There's one this Sunday night. It's at our home. You should come. I mean . . . if you want."

"I'll probably go." Then, afraid he looked too eager, he said more slowly, "I mean, I will if I don't have anything else to do."

Her cheeks turned pink. Then, looking as flustered as he felt, she turned away. "Mrs. Miller, what would you like me to do today?"

"Dust the bookshelves in the library, please. Then, if you have time, I'd like you to mop the floors upstairs."

"Yes, ma'am." Before turning to go, she darted a quick glance his way. But before he could think of anything to say, she turned away.

Caleb couldn't resist following her movements as she gracefully walked out of the room and down the hall to the library.

Mrs. Miller noticed. "She's a nice girl, that Rebecca."

"Yes. I mean, she seems nice."

"So, you two were in school together when you were young?"

"Yes."

"I'm surprised you two never mentioned each other."

"We didn't know each other back then. She looked different. And shy."

"I think she's mighty pretty," said Mrs. Miller.

Oh, she was. She was terribly pretty. And there was something about her eyes that made him curious to know what she was thinking.

But he felt funny saying any of that. So he took another bite of cookie instead.

CHAPTER 29

"You've lost weight, Lilly," her mother said when Lilly was helping her sort and fold baby clothes in the newly painted nursery.

Lilly's hands paused, two tiny nightshirts in her hands. "I know."

"That's not healthy. You know, you never did gain back all the weight you lost after the miscarriage." She paused. "Starving yourself won't fix your problems."

"I know. I just haven't been hungry."

Her mom looked at her worriedly as she pulled out another pair of socks and neatly put them in a drawer. "It's been a month since you broke things off with Robert, but you still seem so down. Are you sure there isn't anything I can do? Do you want to talk about things?"

"There's nothing to talk about." When a look of extreme concern passed over her mother's features, guilt weighed heavy on her. "Mom, thanks for caring. But I don't want you to worry. You've got your own health to worry about."

"I might have another baby coming, but that doesn't mean I'm not thinking about you. Or that I don't want to try and help."

"There's nothing you can do," Lilly said honestly. "I've fallen in love with a man I shouldn't love. One day it won't hurt so bad."

As she picked up a soft quilt and folded it into fourths, her mom murmured, "There's got to be something you can do . . ."

"The only thing that would give me Robert is to become Amish. Mom, I wish I could do that. I wish I could with my whole heart, but I can't. Maybe one day I'll be ready to give my vows to the church, or to that way of life. But right now, I just can't. It's not who I am, and it's not who I think I can be."

"I never thought I'd encourage you to become Amish, but maybe you should speak to the Grabers?" she said gently. "Maybe they can give you some guidance. I really hate to see you so heartbroken."

"It was a talk with them that made me realize that I need to be honest with myself. Not rush into something in order to get what I want." As her voice started to crack, Lilly steeled herself. Tried to at least look like she was in control. "Am I wrong? I thought being strong and not giving in to what I want right now meant I was maturing."

"You're maturing. And, I'm proud of you, I am. I just had hoped that things would be easier for you. That's all."

"Me too," she murmured. "I had hoped after everything I'd been through this year that things would become easier."

Her mother had just squeezed her shoulder when a knock at the front door brought them both to their feet. "It must be a package," she murmured.

Lilly sat listlessly on the braided rug and folded another pair of sleepers as her mother walked to the front door. But when Lilly heard low murmuring instead of the expected open and shutting of the door, she got to her feet and walked down the hall.

And then almost felt her knees give way when she saw who'd come to call. "Robert?"

He stood at the entrance to the kitchen, hat in hand. "Lilly. Hello."

"Hello." As they stared at each other — and her mother stared at them — Lilly felt her face flush. Honestly, could they be saying anything less meaningful at that moment? Or more absurd?

"Lilly, I wondered if perhaps you'd like to come walking with me."

She was afraid. So far, it had taken everything she had to move on. To not think of Robert every waking moment. To not wish that she could be different.

What would happen if she was in his company again? How could she stand it if the same longing to be his girlfriend . . . his fiancée . . . his *wife* hit her just as hard as it had a mere thirty days ago?

Without her saying a word, Robert seemed to understand. "I know it's hard. But, please?"

In spite of her best intentions to remain self-supporting, she looked her mother's way.

With a shrug and a nod, she silently gave Lilly her answer. *It couldn't hurt. And, it might be a good thing.*

"I'll get my coat." Leaving the room, she rushed to her own. As she grabbed her wool coat off the pile of clothes on a rocking chair, Lilly spied her reflection in the mirror.

The woman looking back at her was the exact opposite of the person who'd first moved into the bedroom almost a year ago. Her cheeks weren't as full. The scared look from an uncertain future had been replaced with the quiet knowledge that not everything would ever go her way.

Not even if she hoped and thought positively.

Not even if she prayed really hard.

Sometimes, God took everything out of her hands. He was in charge. It was necessary for her to accept it and move on.

This, of course, was one of those times.

Mindful of Robert standing in the hall and waiting for her, she hurried back. "I'm ready."

"Let's go, then?"

He held the back door open for her as she led the way out into the garage, and then to the driveway. It was close to Thanksgiving now, and the air no longer just hinted of the coming winter, it had a definite frosty edge to it.

Gone were the vivid blue skies and golden leaves that had decorated each day with hope. Now the sky was gray, emphasizing the weathermen's predictions that the first snowfall was likely to arrive that afternoon.

Robert fingered the collar of her coat. "This fabric isn't terribly thick. Will you be warm enough?"

"I'll be fine." Holding up her gloved hands, she tried to smile.

He looked at the cashmere covering her

fingers with misgiving. "Those don't seem too warm, either."

"I'll be fine as soon as we start walking." In actuality, she didn't even feel the cold. Inside, she felt numb — a curious dread had filtered through her body . . . preparing her for his words. For yet another round of disappointment. Actually, everything about him made her ache with regrets.

Just being near him reminded her of her shattered hopes. Of the fact that not all dreams could become realities.

He pointed to the left. "Do you care to walk toward the Yoders' vegetable stand? There's a good path near the road. I fear it might be too chilly to walk across the fields toward the creek."

The walk she'd once told him was her favorite.

"That's fine."

Side by side they set out. Stiff and slow. Though she never would have taken his arm, walking by his side while taking care not to touch him definitely felt awkward.

After a good five minutes, her impatience won out. "Robert, why did you want to see me?"

"Because I couldn't stay away."

"You need to try. Believe me, if I thought I could move in with the Grabers and learn

Pennsylvania Dutch and adopt the *Ordnung,* I would." Every word felt like it was being pulled from her insides. "I promise, I would do all that in a heartbeat. You don't know how hard I've tried to see myself as Amish. But I'm not ready."

He paused. "Lilly, do you still love me?"

How could he even ask? "Of course I do."

"I . . . I still love you, too."

Lilly moved one foot in front of the other. Told herself not to look at him. Not to care so much. Not to feel so much. Soon, she could go back to her room and cry. And then, later, she could smile at the world again. She could pretend that she was fine.

In front of them, the path widened and split. The far side led to a small area with a bench and a small overhang. A school bus stop.

Cupping his hand around hers, he pulled her into the enclosure. Now they were surrounded on three sides by wide slats of wood. Effectively shielded from the outside world. Standing a mere two feet apart. Here, the air was warmer, it mixed with their breath. Heated their cheeks.

"Lilly," he began, his voice gravelly and thick, "I came to see you because I wanted to tell you that I understand."

Knowing he understood didn't stop the

pain. "All right. OK." She stepped back. "Let's go back —"

His hand tightened around hers. Slowly pulled her closer. "Shh," he murmured. Carefully, he pressed his lips to her brow. "Listen, Lilly." When she lifted her chin to meet his gaze, he continued. "And . . . I wanted to tell you that I spoke to my family. And to our bishop." He took a deep breath. "I'm going to leave the church."

Panic slammed her. "No." She knew what he'd be giving up. She knew how solemn his vows to his faith were. How much he loved his community.

Instead of looking relieved, Robert only looked amused. "It's not a choice for you, my Lilly. It was a decision only I could make."

With wide eyes, she watched him raise her left hand and carefully peel off her glove. "You'll be shunned. I can't let you do that. Not even for me."

To her confusion, he chuckled softly before pressing his lips to her bare knuckles. "Oh, Lilly. When will you ever understand how special you are? When will you ever understand how much you are valued? You are worth my sacrifice. Any sacrifice."

She shook her head. No. He was wrong. She wasn't worth that. "Robert —"

"Shh. Please listen. Since you've left, I've tried to go on. But my heart is empty. I'm only twenty-four, but I feel like an old man. I've lost a wife, and now, I've been about to lose a future love. I can't do that."

After removing her other glove, he took her hands and set them between his own. Immediately, his rough, work-hewn palms covered hers and warmed them. Just like they had in the cornfield.

"My life with Grace was everything I'd ever wanted," he murmured. "She was a wonderful woman, and everything I had ever dreamed in a wife." His expression became wistful as he continued. "If she had lived, I know we would have been happy."

"I know that."

Reaching up, he smoothed back her hair. "But I can't remake the past. I can't simply go find another Amish woman and build a marriage again."

"Perhaps in time . . ."

"There's been no one for me after Grace. No one, until I saw you. You have lifted my sorrows and brought light into my life again. Because of you, I'm able to think of a future."

"But leaving the Amish —"

"There's a conservative Mennonite church not far from here. I went and talked to their ministers yesterday."

"Yes?"

"They believe many of the same things that I do. It will be a difficult change, but I think, with God's help, that I can make a life for myself there . . . if I had you."

A Mennonite church? She knew enough about the faith from her employer to know that she could become Mennonite.

Robert continued. "As a Mennonite, you could retain some of your technologies. They would let you have a car. A phone. They would not look upon our marrying as wrong."

"But your family —"

"They are terribly upset," he murmured. "There's disappointment and tears, I'm not going to lie. I don't know what is going to happen. Perhaps I will be completely shunned. Perhaps one day I'll be welcomed back into their homes, at least for a visit."

Very slowly, he lifted her chin with one finger, so that their eyes met. So there could be no mistaking about what he was going to say. "Lilly, I'm willing to accept their rejection if it means I can have you. If I can have you as mine. For a lifetime."

With deliberate care, she pressed her other bare palm against his. Palm to palm. Skin to skin. Together, their hands looked right.

All Lilly had to do was curve her fingers around his and she could grasp hold of his own. They would be joined.

Just as she'd dreamed.

Perhaps some dreams could become real, after all.

And so, she threaded her fingers through his. Then reached up and grabbed hold of his shoulders. Clung. "Yes," she finally said.

His face lit up. "Yes to what?"

She couldn't help but smile. "Yes to everything. To the Mennonite church. To love. To marriage. But most of all — yes to you, Robert Miller."

Without another word, he folded her into his arms. She could feel his chest shudder in relief as she buried her face in his shoulder and smelled his fresh, clean scent.

He loved her. The most amazing man she'd ever met loved her — and was willing to sacrifice everything for a life together.

Closing her eyes, she murmured, "I hope I'll be able to make you happy, Robert. I promise I'll try."

He pushed back a lock of hair, brushing away her fears. "Don't you understand, Lilly Allen? I already know you'll make me happy. Because you already do. I know you'll promise to love me, because you already do."

Very carefully, he leaned back so their eyes could meet. She looked at him with so much love in her eyes, and he murmured, "I know we'll have a lifetime together. A lifetime that will be worth all our sacrifices, because you've already given me so much. You've already promised me a future when you agreed to be by my side. You've already given me what I've longed to have . . . you."

Too overcome for words, she raised her lips to his. And kissed him.

And kissed him again. Just as the first snowflakes of the season fluttered in the air, swirled, and gently cascaded to the ground.

Covering everything with the fresh, clean promise of hope.

Dear Readers,

Ah, Lilly. From the moment I started this series, I felt like she was one of my kids! Time and again, things would happen to her that I hadn't planned to happen. And then, wouldn't you know it, just when I thought her future was set, she would change her mind! Those of you who have teenagers might be able to relate.

As a writer, Lilly has been extremely frustrating. But I've also grown to admire her so very much. She's endured a lot and become strong, and I was very glad to give her a happy ending. I knew Robert Miller was the right man for her. I feel certain that they will have a long and happy life together.

As I write this note, I'm kind of stunned that another series is over. I've loved writing the whole Seasons of Sugarcreek books. Since they took place over one year, I wrote them back to back, with very little time in between. Because of that, by the time I finished this book, I felt like I knew all the places in my series so well. If I could go to the Sugarcreek Inn for coconut cream pie, I would!

I've told a couple of readers that my favorite character in the novels was Anson Graber. That comes from teaching elementary school for ten years, I suppose. Even though a teacher wasn't supposed to have favorites, I always had a soft spot for squirrely little boys. Whenever I wrote about Anson . . . even when he wasn't being very good — I had to smile. Perhaps there has been a character that has become a favorite of yours. If so, I hope you'll let me know.

At the moment, I'm finishing up *Grace,* a Christmas Sisters of the Heart novel. The chance to write this book was really an unexpected gift for me. I've so enjoyed being able to return to the world of the Brennemans, and writing about a very special Christmas in their inn.

Finally, I can't tell you all enough how grateful I am that you pick up my books, give them a try, and pass them to your friends. Hearing from readers always makes my day.

So thank you so much to all of you who have reached out to me. There's never a day that I don't count my blessings. I'll look forward to writing a new series very soon!

With Blessings to you and yours,
Shelley

QUESTIONS FOR DISCUSSION

1. The friendship that develops between the Graber and Allen families is put to the test in *Autumn's Promise*. Frank and Elsa Graber must trust Lilly Allen enough to let her take Caleb to Strongsville. Was asking Lilly to be involved the right thing to do?

2. Why do you think Robert wasn't attracted to another Amish woman? Was it *Lilly* that he was in love with . . . or was it the fact that she was so different from his first wife?

3. What do you think made Robert so appealing to Lilly?

4. How could Robert's family have been more supportive of his wishes? Or, in your opinion, should they have tried harder to keep him away from Lilly? Do you think they'll reach out to him in the future, or completely shun him?

5. Caleb had always thought he didn't fit in the Amish lifestyle. When he visited Lilly's friends in Strongsville, he had the opportunity to "try out" being English. Do you think he should have gone ahead and lived with the Leonards for a month? Do you think he will regret his decision one day?

6. Lilly realizes that though she loves Robert, she ultimately doesn't want to become Amish. Do you think she made the right decision? Or should she have tried harder to conform to the Amish way of life?

7. When Lilly visits Cassidy's home, and finally tells Cassidy about her pregnancy and miscarriage, she realizes that she can't go back in time. She'll never be the person she once was. Can you think of some life experiences that have made you different than the person you once were?

8. What do you think will happen with Lilly and Robert, and their place in the community?

9. Much of the series shows both English and Amish characters reaching out to each other for support. Their bond helps them in innumerable ways. Can you think of a time when an unlikely friendship has brought you

great joy?

10. How do you think the scripture verse from Philippians can be related to your life?

"I do not mean that I am already as God wants me to be. I have not yet reached that goal, but I continue trying to reach it and to make it mine. Christ wants me to do that, which is the reason he made me his." — Philippians 3:12

11. Finally, I referred to the saying below while writing much of the book. How have you lived your life by giving?

"You make a living by what you get, but a life by what you give." — Pennsylvania Dutch Saying

ABOUT THE AUTHOR

Shelley Shepard Gray is the beloved author of the Sisters of the Heart series, including *Hidden, Wanted,* and *Forgiven.* Before writing, she was a teacher in both Texas and Colorado. She now writes full-time and lives in southern Ohio with her husband and two children. When not writing, Shelley volunteers at church, reads, and enjoys walking her miniature dachshund on her town's scenic bike trail.